P9-CCU-417

HIT AND RUN

Also by Lawrence Block

Keller's Greatest Hits

Hit Man ▪ Hit List ▪ Hit Parade

The Matthew Scudder Novels

The Sins of the Fathers ▪ Time to Murder and Create ▪ In the Midst of Death ▪ A Stab in the Dark ▪ Eight Million Ways to Die ▪ When the Sacred Ginmill Closes ▪ Out on the Cutting Edge ▪ A Ticket to the Boneyard ▪ A Dance at the Slaughterhouse ▪ A Walk Among the Tombstones ▪ The Devil Knows You're Dead ▪ A Long Line of Dead Men ▪ Even the Wicked ▪ Everybody Dies ▪ Hope to Die ▪ All the Flowers Are Dying

The Bernie Rhodenbarr Mysteries

Burglars Can't Be Choosers ▪ The Burglar in the Closet ▪ The Burglar Who Liked to Quote Kipling ▪ The Burglar Who Studied Spinoza ▪ The Burglar Who Painted Like Mondrian ▪ The Burglar Who Traded Ted Williams ▪ The Burglar Who Thought He Was Bogart ▪ The Burglar in the Library ▪ The Burglar in the Rye ▪ The Burglar on the Prowl

The Adventures of Evan Tanner

The Thief Who Couldn't Sleep ▪ The Canceled Czech ▪ Tanner's Twelve Swingers ▪ Two for Tanner ▪ Tanner's Tiger ▪ Here Comes a Hero ▪ Me Tanner, You Jane ▪ Tanner on Ice

Also by Lawrence Block

The Affairs of Chip Harrison

No Score ▪ Chip Harrison Scores Again ▪ Make Out with Murder ▪ The Topless Tulip Caper

Other Novels

After the First Death ▪ Ariel ▪ Cinderella Sims ▪ Coward's Kiss ▪ Deadly Honeymoon ▪ The Girl with the Long Green Heart ▪ Grifter's Game ▪ Lucky at Cards ▪ Not Comin' Home to You ▪ Random Walk ▪ Ronald Rabbit Is a Dirty Old Man ▪ Small Town ▪ The Specialists ▪ Such Men Are Dangerous ▪ The Triumph of Evil ▪ You Could Call It Murder

Collected Short Stories

Sometimes They Bite ▪ Like a Lamb to Slaughter ▪ Some Days You Get the Bear ▪ Ehrengraf for the Defense ▪ One Night Stands ▪ The Lost Cases of Ed London ▪ Enough Rope

Books for Writers

Writing the Novel from Plot to Print ▪ Telling Lies for Fun & Profit ▪ Write for Your Life ▪ Spider, Spin Me a Web

Anthologies Edited

Death Cruise ▪ Master's Choice ▪ Opening Shots ▪ Master's Choice 2 ▪ Speaking of Lust ▪ Opening Shots 2 ▪ Speaking of Greed ▪ Blood on Their Hands ▪ Gangsters Swindlers Killers & Thieves ▪ Manhattan Noir

LAWRENCE BLOCK

HIT AND RUN

wm

WILLIAM MORROW

An Imprint of Harper Collins *Publishers*

This book is a work of fiction. The characters, incidents, and dialogue are drawn from the author's imagination and are not to be construed as real. Any resemblance to actual events or persons, living or dead, is entirely coincidental.

FIRST EDITION

Designed by Kara Strubel

Library of Congress Cataloging-in-Publication Data

Block, Lawrence.
Hit and run / Lawrence Block. — 1st ed.
p. cm.
ISBN 978-0-06-084090-7
1. Keller, John (Fictitious character)—Fiction. 2. Assassins—Fiction. I. Title.
PS3552.L63H55 2008
813'.54—dc22 2007022143

---

08 09 10 11 12 OV/RRD 10 9 8 7 6 5 4 3 2 1

For my cousin

PETER NATHAN

Acknowledgments

The author is grateful to Rita Olmo and Beatriz Aprigliano-Ziegler of Fairchild House, whose gracious New Orleans hospitality aided and abetted the writing of this book.

HIT AND RUN

1

Keller drew his pair of tongs from his breast pocket and carefully lifted a stamp from its glassine envelope. It was one of Norway's endless Posthorn series, worth less than a dollar, but curiously elusive, and missing from his collection. He examined it closely, held it to the light to make sure the paper hadn't thinned where a hinge had once secured it to an album page, and returned it to the envelope, setting it aside for purchase.

The dealer, a tall and gaunt gentleman whose face was frozen on one side by what he had explained was Bell's palsy, gave a one-side-of-the-face chuckle. "One thing I like to see," he said, "is a man who carries his own tongs with him. Minute I see that, I know I've got a serious collector in my shop."

Keller, who sometimes had his tongs with him and sometimes didn't, felt it was more a question of memory than seriousness. When he traveled, he always brought along his copy of the Scott catalog, a large 1,100-page volume that listed and illustrated the stamps of the world from the very first issue (Great Britain's Penny Black, 1840) through the initial century of philately and, in the case of the British Empire, including the last of the George VI issues in 1952. These were the stamps Keller collected, and he used the catalog not only for its information but as a checklist, deliberately circling each stamp's number in red when he added it to his collection.

The catalog always traveled with him, because there was no way he could shop for stamps without having it at hand. The tongs were useful, but not indispensable; he could always borrow a pair from whoever had stamps to sell him. So it was easy to forget to pack tongs, and you couldn't just tuck a pair in your pocket at the last minute, or slip them in your carry-on. Not if you were going to get on an airplane, because some clown at Security would confiscate them. Imagine a terrorist with a pair of stamp tongs. Why, he could grab the flight attendant and threaten to pluck her eyebrows . . .

It was surprising he'd brought the tongs this time, because he'd almost decided against packing the catalog. He'd worked for this particular client once before, on a job that took him to Albuquerque, and he'd never even had time to unpack. In an uncharacteristic excess of caution, he'd booked three different motel rooms, checked into each of them in turn, then wound up rushing the job on an impulse and flying back to New York the same day without sleeping in any of them. If this job went as quickly and smoothly he wouldn't have time to buy stamps, and who even knew if there were any dealers in Des Moines?

Years ago, when Keller's boyhood stamp collection rarely set him back more than a dollar or two a week, there would have been plenty of dealers in Des Moines, as there were just about everywhere. The hobby was as strong as ever these days, but the street-level retail stamp shop was on the endangered species list, and conservation was unlikely to save it. The business nowadays was all online or mail order, and the few dealers who still operated stores did so more to attract potential sellers than buyers. People with no knowledge of or interest in stamps would pass their shop every day, and when Uncle Fred died and there was a collection to sell, they'd know where to bring it.

This dealer, James McCue by name, had his store occupying the ground-floor front of his home off Douglas Avenue in Urbandale, a suburb whose name struck Keller as oxymoronic. An urban dale? It seemed neither urban nor a dale to Keller, but he figured it was probably a nice enough place to live. McCue's house was around seventy years old, a frame structure with a bay window and an upstairs porch. The dealer sat at a computer, where Keller figured he probably did the greater portion of his business, and a radio played elevator music at low volume. It was a peaceful room, its manageable clutter somehow comforting, and Keller picked through the rest of the Norway issues and found a couple more he could use.

"How about Sweden?" McCue suggested. "I got some real nice Sweden."

"I'm strong on Sweden," Keller said. "At this point the only ones I need are the ones I can't afford."

"I know what that's like. How about numbers one to five?"

"Surprisingly enough, I don't have them. But then I don't have the three skilling orange, either." That stamp, cataloged as number 1a, was an error of color, orange instead of blue green, and was presumably unique; a specimen had changed hands a few years ago for three million dollars. Or maybe it was euros, Keller couldn't remember.

"Haven't got that fellow," McCue said, "but I've got one through five, and the price is right." And, when Keller raised his eyebrows, he added, "The official reprints. Mint, decent centering, and lightly hinged. Book says they're worth $375 apiece. Want to have a look?"

He didn't wait for an answer but sorted through a file box and came up with a stock card holding the five stamps behind a protective sheet of clear plastic.

"Take your time, look 'em over carefully. Nice, aren't they?"

"Very nice."

"You could fill those blank spaces with these and never need to apologize for them."

And if he ever did acquire the originals, which seemed unlikely, the set of reprints would still deserve a place in his collection. He asked the price.

"Well, I wanted seven-fifty for the set, but I guess I'll take six hundred. Save me the trouble of shipping 'em."

"If it was five," Keller said, "I wouldn't have to think about it."

"Go ahead and think it through," McCue said. "I wouldn't really care to go lower than six. I can take a credit card, if that makes it easier."

It made it easier, all right, but Keller wasn't sure he wanted to take that route. He had an American Express card in his own name, but he hadn't used his own name at all this trip, and figured he'd just as soon keep it that way. And he had a Visa card he'd used to rent the Nissan Sentra from Hertz, and to register at the Days Inn, and the name on it was Holden Blankenship, which matched the Connecticut driver's license in his wallet, on which Blankenship's middle initial was J., which Keller figured would help to distinguish him from all the other Holden Blankenships in the world.

According to Dot, who had a source for credit cards and driver's licenses, the license would pass a security check, and the cards would be good for at least a couple of weeks. But sooner or later all the charges would bounce when nobody paid them, and that didn't bother Keller as far as Hertz and Days Inn and American Airlines were concerned, but the last thing he wanted to do was screw a stamp dealer out of money that was rightfully his. He had a feeling that wouldn't happen, that the credit card company would be the one to eat the loss, but even so he didn't like the idea. His hobby was the one area of his life where he got to be completely clean and aboveboard. If he bought the stamps and avoided paying for them, he was essentially stealing them, and it hardly mattered if he was stealing them from James McCue or Visa. He was perfectly comfortable with the notion of having official reprints on the first page of his Swedish issues, but not stolen reprints, or even stolen originals. If he couldn't come by them honestly, he'd just as soon get along without them.

Dot would have a snappy comeback for that one, he supposed, or at the very least roll her eyes. But he figured most collectors would get the point.

But did he have enough cash?

He didn't want to check in front of an audience, and asked to use the bathroom, which wasn't a bad idea anyway, after all the coffee he'd had with breakfast. He counted the bills in his wallet and found they came to just under eight hundred dollars, which would leave him with less than two after he bought the stamps.

And he really wanted them.

That was the trouble with stamp collecting. You never ran out of things to want. If he'd collected something else—rocks, say, or old Victrolas, or art—he'd run out of room sooner or later. His one-bedroom apartment was spacious enough by New York's severe standards, but it wouldn't take many paintings to fill the available wall space. With stamps, though, he had a set of ten large albums, occupying no more than five running feet of bookshelf space, and he could collect for the rest of his life and spend millions of dollars and never fill them.

Meanwhile, it wasn't as though he couldn't afford six hundred dollars for the Swedish reprints, not with the fee he was collecting for the job that had brought him to Des Moines. And McCue's price was certainly fair. He'd be getting them for a third of catalog, and would have cheerfully paid close to full catalog value for them.

And did it matter if he wound up short of cash? He'd be out

of Des Moines in a day or two, three at the most, and aside from buying the occasional newspaper and the odd cup of coffee, what did he need cash for, anyway? Fifty bucks to cover a cab home from the airport? That was about it.

He shifted six hundred dollars from his wallet to his breast pocket and went back to have another look at the stamps. No question, these babies were going home with him. "Suppose I pay cash?" he said. "That get me any kind of a discount?"

"Don't see much cash anymore," McCue said, and grinned. One side of his mouth went up while the rest stayed frozen. "Tell you what, we can skip the sales tax, long as you promise not to tell the governor."

"My lips are sealed."

"And I'll throw in those Norway stamps you picked out, though I don't guess that'll save you much. They can't come to more than ten dollars, can they?"

"More like six or seven."

"Well, that'll buy you a hamburger, if you don't want fries with it. Call it an even six hundred and we're good."

Keller gave him the money. McCue was counting it while Keller made sure he had all of the stamps he'd bought, tucking them away in an inside jacket pocket, adding the pair of tongs to another, closing the stamp catalog, when abruptly McCue said, "Oh, holy hell! Hold everything."

Were the bills counterfeit? He froze, wondering what was the matter, but McCue was on his feet, walking over to the radio, turning up the volume. The music had stopped and an agitated announcer was interrupting with a news bulletin.

"Holy hell," McCue said again. "We're in for it now."

2

Dot must have been sitting right next to the phone. She picked it up halfway through the first ring and said, "That wasn't you, was it?"

"Of course not."

"I didn't think so. The picture they showed on CNN didn't look much like the one they sent us."

It made him nervous, talking like this on a cell phone. The technology kept improving, to the point where you had to take it for granted that there was a record somewhere of every call you made, and that the authorities could access the information in a heartbeat. If you used a cell phone, they could pinpoint the location of it when you made the call. They kept building better mousetraps, and the mice had to be correspondingly more resourceful. Lately, whenever he had a job, he would buy two prepaid cell phones for cash from a store on West Twenty-third Street, making up a name and address for their records. He'd give one to Dot and keep the other for himself, and the only calls either would make were to the other. He'd called a few days ago, to report his arrival in Des Moines, and he'd called again earlier that morning to say that they'd told him to wait at least one more day, although he could have hit the guy and been on his way home by now.

And he was calling now because someone had just killed the

governor of Ohio. Which would have been noteworthy under any circumstances, given that John Tatum Longford, the best OSU running back since Archie Griffin, who'd gone to law school after he blew out his knee in his one pro season with the Bengals, was personable and charismatic and the first black governor ever to grace the statehouse in Columbus. But Governor Longford had not been in Columbus when a well-placed bullet blew out more than his knee, had not in fact been anywhere in Ohio. The man was a hot presidential prospect, and Iowa was one of those important early states, and the night before Longford had been in Ames, addressing a group of students and faculty at Iowa State University. From there the governor and his party had driven down to Des Moines, where he'd spent the night at Terrace Hill as the guest of the governor of Iowa. At 10:30 the next morning he'd appeared onstage at a high school auditorium, and around noon he'd shown up to address a Rotary luncheon. Then the gunshot, and the race to the hospital, where he was pronounced dead on arrival.

"My guy's white," he told Dot. "And short and fat, like the photograph."

"It was a head shot, wasn't it? I mean the photograph, not what happened just now. So you couldn't really tell that he was short. Or fat, as far as that goes."

"He was jowly."

"Well."

"And you could certainly tell he was white."

"No argument there. The man was white as the ace of clouds."

"Huh?"

"Never mind. What are you going to do?"

"I don't know. I saw my guy just yesterday morning, I was almost close enough to spit on him."

"Why would you want to do that?"

"What I'm getting at is that I could have done the job and been home by now. I almost did it, anyway, Dot. With the gun or with my hands. I was supposed to wait but I thought, hell, why wait? They'd have been pissed but I'd have been out of here, and instead I'm in the middle of a manhunt for a killer they haven't identified yet. Unless there's been something on the news in the last few minutes?"

"I've got the set on," she said, "and there hasn't. Maybe you should just come home."

"I was thinking of that. But when you think what airport security is going to be like around here—"

"No, don't even try. You've got a rental, right? You could drive to, I don't know, Chicago? And catch a flight there."

"Maybe."

"Or just drive all the way. Whatever you're more comfortable with."

"You don't think they'll have road blocks set up?"

"I didn't think of that."

"Of course I didn't do anything, but the ID's fake, and just attracting any attention—"

"Is not the greatest idea in the world."

He took a moment, thought about it. "You know," he said, "the son of a bitch who did this, they'll probably catch him in a matter of hours. My guess is he'll be killed resisting arrest."

"Which will save somebody the trouble of sending a latter-day Jack Ruby to take him out."

"You asked if this was my doing."

"I really knew it wasn't."

"Of course not," he said, "because you know I'd never touch anything like this. High-profile stuff, it doesn't matter how much they pay, because you don't live long enough to spend it. If the cops don't kill you your employers will, because it's not safe to leave you around. You know what I'm going to do?"

"What?"

"Sit tight," he said.

"And wait for it to blow over."

"Or burn itself out, or something. It shouldn't take too long. A few days and either they catch the guy or they know he got away from them, and people stop giving a rat's ass about what's happening in Des Moines."

"And then you can come home."

"I could even do the job, as far as that goes. Or not. Right now it wouldn't bother me to give the money back."

"For perhaps the first time in my life," Dot said, "I feel that way myself. Still, all things being equal—"

"Whatever that means."

"I've often wondered myself. It does get a sentence started, though. All things being equal, I'd just as soon keep the money. And it's the last job."

"That's what we said," he said, "about the job before this one."

"I know."

"But then this one came along."

"It was a special situation."

"I know."

"You know, if it really bothered you, you should have said something."

"It didn't really bother me until a few minutes ago," he said, "when the radio switched from 'The Girl with Emphysema' to 'This Just In.'"

"Ipanema."

"Huh?"

"'The Girl from Ipanema,' Keller."

"That's what I said."

"You said 'The Girl with Emphysema.'"

"Are you sure?"

"Never mind."

"Because why would I say that?"

"Never mind, for God's sake."

"It just doesn't sound like something I would say."

"Call it a slip of the ear, Keller, if that makes you happy. We're both a little rattled, and who can blame us? Go back to your room and wait this out."

"I will."

"And if anything comes up—"

"I'll let you know," he said.

He closed the phone. He was sitting behind the wheel of the rented Nissan, parked at the first strip mall he'd come to since leaving McCue's place. His new stamps were in an envelope in one pocket, his tongs in another, and his Scott catalog was on the seat beside him. He was still holding the cell phone, and he had no sooner put it in a pocket than he changed his mind and took it out again. He opened it and was looking for the Redial button when it rang. The caller ID screen was blank, but there was only one person it could be.

He answered it and said, "I was just about to call you."

"Because you had the same thought I did."

"I guess so. Either it's a coincidence—"

"Or it's not."

"Right."

"I have a feeling that thought was in both our minds from the minute we got the news flash."

"I think you're right," he said, "because when it just now came to me it felt like something I've known all along."

"Day to day," she said, "before Longford made the news, did it feel wrong?"

"It always does."

"Really?"

"Lately, yeah. That's one reason I want to pack it in. You remember Indianapolis? The plan there was that they'd kill me once I took out the target. They put a bug on my car so they'd always be able to find me."

"I remember."

"If I hadn't overheard two of them talking—"

"I know."

"And then the other job for Al, the one in Albuquerque, I was so paranoid I booked three motel rooms under three different names."

"And didn't stay in any of them, as I recall."

"Or anywhere else, either. I did the job and came home. Most of the time everything's fine, Dot, but I'm gun-shy, and I take so many precautions I trip over them. And then when I start to relax, somebody shoots the governor of Ohio."

She was quiet for a moment. Then she said, "Be careful, Keller."

"I intend to."

"Lay low as long as you have to, if you're sure you're in a safe place. Don't even think about doing the job for Al, not as long as there's the slightest chance that this might be a setup."

"All right."

"And stay in touch," she said, and rang off.

3

Was it a setup?

That would explain the delays. His purported quarry, the short fat white guy who was manifestly not the governor of Ohio or anyplace else, was not a terribly difficult target. An hour or so after Keller's plane had landed, the man who'd met it was driving Keller through a tree-lined neighborhood in West Des Moines, near Holiday Park. The driver, a big man with large facial features and a lot of hair growing out of his ears, eased up on the accelerator as they passed a ranch house with compulsively symmetrical shrubbery in front of it. A man in Bermuda shorts and a baggy T-shirt stood on the flawless front lawn, watering it with a hose.

"Everybody else on earth," he said, "sets up a sprinkler and leaves it the hell alone. That jerkoff has to stand there and hold it. I guess he's the kind's got to be in charge."

"Well," Keller said.

"Don't he look just like his picture? That's your guy. Okay, now you know where he lives. Next thing we'll do is drive past his office."

And, in downtown Des Moines, the driver pointed out a ten-story office building, on the sixth floor of which Gregory Dowling had an office. "Except you'd have to be nuts to hit him down here," he told Keller, "with all the people around, and they even got a security staff in the building, and there's traffic to make it tough to get away when the job's finished. You go to his house, catch him watering his lawn, just cram the nozzle down his throat till it comes out of his ass."

"Slick," Keller said.

"Just a manner of speaking. You know where he lives, you know where he works, now it's time to take you home."

Home?

"We're putting you up at this place, the Laurel Inn. Nothing fancy but not too shabby, either, you know? Nice pool, decent coffee shop, plus you got a Denny's right across the road. You're right at an interstate exit, so you're on and off in a hurry. And it's all taken care of, so you got no bill to pay. Charge anything you want to the room, it's on the boss."

The place certainly looked good from the highway. Around back in the parking lot, the big fellow handed Keller a palm-size cardboard folder holding a key card. Only the name of the motel appeared on the key card; the room number, 204, was written on the folder.

"They never told me your name," the fellow said.

"They never told me yours, either."

"Meaning let's keep it that way? Fair enough. Name you're registered under is Leroy Montrose, and don't blame me, 'cause I ain't the one picked it out."

The hair on the man's head was neatly cut and styled, and Keller wondered why his barber didn't do something about the hair growing out of his ears. Keller had never thought of himself as particularly fastidious, but he really didn't like to look at it, all that hair sprouting out of the guy's ears.

"Leroy Montrose, Room 204. Any charges, just sign your name. Well, Leroy's name. You sign your own name, which I guess you like keeping a secret, and they'll just look at you funny."

Keller didn't say anything. Maybe the ear hair functioned like antennae, maybe the guy was getting signals on it from his home planet.

"Thing is," the guy said, "it's good you're here now, but it might be a while before you can go ahead and do your thing."

"Oh?"

"There's a guy has to make sure he's someplace else when it goes down, if you get my drift. And there's a couple other whatchacall variables involved. So what they want you to do is stay pretty close to the room so we can call you and keep you in the loop. Like go ahead or don't go ahead, you follow me?"

"As day follows night," Keller said.

"Yeah? Good way to put it. What am I forgetting? Oh, right. Open the glove compartment. See the paper bag? Take it out."

It was heavy, and he didn't need to open it to know what it contained.

"Two of 'em, Leroy. Okay if I call you Leroy?"

"Feel free."

"Get the feel of 'em, pick the one you like. No rush, take your time."

They were handguns, of course, one a pistol, the other a revolver. Keller didn't much want to handle them, but neither did he want to look squeamish. The pistol fit his hand better, but pistols could jam, which gave the revolver a definite edge.

But did he want either of them?

"I'm not sure I want to use a gun," he said.

"You really like the idea of jamming the nozzle down his throat, huh? Still, you want to keep your options open. They're both loaded. I got an extra clip for the Glock auto somewhere. The revolver, I can send over a box of shells later on."

"Maybe I'll take them both."

"Walk up on him with a gun in each hand? I don't think so. I had to guess, I'd say you look like a Glock guy to me."

That was reason enough for Keller to choose the revolver. He checked the cylinder, noted the four bullets and the one empty chamber, snapped it shut. And for a moment he had a strong and entirely unexpected urge to point the thing at the man with the hairy ears and pull the trigger. Just blow him away and catch the next plane back to New York.

Instead he handed him the Glock, pocketed the revolver. "Never mind the extra shells," he said.

"You don't miss, huh?" Big grin. "I guess a pro is a pro, right? Oh, before I forget, lemme have the number of your cell phone."

Yeah, right. Keller told him he didn't have one, and the man patted his own pockets until he found one and handed it over. "So we can call you. Keep it with you when you go over to the Denny's for a patty melt. I love them things, but you want to tell them to let you have it on rye bread. Makes all the difference."

"Thanks for the tip."

"No problem. Now, the car. You shouldn't have any trouble with it. You got a full tank of gas and she's got eighteen hundred miles before she's due for an oil change."

"That's comforting."

There was more about the car—how to adjust the seats, the tendency of one of the trouble lights to go on for no good reason—but Keller hadn't paid much attention. The fellow took the keys out of the ignition and handed them to Keller, and Keller asked him how he was planning to get home.

"I go home," he said, "and I got my wife to deal with. I'd rather go someplace else, if it's all the same to you."

"I meant—"

"Hell, I know what you meant. See that beat-up Monte Carlo over there? That's my ride, just waiting for me. Now you could go to the front desk if you wanted, but there's no need. Room 204's on the second level, and you can just take those outside stairs right over there."

Suitcase in hand, gun in pocket, Keller mounted the stairs and found his room. He stuck the key in the lock and turned for a look at the Monte Carlo, which hadn't moved. He opened the door and went inside.

It was a pretty nice room, with a good-size television set and a king-size bed. The framed prints on the wall were easy enough to ignore. The air conditioner was set a little on the chilly side, but he left it alone. He sat on a chair for five minutes, and when he drew the drapery aside and looked out the window, the Monte Carlo was gone.

Half an hour later he was across the street in a booth at Denny's, with his suitcase on the seat opposite him. He had a patty melt on rye with a side of well-done french fries, and he had to admit it was pretty good. The coffee was not going to put Starbucks out of business, but it was decent enough for him to take the waitress up on her offer of a second cup.

Now how hard was that? Guy suggests a meal and you follow his suggestion and it's not bad at all. So what's so bad about going along with the program?

But no, the patty melt was where the program ended. They make it easy, he told himself, and you have to make it hard. They supply a decent room at a clean, well-situated motel, and you won't even use the john because you don't want to leave your DNA in it. The only thing he was willing to leave in the room was the cell phone they'd provided—turned off, wiped free of prints, and tucked away under the very center of the king-size mattress. He'd thought about leaving the gun there as well, but in the end he'd decided to hang on to it for the time being, and it was in his suitcase.

He'd returned to the car they gave him, but only in order to wipe any surfaces he might have touched. He triggered the remote on the key fob to lock the car, and had the urge to fling the keys into a handy Dumpster. Could they use the car keys to track him? He wasn't sure, and his sense of contemporary technology was that anybody could do anything, and if they couldn't today they'd be able to tomorrow. Still, he didn't see any reason to toss the car keys just yet, or the room key, either.

He'd walked across the street to Denny's, finished his patty melt and fries and two cups of coffee, and now he used a pay phone next to the men's room to call a taxi. "Going to the airport," he said, and they wanted to know his name. He felt like telling them he'd be the only person in front of Denny's waiting for a cab, but instead he just told them his name was Eddie. "Be ten minutes, Eddie," said the woman on the other end of the line, and the cab showed up in eight.

The girl at the Hertz counter was happy to rent Holden Blankenship a Nissan Sentra. He called ahead on one of the courtesy phones across from baggage claim and booked himself into a Days Inn, and the room was ready for him by the time he drove there. He unpacked, took a shower, turned the TV on, surfed through a slew of cable channels, turned it off again, and stretched out on the bed. But he sat up almost immediately, convinced he'd left the wrong phone in Room 204 at the Laurel Inn.

He found his phone—if in fact that's what it was. It looked all right, but the truth was he'd never really looked at it much since he bought it, and hadn't looked much at the one Mr. Ear Hair had given him, either, and—

He opened it up and hit Redial, and it rang twice before Dot got to it. He relaxed when he heard her voice. They talked for a few minutes, and he brought her up to date.

"I'm in a holding pattern," he said, "and I think I just made things more complicated than they needed to be. They have to let me know when it's okay to do the work, and I just made it impossible for them to contact me."

"If a phone rings and it's underneath a mattress, does it make a sound?"

"Not when it's turned off. I'll have to check the desk for messages."

"Or maybe they can send you signals through the fillings on your teeth."

"If I were any more paranoid, I'd probably worry about that. I'd have to make myself a protective cap out of tinfoil."

"You can laugh all you want," she said, "but they work like a charm."

The days passed slowly. Periodically he checked the Laurel Inn for messages, and on the third day the clerk read a number for him to call. He called, and a voice he didn't recognize asked his name. "Leroy Montrose," Keller said. "I'm supposed to call this number."

"Hang on," the voice said, and a moment later the man with the ear hair came on the line. "You're a hard man to get hold of, Leroy," he said. "You don't answer your phone and you don't check your voice mail."

"You gave me a dead phone," Keller told him. "And no charger. I figured you'd know to call the room."

"Jesus, I coulda sworn—"

"Suppose I just call this number a couple of times a day," Keller said. "That'll work, won't it?"

The man wanted to bring him another phone, or a charger, or both, but Keller managed to talk him out of it. He'd call that number every morning and afternoon, and before he turned in for the night. And, he added, with a little steel in his voice, he hoped it wouldn't be too much longer, because Des Moines was an okay place, but he had things to do back home.

"Probably tomorrow," the fellow said. "Gimme a call first thing in the morning."

But the first thing he'd done the following morning, after a quick breakfast down the street, was find his way back to Gregory Dowling's ranch house in West Des Moines. He'd driven past it once before, just to make sure he remembered where it was, and this time his quarry was out in front again, not watering the lawn but on his knees alongside a flower bed, doing something with a trowel.

Keller had taken the trouble to leave his Days Inn room so that he wouldn't need to return to it. He'd packed his bag, wiped down the few spots he might have touched, and did everything but drop his key at the desk. If he got the go-ahead from his contact, he could take out the target and go straight to the airport. If not, the room would be waiting for him.

Without having planned it, he braked to a stop right in front of Dowling's house, leaned across the front seat, rolled down the window. He couldn't quite bring himself to honk, it struck him as impolite, but he didn't have to; the man had heard the car approach and trotted right over to see if he could be of help. Keller told him he was new in the neighborhood and had managed to get lost trying to find the Rite Aid, and while the fellow was providing elaborate directions, Keller's hand dropped into the pocket where he'd stowed the revolver.

Be nothing to it. Dowling, blissfully unaware, was gripping the window opening with one hand while gesturing expansively with the other. Whip out the gun, point it at him, give him two in the chest. The motor was running, so all he'd need to do was put the car in gear and he'd be around the corner before the body hit the ground.

Or forget the gun and just grab the poor bastard by the hair and the shirtfront. Yank him in through the open window, break his neck, then give him a shove and let him go.

Al might not be happy. But the job would be done, and what could they do, make him come back and do it over?

"Well," Gregory Dowling said, straightening up and stepping back. "If there's nothing else—"

"You've been a big help," Keller told him.

He followed directions to the drugstore—it was as good a place as any to find a pay phone—and called the number. If he'd done that in the first place, he thought, the job would be done by now. Okay, fair enough, he'd make the call now, and if he got the green light he'd go right back and tell the fellow he must have misheard him, and they'd go through the farce again, only this time he'd use the gun or his hands and finish the job once and for all.

He made the call. "No, today's no good," he was told. "Give us a call first thing tomorrow morning."

And he'd done just that, only to get the same message yet again. "Tomorrow," the man told him. "Tomorrow's a sure bet. In fact tomorrow morning you don't even have to check with us, okay? Because it's all set up. Anytime tomorrow, morning or afternoon, you can just go and do what you gotta do."

"We're all set for tomorrow," he told Dot.

"High time."

"You said it. I'll be glad to get back."

"Back to your own bed."

"The bed's okay. Tell you the truth, it's better than my own. I'm overdue for a new mattress."

"The things you don't know about a person."

"What I miss," he said, "is my TV."

"Fifty-inch, hi-def, plasma, flat panel. Did I forget anything?"

"No, and neither did the manufacturer. It's just about perfect."

"You've talked so much about the damn thing I'm gonna have

to get one myself. I feel for you, Keller, having to make do with motel TV."

"What's aggravating," he said, "is there's no TiVo."

"Now there I have to agree with you," she said. "TiVo changed my life. And there you are, poor baby, stuck in Des Moines with all the commercials you used to be able to speed through."

"And I can't pause the thing when I go to the bathroom, or back up when there's a line of dialogue I missed, and—"

"For God's sake, hurry up and come home," she said, "or I'm gonna have to tell Al you need a hardship bonus."

He rang off and started walking over to the TV, then stopped himself. He'd looked up stamp dealers in the Yellow Pages the previous afternoon, and he checked again, and called James McCue to make sure he was open for business. No reason to pack the suitcase this time, as he knew he'd be coming back to the motel, so all he'd done was grab up his Scott catalog and his tongs and head out the door.

That was what, a couple of hours ago? Now the governor of Ohio was dead, and he had to do something and wasn't sure what. If he'd packed his bag and wiped his room down, he wouldn't have to go back to it. But he'd probably be going there anyway, because where else could he go?

4

When he got to the Days Inn he took a slow turn around the parking lot, looking for any sign of police activity, or indeed anyone at all taking a special interest in the place. But it looked the way it always looked, and he parked his car in its usual spot and went to his room.

Inside, he turned on the television set. The assassination of Governor Longford was all over the dial, unless you wanted to watch QVC or the Food Channel. Keller chose CNN and heard a couple of experts trying to estimate the likelihood of riots in Cleveland. The weather, one of them pointed out, was a significant variable. Heat and humidity added up to riot weather, she said, while a cold snap and rain kept folks indoors.

That was sort of interesting, but Keller, stuck in Des Moines, couldn't bring himself to care about the weather in Cleveland. He hung in there while they talked the subject to death, but hit the Mute button in a hurry when they rang in a Nexium commercial.

At least the remote had a Mute button. You couldn't fast-forward, you couldn't pause, and you couldn't reverse, but the one thing you could do was make the damn thing shut up, and he did.

Should he pack?

He wasn't going to try leaving Des Moines, not yet. Whether all of this was coincidence or something a good deal more sinister, he'd be safer holed up than running around in the open. He hadn't done anything, not even what he'd come here to do, but that wouldn't matter to anybody who picked him up with bogus ID and an unregistered handgun just a matter of miles from where Longford had been shot dead.

By two shots from a handgun—that's what someone had been saying, just before they got the weather report from Cleveland, and it just now registered. An unknown assailant brandishing a handgun who'd fired twice at point-blank range and escaped—how, for God's sake?—into the crowd.

A Glock, he thought. A Glock automatic, the gun he'd been offered and turned down. The gun he'd handled.

He could remember the way the grip had fit his hand. And how he'd turned the gun over in his hands, deliberating, before handing it back to the man with the hairy ears. He'd be willing to bet that was the gun they'd used, and that it still had his prints on it. That's why they'd offered him two guns, and the important gun wasn't the one he'd chosen, it was the one he'd touched and rejected.

Well, that really iced the cupcake. All they had to do was pick him up—for anything at all, really—and he was finished. They'd match his prints to the prints on the Glock, and what could he possibly say?

I touched the gun, but I went for the revolver instead, because automatics tend to jam, although this one evidently didn't. And I didn't want to shoot a governor with it, just some mope weeding his lawn, and I never did shoot anybody, so what difference does it make?

Yeah, right.

If his prints were on file, if he'd ever been arrested or ever held a government job, if he'd ever done any of the innumerable things that move them to ink your fingers and record your prints, he wouldn't stand a chance. But he'd led a charmed life thus far, so any prints on the Glock would lead them nowhere for the time being. Until they got their hands on him and got his hands on an ink pad, at which point it was pretty much all over.

Or was he getting ahead of himself here? He didn't know it was the Glock, didn't know that they'd recovered the gun. For all he knew the shooter had taken it away with him, in which case it hardly mattered whose prints were on it. He couldn't be sure that wasn't how it had happened.

Except somehow he did know, just as he'd somehow known all along that this was a setup. And maybe that was why he'd been so ginchy in Albuquerque, all those months ago. There had been something off about Call-Me-Al from the jump. Paying in advance for unspecified services, calling Dot from out of the blue and telling her money was on its way, then calling again to confirm it had arrived and assure her he'd be in touch. And, months later, making contact once more and sending Keller on his way to New Mexico.

It was, he had to admit, not a bad way to hire a hit man. Nobody, not Dot and not the person who did the work, had any idea who Call-Me-Al might be, or where he lived, or anything else about him. So if things went wrong and Keller wound up in a cell, he couldn't get himself a deal by giving up his employer. He could give up Dot, but that's as far back as it would reach, because there was nobody for Dot to give up. Al was out of anybody's reach.

Say you were planning an extremely high-profile assassination. You wanted a patsy, a fall guy, to give some latter-day Warren Commission a plausible explanation of what had taken place.

Keller had never spent a lot of time on conspiracy theories, and was by no means convinced that the official explanations were wrong; it seemed entirely possible to him that Lee Harvey Oswald, acting alone, had shot down John F. Kennedy, and that James Earl

Ray had done the same for Martin Luther King. He wasn't going to bet the rent money that it happened like that, but he wouldn't bet the other way, either. Both subjects seemed unlikely assassins, but was either one of them as wildly improbable as Sirhan Sirhan, the killer so witless they had to name him twice? And there was no question that he'd shot Bobby Kennedy, because they'd caught him in the act.

But never mind what actually happened. If you were orchestrating something like that, a fall guy was a handy thing to have. And the best sort of fall guy would be someone who did this sort of thing for a living. If you wanted to frame someone for murder, why not pick a murderer? Hire him to kill some nonentity, and time it so he's in the right place at the right time, and then frame him for the real killing, the important killing. But don't let him actually do it, because then he might wind up in a position to rat you out. This way, when the cops picked him up, he couldn't say anything because he wouldn't know anything, and the closest he could come to giving a good account of himself would be to start yammering about how he'd come here to Des Moines to kill someone else. Some poor schlump with no criminal ties and no one looking to kill him, some guy whose sole offense was overzealous lawn care.

Wonderful. The cops would love that one. Jesus, if they did pick him up, he'd know better than to try to sell that story. Or, for that matter, any other story he could come up with just now.

He was sitting in front of the television set, his eyes on the screen, but he was too caught up in his own train of thought for his mind to pay any real attention to what his eyes were seeing. None of it registered, until something about the image on the screen forced its way into his consciousness.

It was a picture of a man, though why they were showing it was unclear, as the sound was still muted. Keller didn't recognize the guy, and yet it seemed to him that there was something familiar about him. He was middle-aged, with a full head of dark hair and something furtive about him. Not the face of someone you'd be inclined to trust, and—

He shot out a hand, groped for the remote. By the time he'd triggered the Mute button it was too late, the picture was gone, and the news itself gone with it. They played a commercial, one Keller especially hated, the one with the moth coming in to assure the sleeping woman of eight hours of restful sleep. Any woman he'd ever known, a moth came in and settled on her face, what she'd do was leap up and start screaming, then pick up a broom and chase the thing all over the house.

He looked for a button to push to back the thing up, but this was TiVo-less TV, and you had to watch everything in real time. And he'd missed it, but who said CNN was the only game in town? He began switching channels, getting half-second glimpses of everything from a lacrosse match to a Texas Hold-'Em tournament, from a rerun of *The Match Game* to a hair replacement infomercial, and before he knew it he'd run the table and was back at CNN, staring once again at his own picture on the screen.

Furtive? Is that how he'd seen himself? No he just looked a little tentative, as if he was trying to work out what he was doing there, with his face on national TV for all the world to see.

The sound was on now, and somebody was saying something, but he couldn't take it in; it was all he could do to look at his own unfortunate face and the caption under it.

THE FACE OF A KILLER, it said.

5

The first thing he did was call Dot. After all the years they'd worked together, that was pretty much an automatic reaction. He picked up the phone, hit Redial, and let it ring. Voice mail cut in after the fourth ring, and he sat there with his mouth open for a long moment, then decided it was pointless to leave a message. He closed the phone and sat there, looking at the TV some more.

Ten minutes later he was in the bathroom, taking a shower.

He'd resisted the idea at first, deeming it a waste of time, but what else was he going to do with his time? Waste some more of it staring at the TV, switching channels until he found one that would proclaim his innocence? Hop in the car and make a run for it? Drive over to Dowling's house and strangle him with his garden hose? He'd showered that morning, he didn't really need a shower, but who could say when he'd get the chance to shower again? Maybe he'd be living in subway tunnels and sleeping in his clothes, maybe he'd be hopping freight trains. He might as well stay as clean as possible for as long as he could.

Or was he running a risk by showering? Hair from his head or his body could wind up going down the drain and get caught in the trap, and a CSI crew could recover it and determine his DNA.

But he'd already showered several times in the course of his stay, so the trap was probably overflowing with his DNA.

For a moment he considered opening the drain himself and trying to get rid of the evidence, but then it struck him that DNA was the least of his worries. They already had his fingerprints, so what possible difference could it make if they had his DNA as well? Once they picked him up, once they got their hands on him, he was finished. DNA wasn't going to figure in the equation.

He got out of the shower and stood in front of the sink and shaved. He'd already done so a few hours ago, he could barely feel any stubble even against the grain, but when would he get to shave again? And why not leave a little more DNA in the sink trap, just for the hell of it?

He got dressed, and packed his bag. He might not be going anywhere, not until he figured out what to do next and when to do it, but it wouldn't hurt to be ready to leave at a moment's notice.

His bag was black, like everybody else's, and had wheels and a handle. It was small enough to carry onto an airplane, and would fit easily in an overhead compartment, but nowadays he always checked it because anything as dangerous as a pair of stamp tongs or as potentially explosive as a tube of hair gel would send the airport security people into a frenzy. And when they spotted his Swiss Army knife they'd call out the National Guard.

If he'd known he was going to be checking it all the time, he'd have bought another color. It seemed to him that three out of four bags coming down the baggage carousel were essentially indistinguishable from his, and he'd come to envy the few garishly colored ones that you saw now and then. To make it a little easier to find his own bag, he'd bought a flame-orange device to wrap around the handle, and it helped. Dot had assured him it would serve a dual purpose; it might help keep some hunter from mistaking his suitcase for a deer.

Dot. He picked up the phone, hesitated, then hit Redial. It rang four times and switched him to voice mail, with a computerized voice inviting him to leave a message. Once again he decided against it, and was about to ring off when he noticed an icon on the screen indicating that he'd received a voice mail message himself. It took him a moment to remember how to retrieve it.

"You have one messages," a recorded voice informed him. "First message."

First and only, he thought.

And then there was silence, ten or fifteen seconds of it, enough to make him wonder if there was going to be a message after all. And then a computer-generated voice, completely uninflected and straight out of a science-fiction movie, pronounced a series of words one at a time:

"Ditch. The. Phone. Repeat. Ditch. The. Damn. Phone."

He stared at the phone as he might have stared at a talking dog. It was Dot, it could only be Dot. Nobody else had his cell number, and who else would have repeated the message and inserted *damn* the second time around? But how had Dot managed to turn herself into a robot?

Then he remembered. A neat trick she'd discovered in one of the applications she ran on her computer. You highlighted a piece of text, pressed something or other, and the computer read the words aloud in a voice all its own. *Just. Like. That. One. Robotic. Word. At. A. Time.*

Voiceprints, he thought. That's what she was guarding against. You could beat voiceprint identification by whispering, or at least you used to be able to, but who knew how much better they'd made the mousetrap?

He called voice mail again, listened to the message again, and this time when the voice mail lady offered him the options of repeating or saving or erasing the message, he chose Erase. "Message is erased," she told him, and the little voice mail icon vanished from the screen.

Ditch the phone. Ditch the damn phone.

How? Just toss it?

If someone found it, and if FBI technicians went to work on it, who could say what it would tell them? They could find out the number he'd called and when he'd called it. They couldn't recover the actual conversations, at least he didn't see how they could, but why leave anything to chance?

One bullet would take care of the phone forever, but it might attract unwelcome attention, and at the very least it would reduce his arsenal by a fourth. He should have taken Hairy Ears up on his offer of a box of shells, but at the time all he'd had to be able to do was kill one person. It never occurred to him that he'd wind up running for his life.

He unloaded the gun, weighed the four bullets in his hand, set them down gently on the bed. A revolver was a pretty simple device, and you couldn't make it fire by hitting something with the butt, but enough strange things had already happened today and he didn't want to risk another. He took the unloaded revolver and the treacherous cell phone into the bathroom, wrapped the phone in a towel, placed it on the floor, and smashed it to bits with the gun butt.

He opened the towel and looked at the collections of bits and pieces of what had moments ago been a sophisticated and very useful machine. It was no longer a threat to him, could not lead anyone to him, wherever he might be, or to Dot's house in White Plains.

Nor was it the lifeline it had been, the link to the only person on earth who could help him, or was likely to want to. Well, she couldn't help him now. Nobody could help him.

He was on his own.

6

He was ready when the knock came. The pizza and Coke came to twelve dollars and change, and he had a ten and a five in hand. "Just leave it outside the door," he told the delivery man. "We're, uh, a little on the informal side at the moment. Here you go, fifteen bucks, keep the change."

He slid the bills under the door and watched them disappear. There was a peephole in the door, and he saw the delivery guy straighten up, hesitate for a long moment, and then walk away. Keller waited a couple of minutes, then opened the door and retrieved his meal.

He wasn't hungry, but he made himself eat just as he'd made himself shower and shave, and for a similar reason, because who knew when he'd get the chance again? His face was appearing on every TV screen in America, and when the paper came out it would be there, too. It wasn't a very good likeness, and he'd been blessed with a fairly generic face, with no outstanding features to grab onto, but when a few hundred million people had been exposed to that picture, it stood to reason that one of them would recognize him.

So it wouldn't be a good idea to go to Denny's, say, and treat himself to another of those patty melts.

No, he'd have to stick to food he could have delivered, and that would only work so long as he had a place for them to deliver it to. The only person who'd seen his face at the Days Inn was the clerk on duty when he'd registered, and that had been quick and easy and he doubted he'd made much of an impression. Desk clerks saw hundreds of people every day, and barely looked at them. He himself had only seen one desk clerk this trip, and had entirely forgotten what she looked like, so why shouldn't she have forgotten him as completely?

On the other hand, suppose he were to see her picture, over and over and over. How long would it take before she started looking curiously familiar to him? How long before he remembered who she was?

He ate some of the pizza, drank half of the Coke. The four bullets were still on the bed where he'd put them, and he scooped them up and loaded them back into the gun, leaving an empty chamber under the firing pin. He tried the gun in a pocket, then slipped it under the waistband of his trousers, then put it in the suitcase. And if he needed it in a hurry? What was he going to do, open the suitcase for a quick draw? He got it out of the suitcase and returned it to its place under his waistband.

He didn't want to watch television, but what else could he do? How else would he know when it was time to cut and run?

They kept showing his picture, and he began studying it, no longer interested in what his facial expression suggested or how good a likeness it was, but instead trying to figure out when and where they'd taken it. Not this past week, not here in Des Moines, because he was wearing a khaki poplin windbreaker in the photo, and he hadn't even brought it along this trip, choosing a navy blue blazer instead. He recognized that windbreaker, he'd bought it from a Lands' End catalog two years ago and, while there was nothing wrong with it, he hadn't worn it much.

Albuquerque, he thought. He'd worn it to Albuquerque.

And had he been wearing that burnt-orange polo shirt? That's what he seemed to be wearing in the photo, although it was a little hard to be sure of the color. Had he worn it when he did that other job for Al, when he'd shuttled a man named Warren Heggman out of this world and into the next?

Maybe, maybe not. That wasn't the sort of thing he could remember. But he was pretty sure he'd worn the windbreaker to Albuquerque, and he'd have still had it on when he rang Heggman's bell and punched Heggman's ticket, because he hadn't had time to unpack and change. He'd checked into three different rooms under three different names, but never left his bag in any of them, never even opened it until he was back in New York.

So they were setting him up even then. Taking his picture. They'd probably have done more if he'd given them more time, but he was in and out in nothing flat, so all they had was that one picture of him.

And they'd managed to give it to the authorities. With what sort of story? *"I saw this man running away, and then he stopped and turned and I got this picture of him."* It might not make much sense, but a picture was a picture, and it was something to hand to the media so they could plaster it all over the public consciousness, and maybe it would lead to something.

Did the bastards know his name? They wouldn't have learned it from Dot, and he couldn't think how else they might have found it out. If he'd taken his time in Albuquerque it might have been different, they might have searched his room, might have even tailed him back to New York. He'd flown to Albuquerque via Dallas but took the long way home, through Los Angeles, and it didn't seem likely anyone could have followed him.

If they didn't know his name, or where he lived—

But then the TV caught his attention again, and he found out that they—the authorities, not Al and his hairy-eared associate—knew a little more than they had a few minutes ago.

They had a name to go with the photo.

"Leroy Montrose," the announcer said. The screen showed his photograph, then cut to an exterior shot of the Laurel Inn, then to a shot of Room 204, where a forensics unit looked to be hard at work, dredging the carpet for traces of the elusive Mr. Montrose.

While they kept at it, the off-camera voice informed Keller that a member of the Laurel Inn's staff had recognized the photo as that of a patron who had checked in several days earlier—a neat trick, in Keller's opinion, since he'd never checked in at all, or even passed the desk. He'd gone straight to his room from the parking lot in back via a flight of outside stairs, and he'd left the same way. He'd never passed Go, never collected two hundred dollars, and had never spotted or been spotted by anyone who worked for the hotel, or anyone who was staying there, either.

But then anyone could make a phone call. Anyone could claim to be a hotel employee with a good memory. The saving grace, it seemed to Keller, was that it wasn't going to lead anywhere. They wouldn't find his fingerprints in Room 204, or his DNA, or indeed anything of his other than the cell phone he'd left under the mattress, and who knew if they'd even get that far? And if they did, so what? He'd never used the phone, and had wiped his prints from it, so where could it lead them?

Across the street, he thought.

Across the street to Denny's, where he'd sat at a well-lighted table eating that silly sandwich and fries. He could have used his credit card at Denny's, which would have made things a little bit easier for them, but he'd paid cash, and then what had he done?

He'd called a cab from the pay phone inside the restaurant. And waited inside until the cab pulled up. And got in it and told the driver to take him to the airport.

By now they'd be canvassing stores and restaurants in the immediate vicinity of the Laurel Inn. By now, or within a matter of minutes, they'd have shown his picture to the waitresses and cashiers in Denny's, and somebody would have identified it, and somebody would have remembered that he'd called a taxi. They'd check all the cab companies—they were the government, for Christ's sake, they were the state and local cops and the FBI, they had enough manpower on the case to check everything—and they'd find the driver and know he'd gone to the airport, and they'd hit the car rental desks, and if they'd checked with them earlier they'd check them again, and they'd have the credit card and driver's license he'd used, and they'd lighten up on Leroy Montrose and start looking real hard for Holden Blankenship. That was the name they'd be flashing on TV screens and shouting out over the radio, and the name they'd try on motel clerks throughout the Greater Des Moines metropolitan area.

How long before they got to his Days Inn? How long before they kicked his door in?

By the time they did, he'd better be someplace else.

But where?

7

Two rows over, a man in his thirties got out of an SUV, locked its doors with a remote, plunged his hands in the hand-warmer pockets of his windbreaker, and headed across the asphalt toward one of the entrances to the mall. He didn't look particularly furtive, not to Keller, and the odds were he didn't have anything to feel furtive about. He was younger than Keller, and a littler chunkier in the midsection, and the hair that showed under his baseball cap was longer and lighter. The only point of resemblance, as far as Keller could make out, was the windbreaker.

Keller watched him until he disappeared inside the mall. Then he watched somebody else, a woman pushing a shopping cart, and then he watched a kid whose job it was to roam the lot and collect the shopping carts people had abandoned.

Keller wondered what a job like that paid. Minimum wage, he figured. Not a lot of money in a job like that, and not a whole lot of prestige, either, or much in the way of opportunity for advancement. Still, it had its good points. You weren't likely to wind up with your picture on national television and every cop in the world hunting for you.

Maybe that was his mistake, one he'd made a whole lot of years ago. Maybe he should have picked a career of rounding up shopping carts, instead of one that sent him all around the country killing people.

It was just as well he hadn't driven around too much. The Sentra's gas tank was still a little more than half full. He wasn't sure of its capacity, or what kind of mileage the car got, but if you figured ten gallons left at twenty miles to the gallon then that gave him something like two hundred miles before he needed to gas up.

He'd left his room at the Days Inn just as the day was starting to fade off into twilight, and he'd have liked to have it still darker for the short walk from his room to his car. There was no one around, but he still felt impossibly conspicuous, and he was pretty sure he looked at least as furtive as he had in the photograph, because now he had so much more to be furtive about. He'd tried not to let it show in his walk or in the way he held himself, and either it worked or there was nobody looking at him to begin with, but he reached his car and got in it and got out of there.

He hadn't gone very far. He'd driven directly to this large shopping mall, and had picked a spot that was out of the main stream of traffic without being conspicuous in its isolation. His bag was in the trunk, his gun tucked into his waistband and pressing into the small of his back. The box with the remaining three slices of pizza was on the seat beside him, along with the cup the Coke had come in; he'd rinsed it out, and now it held the broken bits of the cell phone. He could have abandoned them in his room, but decided he'd rather leave the place as empty as he'd found it. And why give them anything to work with?

If he'd had the run of the mall, there was a lot he could have accomplished. A wig or a false beard would look ridiculous (though probably not much more so than the real beard he'd tried, years ago, to grow), but he ought to be able to change his appearance a little bit without calling attention to himself.

Glasses would help. He didn't need glasses, not even for reading, although he had a feeling he would in a couple of years.

If he lived that long—

No, he thought, willing the thought away. He didn't need glasses, not even for reading, but he kept a pair of reading glasses at home for when he put in long hours working on his stamp collection. They were nondistorting magnifying lenses, and all they did was make print a tiny bit larger and more visible. There was no reason to wear them away from his desk, but he didn't get dizzy when he did, and he'd seen how he looked in them. They'd changed the whole shape of his face, and changed his affect at the same time. Glasses were supposed to make you look studious, and he supposed they did, but beyond that they made you look less threatening.

It would help if he had them now, he thought, because this would be a good time to look less threatening. And he could find a pair just like them in any drugstore, they were a standard and unexceptional item, but he couldn't go shopping for them without giving people a look at his face, and that was something he didn't want to do just now.

The same drugstore where he didn't dare buy reading glasses (or sunglasses, which were even better at changing one's appearance, but which had the disadvantage, especially when the sun was down, of looking like a disguise) would also be a source of hair dye and clippers. A short haircut would make him look less like his photograph, and so would a change of color. Both were on the tricky side, and he certainly didn't want to wind up with a cut that was so amateurish as to attract attention, or hair that screamed *Dye Job* at the top of its roots. Better to wait until he figured out how to do it right, and in the meantime a cap of some sort would help.

How hard was that? It was almost more difficult to find a store that didn't sell baseball caps than one that did. They were all over the place, in all colors and with all manner of logos—sports teams, tractors, brands of beer, anything to which your average unthinking lout could proudly proclaim his allegiance. The nonfurtive guy in the windbreaker had been wearing a cap, and Keller wondered if he owed some of his nonfurtiveness to the cap on his head. A ball cap made you look like a regular guy, just like everybody else.

He looked out the window, and there was a guy with a cap, and there was another.

Maybe that was the answer. Stick around, wait for some poor goober in a ball cap to come back to his car, logy and brain-dead after a carbo-laden meal at Applebee's. Bop him on the head (but not too hard, you didn't want him to bleed all over his baseball cap), snatch the thing off his head, and you were in business.

God, would it come to that? The people he typically dealt with had a five- or six-figure price on their heads. All this guy had on his head was a cap, and the price on it was three figures, with two of them coming after the decimal point.

Well, if he couldn't do any better than that, he could follow the two-birds-with-one-stone principle and pick a guy wearing glasses. And they'd better be sunglasses, because otherwise they'd almost certainly have prescription lenses and he'd get dizzy the minute he put them on.

Bop the guy, grab the ball cap, snatch off the sunglasses—and then go through his pockets, because anybody rich enough to afford a cap and shades probably had fifteen or twenty bucks in his pocket, and, along with everything else, Keller was running out of money.

But he didn't go looking for a man with a cap and sunglasses. He stayed in his car and listened to the radio.

He had it tuned to WHO, an AM station right there in Des Moines, one that billed itself as offering "a well-balanced mixture of news and good old American talk radio." According to the labeling laws, you were supposed to list the ingredients in order, according to the relative proportion of each in the product. If WHO had been playing by the rules, they'd have to call it "a well-balanced mix of commercials, news, and good old etc." And a person would be within his rights to question the use of the word *well-balanced*.

The trouble with radio, Keller had come to realize, was that you couldn't mute it. You could turn it off when a commercial aired, but then how would you know when to turn it on again? Well, you wouldn't. About the best you could do was lower the volume when a commercial came on and raise it again when it ended, but that was really more trouble than it was worth, especially in light of the fact that, more often than not, one commercial ended only to be followed by another.

Between the commercials, though, what got said was pretty interesting. The news was centered almost entirely upon the John Tatum Longford assassination and the ensuing manhunt for Leroy Montrose aka Holden Blankenship.

And so, not too surprisingly, was the talk radio. That was the topic of choice for the great majority of the callers, and those few who got through wanting to discuss something else got short shrift from the host, who was far more interested in the ramifications of the shooting. His callers had a variety of points of view on the subject; while nobody came out and said it was just as well that Longford was permanently out of the running for the presidency, it was clear some of them felt that way, just as others saw the man as a tragic victim right up there with a King and a pair of Kennedys.

And, as with those earlier assassinations, the conspiracy theorists were already sharpening their blunt instruments. Montrose/Blankenship, they were quick to assert, was as much a victim as the Ohio governor, an innocent man conveniently on the scene to divert suspicion from the real killers. The several callers who took this stance all agreed on this much, but here their scenarios diverged as each found a different cabal to blame for hatching the plot in the first place. One woman had the whole thing linked to the forcible inoculation of young girls with "that alleged anticancer virus," while another saw it as part and parcel of the whole pro-abortion campaign. A man with a tobacco-raddled throat was sure the use of a handgun smacked of a campaign to discredit the NRA, and by the time he was through, Keller was alarmed to realize he'd been nodding along in agreement.

It was almost comforting that there were people who thought he hadn't done it, although their tendency to tag him with phrases like "pathetic dupe" and "hapless moron" didn't thrill him. What was a little disquieting, though, was that every last one of the folks on his side, if you wanted to call it that, came off sounding absolutely barking mad.

The actual news wasn't a whole lot more comforting. It hadn't taken the cops long to follow the route Keller had already sketched out for them in his mind, from the Laurel Inn to Denny's to the cab and the airport and the Hertz counter, and at that point he began to hope they'd get to the Days Inn in a hurry and spend a lot of time there.

Because now that they knew what kind of car he was driving, and knew the number on its license plate, it hardly mattered whether he was driving or parked. Either way it was just a matter of time before they found him, and probably not very much time at that.

He couldn't just walk away from the Sentra. He needed a car, and he couldn't rent another to replace this one. He could probably steal one, he'd learned long ago how to pop a door lock and hot-wire an ignition, and those skills of one's youth were like swimming and riding a bicycle. Once learned, they were never forgotten.

Which was to say he'd have no trouble stealing a 1980 Chevy, say. His Swiss Army knife was enough to cope with a car of that vintage. But automobiles had changed since he'd learned how to steal them, and they had computers now, and security devices that could lock the steering wheel if they sensed that something illicit was going on. What was he going to do, look for an old car?

The kind of car he knew he could steal would probably break down after a few hundred miles. Even if it held up, it would be conspicuous. That was one great advantage of the car he had now—it was pretty ordinary in appearance, and at least in Des Moines it was as common as dirt. Driving around, it had seemed as though one in ten cars was the same make and model as the one he was driving, and the greater portion of them seemed to be the same color, too, a kind of indescribable hybrid of beige and gun metal. He had no idea what the manufacturer called the color, but suspected it was something abstract, like Seabreeze or Perseverance, that managed to sound okay without narrowing things down too much. Whatever you called it, the Nissan people had used it on half the cars they sold that year, and they'd evidently found a lot of takers for it in Iowa.

In fact—

Wasn't that a car just like his up ahead in the next row? It was hard to tell in this light, but it was definitely a Sentra, and the color looked right. Was this an opportunity? It certainly felt like an opportunity. He could leave his car and take this one, if he could break in and hot-wire it. Or, even better, he could just—

He could just forget the whole thing, because while he was looking at the car its lights flashed on and off. There was an instant when he thought the car was winking at him, trying to get his attention, but a second later he realized it was simply signaling its response to its owner, who had just unlocked its doors with her remote control. And he watched as she loaded her purchases into its trunk and opened the door on the driver's side and settled in behind the wheel.

If he'd beaten her to it, if he'd switched his car for hers, it wouldn't have done him any good. She'd have realized the deception as soon as she returned to her car, and in no time at all the police would have a new plate number for him. And they might have more than that, if her car had a GPS unit in it.

Oh, hell. Did his?

It stood to reason that the rental car companies would put something in their cars in case they lost track of them. He didn't know that they did, but he knew some long-haul trucking firms equipped their rigs in that fashion, to guard against the occasional amphetamine-crazed driver on his way from Little Rock to Tulsa suddenly deciding he'd be happier in San Francisco.

He really had to do something. And he had to do it in a hurry, and it had better be something that wouldn't just substitute one peril for another.

He turned off the radio—it was just making it harder to concentrate—and he took a bite of pizza and wished he had some Coke left to wash it down.

And then it came to him. He forced himself to sit still, forced himself to chew the pizza and swallow it, forced himself to wait while he thought it through to make sure it was sound. And, when he decided he couldn't see anything wrong with his idea, he turned the key in the ignition and put the car in gear.

8

The third time was supposed to be the charm.

The best place to find a car that no one would return to in a hurry, he'd decided, was the long-term parking lot at Des Moines International. And that was also the best place he could think of to abandon a car; whoever found it would figure he'd somehow slipped past them and caught a flight somewhere.

And this was a good time of day to be driving around the long-term lot. There were still flights arriving and departing, so the lot wasn't entirely deserted, in which case he'd have been apt to attract attention. But the peak hours for air traffic in and out had passed, so he was less likely to pick a car that someone would be coming back for anytime soon.

What he wanted was a car just like his. He didn't need to start it, because he wasn't going to drive it anywhere, but he'd have to be able to get into it. He could probably manage that with his knife; failing that, he could break a window. But maybe there was a better way.

He tried three times without success, pulling up behind a parked Sentra, pointing his own remote device at its rear and pressing the trunk release. He didn't think for a moment that every Nissan Sentra would respond to the same remote, but there were only so many frequencies, and sooner or later he almost had to get lucky.

Except he didn't have forever. Eventually he'd run out of Sentras, if he didn't run out of time first. One more, he told himself, hoping the fourth time would be the charm, pulling up to the fourth car, putting his own car in park, removing the key from the ignition, putting it back, starting the car so he could lower the window, then retrieving the key again—you'd really think, wouldn't you, that he could have remembered to lower the window first, or left it down after the previous attempt?—and aiming the remote at the other car's trunk, and pressing the button and holding it, because it wouldn't open right away, you had to keep the thing pointed at the trunk and hold the button down for a few seconds, and what difference did it make because it wasn't going to work anyway . . .

Except this time it did.

He had to act quickly now. First thing he did was open his own trunk (with a button on the dashboard, so he didn't have to screw around with the remote). The trunk of the new Sentra was half full of stuff, and without paying any attention to what it was, he transferred everything but the spare tire to his own trunk. There it could keep his black suitcase company.

He used a rag to wipe down the inside of the now-empty trunk, then closed both trunks and used the remote to unlock the doors. It had worked on the trunk, so he wasn't surprised when it worked on the doors, too, but it was a relief all the same, because he'd pretty much given up expecting anything to go right.

He emptied the glove compartment, gave it a wipe, and replaced its contents with the Hertz folder and operator's manual from his own car. There were maps of Iowa and, less predictably, Oregon, in the door pocket of the new car, and he collected those, along with a couple of losing lottery tickets from the floor and a supermarket receipt from the back seat. When the car's interior was empty, he wiped the surfaces that were likely to have accumulated prints, not to get rid of his own—he'd been careful not to leave any—but to erase the more obvious traces of the car's owner.

They'd given him a claim check when he entered Long-Term Parking, and he'd stuck it in his breast pocket. But the owner of the other Sentra had guarded against misplacing his own claim check, and left it under the clip on the sun visor. Keller, who hadn't even thought about that aspect of things, promptly switched checks.

But could he afford it? If he used his own check he'd pay the minimum, which was just a couple of dollars. But if the other guy had left the car for a week or two, the charges could eat into the small amount of cash he had left.

He checked, and the thing had a time and date stamped on it. It had been parked less than twenty-four hours earlier, so at most it would cost him an extra five dollars, and he decided it was worth it. He left his original tag under the visor, kept the new one in his pocket.

And he substituted a few touches of his own. The pizza box (minus the two remaining slices, which could remain on the passenger seat of his car, because he still didn't know where his next meal was coming from) found a place on the passenger seat of the new car. The fragments of the cell phone went in the new car's trunk, and he drew a certain grim satisfaction from the image of all the FBI's horses and men knocking themselves out reassembling the thing. The cup that had once held Coca-Cola before it had held the ruined phone was now empty, tossed for verisimilitude onto the floor in back.

What else?

Well, he hadn't gotten around to the most important thing of all. But the two cars didn't have to be close to each other for the next step, and he'd be better off getting his own car out of the way. He started it up, found a place to park it, used his Swiss Army knife to remove the front and rear license plates, hunkered down in the shadows while a car crept by, and then carried them to the other car. He switched the plates, returned the new set to the original car, attached them, and drove off, wondering what he'd forgotten.

He couldn't think of a thing.

Could it work?

Well, it seemed to him that it had a shot. For a while, anyway. The minute he left the long-term lot, he was no longer in a car of interest to the authorities. Well, the car was still of interest to them, it was the same car he'd been driving all along, but they didn't know that, because it had a different license plate on it.

He could have switched plates with any car. It didn't have to be the same make and model as his, nor did it have to be stashed in a lot at the airport. But that would only shelter him until the car's owner noticed the switch, or got pulled over by someone who recognized the plate. As soon as that happened, the police would have a new plate number to look for, and he'd be back in their sights all over again.

But if this worked, he'd have some breathing room. Because he wasn't just giving them the old plate, he was providing a car to go with it. They'd find the car, with his rental papers in the glove box. They'd find the smashed-up phone, and they'd probably get a print off the pizza box, and what conclusion would they draw? That he'd switched cars? That he'd switched plates and kept the same old car?

No, they'd almost certainly assume that he'd come to the airport because it was in fact an airport, with the intention of getting on a plane. And they'd have a tough time establishing unequivocally that he hadn't somehow managed to slip through Security and do just that.

Eventually, of course, the real owner of the Sentra would return. But he wouldn't find his car, because they'd have long since hauled it away and very likely stripped the thing down to the chassis, until it would be about as easy to put back together as the cell phone.

So what would he do? After he'd looked all over the lot for it, and very likely cursed a blue streak, what would the guy do?

Report it as stolen, most likely. And the police would add the vehicle to the national hot car list, where it would have thousands of others for company. That meant that police officers all over the country would be looking for it, but it didn't mean they'd be looking very hard. If he was in an accident, if he got stopped for speeding, someone would run the plate and determine that the vehicle was stolen. But if he was just driving around and minding his own business, nobody would give him a second glance.

It would be just as well, though, to point them toward the Sentra sooner rather than later. It would probably be at least a day or two before the owner returned, but that wasn't the only reason to get things moving. As soon as they identified the car and followed their noses into the airport terminal, they'd get out the word to stop searching for the car, and all Nissan Sentras, including the one he was driving, would stop attracting untoward attention.

So should he call it in?

Caller ID, a staple on every 911 line, would immediately pinpoint the pay phone he called from. He'd be long gone before anybody could stop by to ask questions, but was there a better way?

The station had a toll-free number, and it had imprinted itself on his memory somewhere in the course of the few hundred times they'd announced it. He picked a pay phone at the far end of a strip mall with all its stores closed for the night. When a man with a good radio voice said, "WHO, Central Iowa's leader in news and opinion, you're on the air," he took a breath and said, "Hey, is there a reward for spotting that car everybody's looking for? On account of I just seen it out by the airport."

"You should have had your dial set to 740," the fellow said. "They found the car, and we had it on the air a full five minutes ago. You missed the boat, hoss."

He said, "So do I get the money or not?" and heard a short bark of laughter before the phone clicked in his ear.

"I guess that's a no," he said out loud. And got back in the car and started driving.

9

One moment he was dreaming, some variant on a dream he'd had off and on his whole life, the one where he was naked in public. It wasn't a difficult dream to interpret, and had been one of the first things he and his therapist tackled in that long-ago failed experiment in self-discovery. But he still dreamed it every once in a while, and after all these years a sense of recognition took a lot of the edge off the dream. *Oh, you again*, he'd think, and then sink back into the apparent reality of the dream.

This time the dream was suddenly over and he was as suddenly awake, with no real memory of the dream and no other evidence that he'd been asleep. He was sitting upright behind the wheel of his car, and he kept his eyes closed while he got his bearings. He had the awful feeling that the car was surrounded by men with drawn guns, men who were just waiting for him to open his eyes. But they would go on waiting as long as he pretended to be asleep, so that's what he had to do, just sit there with his eyes shut, his breathing regular and shallow.

He opened his eyes. There was nobody standing anywhere near the car. A pickup truck was parked at an angle half a dozen spaces away, its engine idling, and there was a big RV clear down at the other end of the strip, which he seemed to remember from when he pulled off the road and parked. Other than that the place was deserted.

He was in a rest area off U.S. Route 30 west of Cedar Rapids. He'd taken I-80 out of Des Moines, then decided he'd rather stay off the interstate, at least until he was out of Iowa. The map had shown him what looked like a good road angling northeast toward Marshalltown, and he took it as far as Route 30 and aimed himself at Cedar Rapids. From there he'd have a choice of a few routes—northeast to Dubuque, where he could cross the Mississippi into southern Wisconsin, or stay on 30 east to Clinton and cross into Illinois, or another road that angled between those two. He didn't think it mattered much which route he chose, but the one thing he wanted to do was get out of Iowa and into either Illinois or Wisconsin as soon as possible. And it looked as though he could do that without having to fill the gas tank.

What he hadn't taken into account was fatigue. It wasn't that late, and he hadn't gotten up that early, but the stress he'd been under had evidently taken its toll, and he started yawning and felt himself losing concentration well before the approach to Cedar Rapids. He tried to shake off the tiredness, and thought about stopping somewhere for a cup of coffee, but the whole point was not to stop before he had to and not to expose himself to human eyes if he could possibly avoid it. Besides, he knew coffee wasn't going to do it. The last thing his body wanted was a stimulant. What it was crying out for was a chance to shut down for a while.

The rest area, when he came upon it, was a godsend. A sign announced that it was closed from two to five A.M., and that violators would be prosecuted. He'd heard somewhere that rules like that were designed to keep prostitutes from working the area, setting up shop and hailing passing truckers on their CB radios. Keller, who couldn't imagine how either of the parties involved, the hookers or the truckers, could be quite that desperate, also couldn't figure out what business it was of anybody else's. But he gathered that an ordinary motorist closing his eyes for a couple of hours wouldn't get bothered, and the presence of the trailer at one end of the rest area and a couple of cars at the midpoint suggested he wasn't alone in this conclusion. So he'd found a place to park, far away from the others, and he'd shut down the engine and locked the doors, and then he closed his eyes, figuring twenty minutes or a half hour would have him as good as new.

He hadn't bothered to check the time when he called it a night, but it couldn't have been much later than one or two, and it was just past five now, so he'd slept three or four hours. That was time he couldn't afford to spend standing still, but on the other hand he had clearly needed the rest. Now he could get back on the road. Or, even better, he could think things through with a sleep-refreshed brain, and *then* he could get back on the road.

He looked at the map, decided he'd do best to stay on 30. That was the most direct route. Earlier, Dubuque had held some appeal for him because he'd at least heard of it, which wasn't true of Clinton. Now, in the cool light of day, or what would be the cool light of day in an hour or so when the sun came up, he could see that the most important thing was to get across a state line, not to pass through a town he'd heard of. (And it wasn't as though he'd heard anything particularly alluring about Dubuque. In fact, the only thing he could recall about it was the advertising slogan *The New Yorker* magazine had used back when he was a boy. *Not for the Old Lady from Dubuque,* they'd boasted, which had had the effect of making the magazine sound wonderfully sophisticated, while no doubt pissing off any number of old ladies and Dubuquers.)

How you do go on, he thought to himself, only the voice he could imagine speaking those words was Dot's. He wished he could hear her voice now, saying those words or almost any others. She was the only person he ever really had a conversation with. He didn't spend his days in stony silence, he'd exchange a few words with his doorman, banter with the waitress in the coffee shop on Lexington Avenue, talk about the weather with the guy at the newsstand or discuss the fortunes of the Mets and Yankees, Nets and Knicks, Giants and Jets—depending on the season—with guys he ran into at the gym or in a bar or waiting for an elevator.

But he didn't really know anybody except Dot, and hadn't let anyone else know him. It was rare that he went more than a couple of days without talking to her. And now she was the one person he couldn't call.

Well, actually, she was one of the several hundred million people he couldn't call, because he couldn't call anybody. But she was the one person he wanted to call and couldn't, and it bothered him.

And then he heard her voice in his head. It wasn't uncanny, it wasn't some eerie visitation, it was just his own mind pretending to be Dot and telling him what it thought she would tell him. *You damn near threw your back out shifting all that crap from one trunk to the other,* the voice said. *Don't you think you ought to at least see what you've got?*

Whoever's idea it was, his or Dot's, it wasn't a bad one, and this was the perfect time to do it, with no one around to take an interest in him or what he was doing. He popped the trunk and pulled out a cardboard carton that he'd shifted intact and unexamined from one trunk to the other. He sorted through it now, and if he made it all the way to the ocean it might prove useful, because it was all stuff for the beach—little toy buckets and sand shovels, bathing suits, beach towels, and a Frisbee. That last wasn't exclusively for the beach, you could throw a Frisbee just about anywhere, as long as you had somebody to throw it to. If he had to throw it, he supposed he would throw it away.

And why not toss the whole carton? There was a trash bin just steps from his car, and was there any reason to keep any of this junk? He hoisted it, headed for the bin, then changed his mind, returning to the car and distributing items from the carton on the back seat and floor. A blue and yellow plastic bucket here, a red shovel there. It would be good camouflage, he told himself, because anybody taking a quick peek at the car's interior would know he was looking at the car of a husband and father, not an assassin on the run.

Unless they just figured him for a pedophile . . .

Back to the trunk. There was a metal tool chest of the sort he supposed most men carried in their cars, tricked out with all manner of tools and gadgets, not all of which he was able to identify. Some, he was pretty sure, had to do with fishing; he recognized lead sinkers and plastic floats, as well as a couple of lures with hooks attached, one shaped like a minnow, the other looking for all the world like the little spoons employed by cocaine users. For an instant he let himself imagine some pie-eyed fish, nostrils dilated in glorious anticipation, taking a deep sniff and getting hooked through the gills. Which, metaphorically, was what was supposed to happen to people, though he had no firsthand experience in that area. If Keller was addicted to anything it was to stamps, and they had never been accused of burning holes in anybody's septum.

Though they could certainly burn a hole in a man's pocket. The last purchase he'd made (aside from the pizza, the one remaining piece of which would serve as his breakfast as soon as he finished inventorying the trunk) was five Swedish stamps for $600, abruptly reducing his cash on hand to $187 plus the change in his pocket. Since then, the pizza had claimed $15 and the airport parking lot $7, and he had to buy enough gas to get him halfway across the country. Figure fifteen hundred miles, probably more with the inevitable to-ing and fro-ing, call it twenty miles to the gallon at $2.50 a gallon, and what did that come to?

He ran the numbers in his head and kept coming up with different answers, and finally he took out a pen and a scrap of paper and worked it out. The number he wound up with was $187.50, which seemed high to him, and especially so in view of the fact that it was twenty-two dollars more than he had to his name.

And he would need money for food. He'd worked out a way to buy food without giving anyone a good look at him, but he'd still have to part with cash. And sooner or later—and it had better be sooner—he was going to have to buy a baseball cap, and some product to change his hair color, and some implement he could use to give himself a haircut. (There was a pair of pruning shears in the tool chest, and if he'd been a rosebush they might have worked just fine, but he didn't think they'd do a good job on a human being.) The places that sold the things he needed almost always took credit cards, but if he used one he'd be in worse shape than he was now.

If he had hung on to the $600, he'd be okay. He'd still have problems, and they might well prove insoluble, but running out of money wouldn't be one of them.

Instead, he had five little pieces of paper. Once they could have been used to mail a letter, if he'd happened to be in Sweden and if there happened to be somebody he wanted to write to. Now they weren't even good for that.

He felt like Jack, the young genius who'd traded the family cow for the magic beans. As he remembered the story, everything turned out all right for Jack in the end.

But that, he reminded himself, was a fairy story.

10

Two hours later he crossed the Mississippi at Clinton. A few miles into Illinois, with the gas gauge zeroing in on the big E, he pulled up to one of the full-service pumps at a gas station. They seemed to be in the middle of the local equivalent of rush hour, which struck Keller as all to the good.

The attendant looked to be just out of high school, and trying to come to terms with the prospect of spending the rest of his life on the outskirts of Morrison, Illinois. He had earbuds and looked like an intern with a stethoscope, but Keller could see the iPod in the bib pocket of his overalls, and whatever he was listening to was evidently more interesting than Keller.

He'd lowered the sun visor and positioned it to block the upper half of the side window, which gave the kid less of a view of his face. He asked for forty dollars' worth of regular; he'd have just as soon filled the tank to the brim, but didn't want to have to wait for change. The kid got things going, then came back to ask him if he wanted the oil checked. Keller told him not to bother.

"I had one just like that," the kid said. "That li'l bucket? With the yellow puppy dogs on it? For the beach, you know?"

"My kid's crazy about it," Keller said.

"Wonder what ever became of it," the kid said. He went away, and the next thing Keller knew he was wiping the windshield and making a surprisingly thorough job of it. Keller wanted to tell him to skip that, too, but then the boy would have to wonder what Keller was doing in the full-service section if he didn't want any service. He let him continue, and studied the road map, shielding his face with it.

He wiped the rear window, too, and when he'd finished he came over to the driver's side and Keller handed him a pair of twenties. He thought of offering him a third twenty for his cap, which said *OshKosh B'Gosh* in flowing script that matched the logo on his overalls.

Yeah, right. Or maybe he could trade him the beach bucket for it. A good way to avoid attracting attention.

He'd have welcomed the chance to pick up a few things in the station's convenience store. Or use the men's room. But he had the tank filled, or mostly filled, and that was going to have to be good enough for now.

He kept going eastbound on Route 30, holding the car to fifty-five miles an hour on the stretches of open road, and slowing to the posted speed limit whenever he came to a town. Right after he crossed I-39 he spotted a Burger King with a drive-up window, and he ordered enough burgers and fries and shakes for a whole family. He didn't get a look at the server, and didn't think anyone could have gotten a look at him, and in no time at all he was back on the road.

The next town he came to was called Shabbona, but before he got to it he saw signs for Shabbona State Park, and there he was able to eat at a picnic table and use a restroom, all without encountering another human being.

There was a pay phone, and he was tempted.

According to the radio news, his license plate switch had been successful; the prevailing opinion was that Holden Blankenship had somehow managed to board a plane at Des Moines International Airport. Predictably, there had been sightings. A woman who'd flown from Des Moines to Kansas City was certain she'd spotted Blankenship in the flight lounge adjoining hers, waiting for a Continental departure to Los Angeles. She'd been this close to saying something to somebody, she'd told reporters, but they were boarding her flight and she was anxious to get home.

Other helpful citizens reported catching glimpses of the elusive assassin in locales ranging from small towns in Iowa to large cities on both coasts. A man in Klamath Falls, Oregon, swore he'd seen Blankenship "or his twin brother" standing in front of that city's Greyhound bus terminal, dressed like a cowboy and twirling a lariat, with a six-shooter on each hip. Keller had never dressed like a cowboy or twirled a lariat, nor could he recall a visit to Klamath Falls. But he had been in Roseburg, Oregon, and remembered it well. It seemed to him that Roseburg wasn't all that far from Klamath Falls, and he had a map of Oregon in his door pocket, and was reaching for it to check the precise location of Klamath Falls when he reminded himself that he really didn't care where the town was. He wasn't going there, after all, wasn't even heading in that direction, so the hell with it.

Suppose he used the phone. He couldn't call Dot's cell phone, which he presumed had received much the same treatment he'd given his. But he could call her land line.

To what purpose? She wouldn't be there. Al might or might not know Keller's real name, and where he lived, but he knew Dot's phone number. He'd called it a couple of times. And he knew her address, having sent FedEx parcels to it, some of them containing cash.

And Dot would know that he knew, and act accordingly. *Ditch.*

The. Phone. Repeat. Ditch. The. Damn. Phone. She wouldn't have sent that message if she hadn't had a good read on the situation, and in that case she'd know what she had to do, which was Get Out of Dodge.

So if he called her, no one would answer. Unless the cops were there, or Al's people. If the cops were on the scene, and he called, they might be able to trace it. Al's minions probably couldn't, but he didn't want to talk to them any more than he wanted to talk to the cops, so what was the point of calling?

And he didn't have enough change for a call, anyway. What was he supposed to do, bill it to his home phone? Reverse the charges?

By sticking with Route 30, he managed to bypass Chicago to the south. He liked the highway well enough. The traffic never got all that heavy, and the big trucks mostly kept to the interstate. Towns came along just about often enough to break the monotony of endless highway driving. And there were plenty of places along the way that would have made interesting stops, if he had been able to stop anywhere. But he knew better than to risk it, and drove on past antique shops and nonchain restaurants and all manner of roadside attractions. Someday, he thought, he'd have to drive this road again, when he wasn't in a hurry, when he didn't have a compelling need to avoid human contact, when he was able to lead again the life he'd led back in the old days, when John Tatum Longford still had a pulse.

But would it ever be like that again?

For hours he'd avoided that thought, holding it at bay, keeping it shunted aside on the shoulder of the highway of thought. But it was there now and he couldn't blink it away, couldn't keep from taking a cold-eyed look at it.

One last job. Why couldn't he have told Dot to turn it down?

■ ■ ■

He'd come back from what was supposed to be his final business trip. Before he left, he'd sat down in Dot's kitchen while her fingers did their little dance on the keyboard of her computer. She paused, studied the screen, then looked up to advise him that his net worth, as of the stock market's close the previous day, was just slightly in excess of two and a half million dollars. "You figured you needed a million to retire," she reminded him, "and I didn't say anything, but when I ran the numbers it seemed to me that you ought to have double that to retire in comfort. Well, you've got that and more."

Two years ago, the Indianapolis job had supplied him with some inside information, and she'd opened a trading account to take advantage of it. One thing had led to another, and she'd been investing their money ever since. It turned out to be something she was good at.

"That's amazing," he told her.

"Well, I've been lucky, but I do seem to have a definite knack. And most of what you've earned since then, most of what we've both earned, has gone right into the market, and all of that money has just kept on making more money. No wonder the Chinese have taken up capitalism, Keller. They're no dummies."

"Two and a half million dollars," he said.

"You could fill up every last space in your stamp collection."

"There are individual stamps," he told her, "that you couldn't buy for two and a half million. Just to keep the whole thing in perspective."

"Why would we want to do that?"

"But it's still a lot of money," he allowed. "If I spend a hundred thousand dollars a year, it should last twenty-five years. I'm not sure I'll last that long myself."

"A healthy clean-living boy like you? Of course you will, but don't worry about running out of money in twenty-five years, or even in fifty."

And she'd outlined what she planned to do, as soon as he gave her the go-ahead. He hadn't followed too closely, but the gist of it was that she'd invest the greater portion of his capital in municipal bond funds, yielding 5 percent tax-free, and the rest in stock funds to hedge against inflation. She could set it up so that they'd send him a check every month for $10,000 and never deplete his capital.

"There are people who would kill for a deal like this," she told him, "but then you've already done that, haven't you, Keller? Do this one last job and you can put your feet up and play with your stamps."

He'd pointed out, not for the first time, that one didn't play with stamps, one worked with them, and added that, call it work or play, he never put his feet up while he was so engaged. And he said, "One last job."

"You say it as if there should be organ music playing. Dum-de-dum-dum."

"Well, isn't that how it works? Everything goes fine until that one last job."

"The trouble with that big TV," she said, "is that you watch too much garbage just because it looks so pretty. Nothing's going to go wrong."

And nothing did, remarkably enough, and he came home relieved and relaxed, only to find out that Call-Me-Al, who'd sent along a substantial cash payment on account some months previously, now had something for him to do.

"But I'm retired," he'd said, and she didn't argue the point. She'd long since credited his share of Al's advance payment to his account, but she could deduct it, and find some way to send it back along with her own cut. Except she didn't know how she could go about doing that, because she didn't have a clue where to send the money. All she could do was wait until Al got in touch, demanding to know what was taking so long, at which time she could explain that her guy was dead or in jail, because they never believed anybody retired from this business, and he could tell her where to send the money.

Couldn't she find somebody else? That way there'd be no refund required.

"Well, I thought of that," she said. "But it's been ages since I worked with anybody but you. Once you decided you wanted to work as much as you could so you could fatten up your retirement fund, I started giving you everything that came in. One time I left a client hanging so you could do his job after you came back from the one you were working."

"I remember."

"Not too professional, but we got away with it. I let everything else go, because I'd already decided that the day you retire is the day I hang it up myself."

He hadn't known that.

"And he specifically asked for you, if that matters. Al. 'Please use the chap who did such nice work in Albuquerque.' Isn't it nice to be appreciated?"

"He said chap?"

"Chap or fellow, I forget which. This was in a note, along with the photo and the contact information. He didn't call this time. In fact it's been so long since I heard from him by phone I forget what his voice sounds like. I've probably got the note somewhere, if it matters."

He shook his head. "I guess the simplest thing," he said, "is to go ahead and do it."

"I don't want to push you into it, but I have to say I think you're right."

The simplest thing. Couldn't be simpler, could it?

11

He'd bought a whole day's worth of food at the Burger King, but he'd been thirsty to begin with and the salty food made him thirstier. And the shakes, almost too thick for the straw, didn't help much. On the way into Joliet—a town he knew only as the home of a state penitentiary, which struck him as an even worse way to be famous than Dubuque's—he spotted a strip mall and pulled in. There was a bank of vending machines out in front of the coin laundry, with no end of sweet and salty things that he didn't want, but the Coke machine also offered sixteen-ounce bottles of water. He fed it ten dollars and got four bottles of what the label assured him was pure natural spring water. It was the same price as the soft drinks, and all they had to do was bottle it. They didn't have the expense of adding sugar or artificial sweetener or flavorings or caramel color or really anything at all. On the other hand, it was pure and natural, which was more than you could say for the other offerings, so you really couldn't complain about the price.

When Keller was a boy, the only time he ever saw water in a bottle was on his mother's ironing board; the bottle had a cap with holes punched in it, and she'd sprinkle some water on whatever she was ironing, for reasons Keller had never quite understood.

Keller, like everyone he knew, drank water from the tap, and it didn't cost anybody anything.

Then there came a time when stores began to stock bottled water, but the only people who bought it were the kind of people who ate sushi. Now, of course, everybody ate sushi, and everybody drank bottled water. Outlaw bikers, guys with equal space on their bodies for scars and tattoos, badass bruisers who opened beer bottles with their few remaining teeth, all had their little bottles of Evian to wash down their California rolls.

Keller sat in his car and drank one of the bottles in a few long swallows. On the far side of the coin laundry, next to the Chinese restaurant, was a wall-mounted pay phone. Keller couldn't swear to it, but it seemed to him that you didn't see as many pay phones as you used to, and he supposed it was just a matter of time before they disappeared. Everybody had a cell phone nowadays. Pretty soon you'd have to have a cell phone, either that or learn how to send Indian smoke signals.

The hell with it. He got out of the car, walked over to the phone, dialed Dot's number. The vending machine had given him all his change in quarters, and he actually had the $3.75 the robotic voice demanded for the first three minutes. He loaded the coins into the slot, heard that *coo-wheeeet* sound it made when it couldn't put a call through, followed by a recording telling him the number he had dialed was not a working number. The phone gave him back his quarters.

He tried it again, on the slim chance that he'd misdialed, and the same voice told him the same thing, and once again he got his quarters back.

Well, he thought, evidently she got out, which was all to the good. But would she take the time to disconnect the phone? Would she even want to disconnect the phone? Wouldn't it be better as well as simpler to leave the phone alone, so that anyone trying to get to her would waste time looking for her at home?

Too many questions, and no way to answer them.

He stopped for gas a couple of hours after he crossed into Indiana. The station was small, just a couple of pumps in front of a Circle K convenience store, and they were all self-service. You dipped your credit card, filled your own tank, wiped your own windshield, and drove off without ever seeing or being seen by another human being.

But not if you had to pay cash. Then you had to go inside first and pay the girl behind the counter, and she would program the pump to dispense whatever you'd paid for.

He'd driven in and out of a similar situation fifty miles back, unwilling to risk giving an attendant a look at his face. Now the tank was getting low, and even if he managed to find a full-service pump, that didn't mean whoever pumped the gas for him wouldn't take a good look at him while he was at it. He'd been lucky with the young fellow in Morrison, but it wasn't as if he'd latched onto some magic formula.

But he wouldn't buy forty dollars' worth this time. He'd had time to think about it, and what he'd decided was that people who paid out that much money for gas all at once did so with a credit card. The ones who paid cash didn't part with more than ten or twenty dollars at a time. Pay forty and they might remember you, and Keller didn't want to be memorable.

CASH CUSTOMERS PAY INSIDE FIRST THEN PUMP, the hand-lettered sign said, and the message, even without punctuation, was clear enough. Keller, who'd shucked out of his blazer earlier, put it on now. He figured it made him look just a little more respectable and just a little less deserving of a long look; more to the point, it covered the revolver riding in the small of his back. And he wanted the gun there, because he might have to use it.

He got a twenty from his wallet and had it in his hand when he entered the store. Stores like this got robbed all the time, and he knew some of them had security cameras installed, and wondered if this one did. In the middle of rural Indiana?

Oh, the hell with it. He had enough to worry about.

He entered the store, and the girl was all by herself, reading *Soap Opera Digest* and listening to a country station. Keller slapped the bill down, said, "Hi there twenty dollars' worth pump number two," all in one uninflected gush of words, and was on his way out the door before she could lift up her eyes from her magazine. She called out to him to have a nice day, which he took for a good sign.

Of course she could be doing a double take now, he thought as he pumped the gas. She could be thinking that he looked familiar, and deciding just why he looked familiar, and he could see her jaw dropping and the sense of civic purpose coming into her eyes as she grabbed for the phone and dialed 911.

Keller, how you do go on.

Sixty dollars so far for gas, fifteen for burgers and fries and shakes, ten for bottled water. His bankroll was half of what it had been that morning, just eighty dollars and change. He had burgers left, which were marginally edible cold, and he had french fries, which weren't. And one full shake, which had melted but still wasn't what you'd call liquid. He could, he supposed, live on that all the way back to New York. If he was hungry enough he would eat it, and if he wasn't that hungry it meant he didn't need it.

But the Sentra's requirements were less flexible. He had to keep gas in the tank, and even if OPEC flooded the market with oil, he was going to run out of money before he ran out of highway.

There had to be an answer, but he was damned if he could see it. He'd reached a point where his problems didn't have solutions. Even if the skies opened up and showered him with ball caps and clippers and hair dye, even if he was suddenly blessed with the ability to transform his facial features into those of a different person entirely, he'd be broke, stranded somewhere in eastern Ohio or western Pennsylvania with the philatelic equivalent of a handful of magic beans.

Could he sell the stamps? They had been a genuine bargain, if not precisely a steal, at $600. Could he offer somebody else an even greater bargain and get half his money back for them? What, knock on doors? Go through small-town phone books, looking for stamp dealers? He shook his head, dazzled by the sheer impracticality of the idea. He stood a better chance of pasting the stamps on his forehead and mailing himself to New York.

Other courses of action suggested themselves, and fell equally short. A train? The railroads had pretty much given up on the job of transporting people, although they still ran passenger trains from Chicago to New York and up and down the eastern corridor. But he wasn't sure where he might go to catch a train, and even if he worked that out, it would cost him more money than he had. He'd taken the Metroliner to Washington a while ago, and it was certainly a nice way to travel, and you went from midtown to midtown and didn't have airport security to contend with, but it wasn't cheap, not by a long shot. And now they'd changed its name to the Acela Express, which nobody could pronounce and hardly anybody could afford. If he didn't have gas money, he certainly didn't have train money.

The bus? He couldn't remember the last time he'd been on an intercity bus. He'd traveled by Greyhound one summer during high school, and recalled a jarringly uncomfortable ride in a crowded vehicle full of people smoking cigarettes and drinking bottled whiskey out of paper bags. The bus would have to be inexpensive, because otherwise nobody would willingly ride it.

But it was far too public for a man with his picture on the

nation's TV screens. He'd be cooped up for hours with forty or fifty people, and how many of them would take a look at his face? And, even if they didn't make the connection right away, there he'd be, with no place to hide, and there they'd be, with plenty of time to think about things, and what were the odds that one of them wouldn't put two and two together?

No bus, no train. A voice on the radio, pondering his apparent escape via the Des Moines airport, had theorized that Montrose/Blankenship might have made his way across the tarmac to the area where the private planes landed and took off. He might have had a plane stashed there, with a confederate to fly it, or he might even have possessed the skills to fly it himself. Or, the fellow had gone on to suggest, the desperate assassin might have hijacked a private plane, taking the pilot hostage and forcing him to fly the plane to parts unknown.

Keller had welcomed the notion, because it was so wonderfully ludicrous that it had given him a laugh when he'd sorely needed one. Now, though, he wondered if it was such a bad idea after all. There were small private airports all over the country, with dinky little planes landing and taking off all the time. Suppose he found one, some single-runway operation out in the boondocks. And suppose he bided his time and waited until some hotshot bush pilot had his plane all fueled and ready to go, only to have Keller, the desperate assassin himself, stick a gun in his face and demand to be taken to the corner of East Forty-ninth Street and First Avenue?

Well, maybe not.

The motel was a Travelodge, on the edge of a town the name of which he hadn't bothered to notice. He'd pulled around to the rear of the lot like a registered guest on the way to his room, chosen an out-of-the-way parking spot, and cut the lights and engine. He sat behind the wheel, eating one of the cold burgers and drinking water, and watched a man and woman get out of a square-back Honda and walk a short distance to a ground-floor unit. They didn't have any luggage, Keller noted, and the inference he drew from this was strengthened when the man extended a hand and grabbed the woman by the butt. She swatted his hand away, but when he replaced it she let him keep it there, and the hand stayed in place until he needed it to unlock the door. Then they disappeared into the room.

Keller envied them, and less for what they were about to do than for having a room to do it in. He had no idea what this Travelodge got for a room, but it had to be at least fifty dollars, didn't it? All that money, and they weren't even going to sleep there. They were married, he was fairly certain, but not to each other, and they were going to roll around on rented sheets for an hour, two at the most, while Keller was destined to spend another night sleeping in his car.

Was there an opportunity here? Suppose he waited until they finished. Would they lock the door after they left? He somehow doubted it would be their top priority, and they might leave it ajar, in which case he could walk right in the minute they were out of sight.

And even if they locked it, how hard would it be to get in? He had his Swiss Army knife, and if it wouldn't get him through the lock he could try kicking the door in. This was a roadside motel, not Fort Knox.

As far as the management was concerned, the room was rented for the night. Even if they suspected the room had been vacated, they couldn't hand it out again until the maid had serviced it. Judging from the number of cars in the lot, the place was half empty, so that left them with plenty of other rooms to rent. Keller could be in and out of this one without anyone ever knowing he was there.

He could catch a couple of hours of real sleep in an actual bed. God, he could take a shower.

Waiting wasn't that easy. He couldn't turn his mind off, and it kept telling him he was wasting time, that he ought to be back on the highway knocking off the miles.

And how did he know they'd be leaving anytime soon? Maybe they were travelers, too tired from a long day on the road to bother hauling their luggage inside. She'd been carrying a purse, and that might hold all she needed until they had a chance to go out to the car for their bags in the morning. That seemed a little odd to Keller, but people did odd things all the time.

He went over to their car, and there was nothing in the back seat, but they could have stowed their bags in the trunk, as he'd done with his. Their car carried an Indiana plate, but did that necessarily mean they were local? Indiana was a pretty big state. He couldn't say exactly how big it was, or where he was in it, because the only maps he had were for Iowa, where he didn't intend to return, and Oregon, where he wouldn't be going, either, the considerable allure of Roseburg and Klamath Falls notwithstanding. But he knew Indiana had some size to it. It might not be Texas, but it wasn't Delaware, either.

He returned to his car. They were probably local, he had to admit, but they might still stay until morning. Say he lived with his parents, and she had a roommate. They'd need a place to be together in private, but they could stay all night in it without making trouble for themselves. And here he was, sitting in his car, staring with eyes that kept wanting to close at a door that might not open until dawn.

When the door did open, he checked his watch and was surprised to note that they'd only been in there for a little under an hour. The guy emerged first, and stood there in the doorway, holding the door for the woman, then giving her another proprietary pat on the rear as she passed. They were dressed as he'd seen them before, and there was nothing in their appearance to indicate they'd spent the preceding fifty minutes doing anything more adventurous than watching Indiana's own David Letterman, but Keller suspected otherwise.

C'mon, he urged them silently. *Leave the door open.*

And for a moment he thought they were going to, but no, the son of a bitch had to reach for the handle and pull the thing shut. They walked toward their car, and then the guy held up something, a white card of some sort, and offered it to the woman. She backed away, holding up her hands as if to ward the thing off, and he reached to tuck it into her purse, and she grabbed it away from him and threw it at him. He ducked and it sailed over his shoulder, and they both laughed and walked the rest of the way to their car, his hand on her behind once again, and Keller watched where the white card landed because now he knew what it was.

The room key, of course. *Here, honey, a little souvenir of the evening. Let me just tuck it in your purse.* Keller picked it up and brushed it off, tried it in the lock, opened the door. Then he went back for his suitcase and wheeled it to his room, just like any legitimate tourist.

12

He had done what he could to prepare himself for the prospect of sleeping on the fun couple's sheets, but it turned out he didn't have to. The room was furnished with twin double beds, and they'd only used one of them—and used it thoroughly, from the evidence. Keller covered that bed with its spread and turned down the other one. He treated himself to a shower, then slipped between the sheets and closed his eyes. He'd hung the DO NOT DISTURB sign on the door, but had he also remembered to lock the door so it couldn't be opened from outside? He was trying to remember, and thinking he ought to go check, and before he knew it he was asleep.

He was awake before the maid started her rounds. He had another shower, and shaved, and put on clean clothes. He had one more change of underwear in his bag, and a clean pair of socks, and after that he'd have to start recycling the dirty ones, because he couldn't afford to wash his clothes or buy new ones.

Two and a half million dollars in investments and he couldn't afford underwear.

Nobody was going to dust the room for prints, but he wiped it down anyway, out of habit. Back in the Sentra, he ate the last hamburger and drank some bottled water and pretended he'd just had a hearty breakfast. He threw out the cold french fries, the cement milkshake.

He started the car, checked the gas gauge. He would be needing gas soon, and he supposed he could spare a twenty.

At first glance, he wasn't entirely certain the gas station was open, or even still in business. The basic setup was fairly standard, a pint-size convenience store with a couple of pumps out in front, an air hose and a pay phone off to one side. The only vehicle in sight was a tow truck parked around back.

Was anybody home? Keller pulled up to the pump, where a home-made sign instructed all customers, cash or credit, to pay inside before pumping gas. Something felt off to Keller, and he thought about driving on to the next station, but he'd already passed up a couple of opportunities, and pretty soon he'd be running on faith and fumes.

He patted his hair down, put on his blazer and made sure it concealed the gun in the small of his back. Why couldn't the happy fornicators at the Travelodge have left something useful, along with a set of spectacularly soiled sheets? A baseball cap, say, or a bottle of hair dye, or a few hundred dollars and a collection of live credit cards.

Keller had a twenty in hand when he cleared the threshold. Behind the counter sat a stocky man with a broad forehead and a nose that had been broken at least once. Iron-gray hair cut short enough for boot camp showed around the edges of a baseball cap on which an embroidered Homer Simpson held up a mug of beer. The man was reading a magazine, and Keller would have bet anything it wasn't *Soap Opera Digest.* Nor did he seem to find his magazine as gripping as the girl had found hers, because he looked up from it before Keller could open his mouth or put the money on the counter.

"Help you?"

"Twenty dollars' worth of regular," Keller said, and handed him the bill.

"Hang on a second," the man said, catching Keller just as he was turning around. He turned back, and the man was taking a good look at the twenty. Jesus, was there anything wrong with it?

"Been some funny twenties around lately," the man said. "This here looks to be okay."

Keller would have said he'd just made it himself, but couldn't count on the man recognizing it for a joke. "It came straight out of an ATM," he said instead.

"Is that a fact."

Suspicious old bastard. Keller said, "Well, if everything's okay," and started for the door again, but the voice stopped him in his tracks.

"No, hold it right there, son. And turn around slow, you hear?"

Keller turned, and was not surprised to see the gun in the man's hand. It was an automatic, and looked like a cannon to Keller.

"I'm not too good with names," the man said, "but it seems like you've got a few of them, and who's to say any of 'em's the right one? Keep your hands where I can see 'em, you understand?"

"You're making a mistake," Keller said.

"Your damn picture's all over the place, son. And if I'm not much on names I'm pretty good on faces. Bet there's a pretty decent reward on you."

"By God," Keller said. "You think I'm the son of a bitch who shot that man in Iowa."

"Shot that high-stepping coon," the man said. "Well, if you had to gun somebody down, I got no problem with the choice you made. But that don't mean God gave you the right to do it."

"I know I look like him," Keller said, "and you're not the first person to notice the resemblance, but I'm not him and I can prove it."

"You just save your story for the law, why don't you?" And the hand that wasn't holding the gun reached for the phone.

"I'm not him, I swear it," Keller said.

"What did I just say? You got an explanation, there's men with badges'll be happy to listen to everything you got to say."

"The law's after me," Keller said, "but for something else."

"How's that?"

"Alimony and child support. Long story short, she's a cheating bitch and the kid's not mine, and we even proved that with DNA tests and the courts still say I gotta support him."

"You must have had some lawyer."

"Look, let me prove it, okay? I'm just going to get something from my pocket, okay?"

And without waiting for permission he drew the gun and put two bullets in the guy's chest before he could get off a shot.

13

The impact had knocked the man backward, and he'd tipped his chair over and gone to the floor with it, losing his Homer Simpson cap on the way down. Keller went around the counter and checked him, but it was just a formality. Both bullets had entered the left side of his chest, and at least one of them had found his heart, and that was that.

Keller's ears were ringing from the gunshots, and his hand ached a little from the revolver's recoil. He straightened up, glanced through the window. There was a car parked at one of the pumps, and that was disconcerting for the second or two it took him to realize that it was his car, right where he'd parked it.

The dead man was still holding the gun, his finger on the trigger, and Keller had heard stories of men firing guns long after their own death, their trigger fingers curling at the onset of rigor mortis. He wasn't sure it ever happened, and it might even have been a plot element in a comic book he'd read as a child, but in any event he wanted the gun. It was a SIG Sauer automatic with a fully loaded fifteen-shot clip, and his own revolver was down to two bullets, and had just been used in a homicide. The SIG wasn't as huge as it had looked, there was nothing like having a gun pointed at you to make it increase dramatically in size, though it was in fact a little larger and heavier than the revolver. He tried it where he'd been carrying the revolver, and it rode there just fine, and he figured that closed the deal.

He wiped his prints from the revolver and put it in the dead man's hand, shaping the still-warm hand to the butt and slipping the forefinger inside the trigger guard. No one was terribly likely to buy the idea that the old guy had shot himself twice in the heart, but it seemed as good a place as any to stow the revolver, and at the very least it would give somebody something to think about.

He looked for a cash register and didn't see one. There was an old wooden Garcia y Vega cigar box on the counter, and that turned out to be where the fellow kept cash and credit card slips. The cash was all fives and singles, with a couple of tens in the mix. No wonder he'd looked long and hard at the twenty, Keller thought. It was probably the first one he'd seen all month.

He didn't particularly want to touch the dead man, but he wasn't squeamish, either, and from the right-hand hip pocket of the man's camo jeans he drew a leather wallet with a design embossed on it, a design so worn and weathered that Keller could barely make out what it was. He could see it was a crest of some sort, and it looked familiar, but he couldn't place it.

Inside the wallet, he found the very same crest on the card that identified its owner, Miller L. Remsen, as a member in good standing of the National Rifle Association. Guns don't kill people, Keller thought. Sticking your broken nose in other people's business, that's what kills people.

Remsen's Indiana driver's license had his middle name as well, which turned out to be Lewis. It had his date of birth, and Keller worked it out that he was seventy-three, and would have turned seventy-four in October, if he hadn't decided to be such a good citizen. There were cards for Social Security and Medicare, and a couple of very old pictures of children, smiling bravely for the school photographer. By now those children very likely had children of their own, but if so Remsen didn't have pictures of them.

The wallet held cash, including two fifties and a batch of twenties and adding up to just over three hundred dollars. There were two credit cards as well, both in the name of Miller L. Remsen, but the Citibank Visa card had expired. The other was a MasterCard issued by CapitalOne, and it was good for another year and a half.

He pocketed the bills and the valid credit card, wiped everything else he'd touched and put it back, then returned the wallet to the dead man's pocket. He opened the cigar box again, hesitated, then scooped up the small bills.

Something registered, something he caught out of the corner of his eye, and he looked again and saw it—on the ceiling, at the juncture of two walls. A security camera, and who would expect it in a run-down operation like Remsen's? But they were everywhere these days, and when the cops found the body they'd check the camera, and he couldn't let that happen.

He stood on a chair, and climbed down a few minutes later shaking his head. The camera was mounted there, all right, but there was no tape or film or battery in it, and no wires connecting it to a power supply. It was like one of those decals announcing the presence of a burglar alarm system. A scarecrow, that's all it was, and Keller wiped his prints from it and left it there to do its job.

The items on sale in the tiny store area didn't amount to much, and most of them were auto parts or accessories of one sort or another. There were cans of motor oil, wiper blades, engine additives. He grabbed up a pair of six-foot bungee cords, thinking they might come in handy sometime, though he couldn't guess for what. Remsen sold all manner of snacks, too, packages of chips and Slim Jims and those cracker-and-peanut-butter sandwiches, and he thought those might come in handy, too, and then decided to pass. All of the snacks looked as though they'd been there since the Carter administration. He left them where they were.

A door led to a bathroom, which was about as bad as he'd expected. He closed it quickly and opened another door, which led to a ten-by-twelve room that had evidently served as Remsen's living quarters. There was a stack of magazines, all involving guns or hunting or fishing, and there were three hardcover Ayn Rand novels, and, most disconcertingly, there was, in Remsen's bed with its head on one of the two pillows, an inflatable doll, which the man had outfitted with a rubber mask. The face was vaguely familiar, and after a moment Keller realized it was supposed to be Ann Coulter. Keller thought that was just about the saddest thing he'd ever seen in his life.

Something else was bothering him, and it took him a minute to realize what it was. Not the fact that he'd killed the man—he'd killed any number of men, and none of them for a more compelling reason. This guy had it coming, which was more than he could say for a lot of the men and women whose names belonged in the memoir Keller would never dream of writing. Often in the past he'd used a trick of mental gymnastics in order to diminish the memory of a killing, but he wouldn't have to do that in Remsen's case because it wouldn't bother him a bit.

But what did bother him was something he had never done before. He was robbing the dead.

Keller had always wondered what was so terrible about robbing the dead. Compared to, say, robbing the living. Once you were dead, how could you possibly care what became of the watch on your wrist or the ring on your finger? There were, as the song said, no pockets in a shroud, and it was pretty generally acknowledged that you couldn't take it with you, so why not rob the dead? It wasn't like necrophilia, which was flat-out disgusting; it was simply a matter of making use of that which was no longer of any use to its owner.

It was still stealing, of course, since the dead might be presumed to have heirs, so you'd be stealing from them. That said, there were men of whom it was said that they would steal a hot stove, who would draw the line at going through a dead man's pockets. Keller didn't get it, and now that he thought about it he decided society had imposed the taboo out of necessity; if it weren't such an awful thing to steal from the dead, why, everybody would do it.

So it gave him a turn, but once he'd had a chance to sort out his thoughts, it stopped bothering him. And he wasn't taking a watch or a ring, nothing personal. Just some cash and a credit card, both of which he needed desperately.

Outside, he went to his car and filled the tank, and he didn't stop at the twenty-dollar mark, either. The Sentra drank deeply and settled down on its tires, like a heavy man sitting back after a big meal.

Remsen's sign was still hanging on the pump, advising cash and credit customers alike to pay before they pumped their gas. He replaced it with one he'd lettered at the counter, using what was very likely the same Magic Marker Remsen had used. CLOSED FOR FAMILY EMERGENCY, he'd printed in block caps. HELP YOURSELF AND PAY ME LATER. He somehow doubted that anyone who knew Remsen at all well would believe he'd display such trust in his fellow man, but who was going to argue with a free tank of gasoline? They'd all help themselves, he figured, and some of them might even pay for it later.

Back inside, he flipped the sign in the window from OPEN to

CLOSED. He turned off lights, rearranged the scene behind the counter so that the body would not be visible from outside, walked to the open door and pushed the button that would lock it, and stepped across the threshold. And stopped there, one foot outside and one foot in, because it was almost as if he could hear Miller Remsen's voice, halting him in his tracks.

Hold it right there, son. Where do you think you're going?

He didn't want to go back behind the counter, but he knew he had to. Hadn't he already established that he wasn't squeamish? So why draw the line now?

He braced himself, then reached for the Homer Simpson cap. He didn't have to remove it from Remsen's head, it had already fallen off on its own, so all he needed to do was pick it up, which wasn't really all that hard, and then put it in place on his own head, which wasn't all that easy.

In the car he checked his reflection in the rearview mirror. It seemed to him that the cap helped. The adjustable strap was a little loose, he'd noticed that Remsen had a pretty large head, and he tightened it a notch, and that was better. And he tugged at the brim so that it covered a little more of his forehead, and that was better, too.

He had a dead man's gun pressing into the small of his back and a dead man's money and credit card in his pocket, and he'd filled his tank with a dead man's gas. And now he had a dead man's baseball cap on his head.

It was a curious development, all in all. But now it was beginning to look as though he might make it back to New York after all.

The drive-up window at Wendy's was even less threatening than the one at Burger King. He ordered a couple of burgers and a green salad, and ate them in the car a few miles down the road. He drove through the rest of Indiana and all the way through Ohio and a couple of miles of West Virginia, and he was across another state line and into Pennsylvania before he needed to stop for gas. He picked a big truck stop, pulled up to a self-service pump, and used Remsen's credit card.

There was a moment when he realized another motorist was looking at him with interest, and he didn't know what he would do; there were people all over the place, and he couldn't shoot the guy and take off. He looked back at him, and the fellow—he couldn't have been more than twenty-five—gave him a big grin and a thumbs-up.

Why, for God's sake?

"Man, Homer's the bomb," the guy said, and Keller realized he'd been looking not at his face but at his baseball cap, and was expressing his approval of Homer Simpson, or endorsing Homer's enthusiasm for beer, or whatever.

Until that moment Keller had been having mixed feelings about the cap. It unquestionably served to render him less identifiable, which was good, but at the same time it drew attention all by itself, which wasn't. A John Deere cap, a Bud Light cap, a Dallas Cowboys cap—any of those would have offered a degree of invisibility which Homer, embroidered in Day-Glo yellow on a royal blue field, did not begin to provide. He'd even thought about cutting the threads and picking out the embroidery, taking Homer and his mug of suds out of the picture altogether.

But now he was beginning to be just as glad he'd held off. Homer drew attention, as he'd feared he might, but in this instance he'd drawn that attention not to Keller's face but away from it. The more people noticed Homer, the less attention they paid to Keller. He was just a dude with Homer on his cap, and he'd be sending out the subliminal message that he was safe and unthreatening, because how dangerous was the sort of yokel who'd walk around with Homer Simpson an inch or two north of his eyebrows?

14

Somehow in the course of skirting the city of Pittsburgh, he managed to lose Route 30, and signs indicated that he was approaching the Pennsylvania Turnpike. It would get him to New York, but he seemed to recall having heard that the state troopers on the Pennsy Pike were hell on speeders. That bit of information might have been twenty years old, if it was ever true in the first place, and he hadn't exceeded a speed limit since he left Des Moines, but according to another sign, the road he was on would get him to I-80, and that's where he headed.

Before his encounter with Remsen, he'd have had a more compelling reason to pick I-80. It was free in Pennsylvania, while the Pennsylvania Turnpike was a toll road. When he'd been hoping to stretch his gas money so that it would get him home, it was worth driving out of one's way to escape a highway toll. But now he had money in his pocket, and the worst thing you could say about a toll booth was that it would give one more person a quick look at his face.

It took him longer than he'd expected to get to the interstate, and he was glad when a rest area provided a chance to stop. He needed a restroom, and while he was there he checked his reflection in the mirror and couldn't take his eyes off Homer Simpson. Did the image have to be so bright? Maybe he could rub a little dirt on it, tone it down some.

He left it alone, had a look at the map mounted on the wall outside, then returned to his car and sat there, trying to decide if he could make it all the way back to the city in one shot. He probably had enough gas, though there was no point in taking the chance of running out, say, in the middle of the George Washington Bridge, not when Miller Remsen was ready and willing to fill up the tank for him.

What he had to decide was whether to spend another night on the road. A few hours in a real bed had spoiled him, and the idea of trying to sleep in the car was unappealing now. How far was he from the city? Seven, eight hours? More, with stops for gas and food?

At a rough estimate, he calculated that he'd hit the city around three or four in the morning if he drove straight through. That might not be a bad time to turn up at his apartment. There'd be fewer people on the streets, and the ones who were out and about at that hour were apt to be too drunk to notice him, or to remember if they did.

A line of thought tried to intrude, and his mind deliberately pushed it aside . . .

If he drove straight through, he thought, he'd arrive tired and worn out, and was that the best way to land on his own doorstep? He'd want to crawl into bed the minute he got through the door, and he wouldn't be able to, because he'd have tons of things to do. Never mind the mail, which always piled up when he took a trip. There'd be plenty of other things demanding his immediate attention. There always were.

That thought again, and again he never let himself become entirely conscious of it, warding it off almost without effort.

He switched on the radio for the first time since he'd left Remsen's place, but he was in the mountains now and the reception was bad. The only station he could pick up was playing music, and the static was so heavy he couldn't even tell what kind of music it was.

He switched it off. It seemed unlikely that they'd have discovered Remsen's body. The sign he'd left would explain the man's absence, and they'd need a compelling reason to break down his door and look around inside. The man lived alone, and if he had a friend in the world, Keller hadn't seen any evidence of it.

He glanced over at the squat brick building that housed the restrooms and vending machines. Alongside the entrance he'd noticed a coin box with copies of *USA Today,* but hadn't thought to pick one up. It struck him now that it might not be a bad idea to find out what was happening in the world, especially since the radio wasn't going to do much for him for the next few hours. He opened the door and got out of the car, and a big SUV picked that moment to pull into the rest area and park right in front of the little brick building, and its doors opened to let out two adults and four small children, all in a hurry to use the john.

Far too many people all at once. He got back in his car. The paper could wait.

He got on the road again and thought about the man he'd killed in Indiana. There might be another crusty old fart who went hunting and fishing with Remsen, or came over and played gin rummy with him, and sooner or later somebody would pop the door and find the body, but by then he'd have long since ditched the man's credit card—and the Sentra as well, as far as that was concerned, because he'd be back in New York, where you didn't need a car and had to be crazy to own one.

Whether he made it in one day or two, whether he drove straight through or found a place to sleep, he'd be back in New York in a matter of hours. Out of harm's way, and safe at home.

A sign advertised a restaurant at the next exit, boasting that the place offered Pennsylvania Dutch home cooking. Keller found the prospect irresistible, although he wasn't quite sure what the Pennsylvania Dutch cooked at home. Nowadays, he thought, they probably brought something home from the Grand Union and popped it in the microwave just like everybody else, but he guessed the restaurant harkened back to a simpler era. He took the exit, found the restaurant, pulled into the parking lot, and wondered what the hell he thought he was doing.

Because it was a regular walk-in-and-sit-down restaurant, where you sat at a table and ordered from a menu, and the waitress brought your food to you. And she got a look at you, and so did the other customers, and that was precisely what he'd gone to great lengths to avoid, ever since his face first turned up on the television screen in the Days Inn back in Des Moines. True, he had a baseball cap now, but it wasn't as though he was hiding behind an Ann Coulter mask. His face was still out there for all the world to see.

He put the car in gear, backed out of the lot, and found a Hardee's with a drive-up window. He picked up his food, parked a dozen yards away, ate it, dropped his trash in the can, and found his way to the entrance ramp and back onto the interstate.

Now what was all that about? The mouthwatering prospect of shoofly pie and apple pandowdy? Had his appetite somehow taken over for his brain?

He thought about it, and figured out what it was.

He was in Pennsylvania, and a lot nearer to home than to Iowa. And the closer he got to New York, the safer he felt. Add in the sense of security that came with having money in his pocket, and the way his baseball cap had smoothed the way for him the last time he filled the gas tank, and he had evidently come to believe he had nothing to worry about.

Soon, he thought. Soon he'd be home. But he wasn't there yet.

A couple of hours later, he managed to convince himself that the motel wasn't nearly as risky as the Pennsylvania Dutch restaurant.

There would be no other patrons involved, for one thing. The only person he'd see would be whoever checked him in. And he'd be wearing the baseball cap with the brim down over his forehead, and he'd have his head lowered while he filled out the registration card. And the motel was an independent, not affiliated with a national chain, and that increased the odds that the owner-operator would be an immigrant from the Indian subcontinent. In fact, he'd probably be from Gujarat, and the odds were good that his surname would be Patel.

For years now, people from the Indian state of Gujarat, most of them named Patel, had been buying American motels all over the country. It seemed likely to Keller that there was at least one training academy in Gujarat's main city, whatever they called it, devoted to schooling ambitious locals in motel management. *Our topic today, good students, concerns the proper placement of the mint upon the pillow. Tomorrow we will discuss the paper band proclaiming the toilet to be sanitized for your protection.*

If Keller's face was an unremarkable one, rarely warranting a second glance, wouldn't it be even less remarkable to someone from a significantly different ethnic background? Keller wasn't overly given to racial or ethnic stereotypes, and had never been one to say that all Asians or Africans looked alike, but there was no dodging the fact that, when he got an initial look at someone racially different from himself, what he saw first and foremost was that difference. He saw a black man, or a Korean woman, or a Pakistani; later, through familiarity, he was better able to make out the individual.

And, if you were a man or woman from Gujarat, wouldn't it work in about the same fashion when you looked over the counter of your motel at a white American? Wouldn't you see *what* your prospective customer was before you saw *who* he was? And, since all you had to do was run his credit card and hand him a room key, would there ever be any reason for you to pay attention to any more of him than you saw on first glance?

Keller decided to risk it.

There was no one at all behind the desk when Keller opened the door to the motel office, but he didn't need to see anybody to know that his first assumption was correct. The owners were from India, if not necessarily from Gujarat. The rich smell of curry left no room for doubt.

It was not an aroma you expected to encounter in the hills of central Pennsylvania, and it had an even stronger effect upon Keller than had the phrase *Pennsylvania Dutch home cooking.* Here was a smell that promised everything that had been missing from all those fast-food hamburgers and fries. Keller wasn't hungry, he'd eaten not that long ago, but hunger was somehow beside the point. He wanted to find the source of that wonderful bouquet and roll around in it like a dog in carrion—an image, he reflected, that flattered neither himself nor the food, but even so—

He broke off the thought when the tinkling of a beaded curtain heralded the arrival of a young woman, dark-skinned and slender, dressed in a white blouse and plaid skirt that might have been the uniform of a parochial school. She was almost certainly the daughter of the proprietors, and she was very pretty, and in other circumstances Keller might have allowed himself some light flirting. At the very least he might have commented on how good the food smelled.

But not now. All he did was ask about a room, and all she did was tell him the price was $39, which struck him as perfectly reasonable. If she looked at him at all, at his face or at Homer's, he never saw her do it. He was just a burdensome duty to be dealt with as quickly as possible, before she got back to polishing the essay portion of her application to Harvard.

He filled out the card she gave him, making up a name and address, leaving the space for his car's make and license number blank. They always had a space for it on the card, but they didn't seem to care if you filled it in or not, and this girl, who wouldn't have noticed if he'd registered as Mahatma Gandhi, was no exception.

He paid cash, because his credit card was in Remsen's name and he'd already signed in as somebody else. He could have used Remsen, the name would be safe for days if not weeks, and by tomorrow he'd be back in New York and none of this would matter. But he had the money, so what difference did it make?

She asked him if he would want to make phone calls, because then he would need to leave a deposit, or allow her to take an imprint of his credit card. He shook his head, picked up his room key, and filled his nostrils for one last time with the sweet smell of curry.

15

After all he'd gone through to get his hands on it, he managed to walk halfway to his car the next morning before he realized he'd left his baseball cap in his room. Fortunately he'd also forgotten to leave the room key on the dresser, so he was able to let himself in and retrieve the cap. With Homer on his forehead, rather like a Valkyrie on the prow of a Viking warship, he felt ready to face the world.

He drove a few miles, stopped to top off the gas tank for what would be the final time, drove some more. The phrase *safe at home* echoed in his mind like a mantra. All he needed to do was get into his own apartment and lock the door behind him and he'd be locking out his life as a fugitive and everything that went with it. And, because he was retired now, with no *one last job* looming in front of him, he'd be locking all of that out forever. He'd have his stamps, he'd have his enormous state-of-the-art TV, he'd have his TiVo, and he'd have all the other aspects of the life he'd arranged for himself within easy walking distance—his regular deli, his favorite restaurants, the newsstand where he bought the *Times* every morning, the laundry where he dropped it off dirty in the morning and picked it up clean at night. He didn't suppose it was a terribly exciting life, centering as it did upon such sedentary and solitary pursuits as television and stamp collecting, but excitement had lost its charm for him over the years, if it had ever had any to begin with, and he found it thrilling enough to bid a few dollars on a stamp on eBay and see if some bastard pounced on it before time ran out. It was low-stakes excitement, no question, but that was plenty.

That errant thought was trying to break through again, struggling to rise to the surface. It was like something barely glimpsed out of the corner of your eye. You knew you'd catch sight of it if you turned your head, and that was all it took to keep your gaze fixed straight ahead.

His breakfast, picked up without incident at a drive-up window, consisted of two Egg McMuffins and a big cup of coffee. Just before exiting the interstate he'd seen a sign for a rest area five miles ahead, so he drove there and parked under a tree. He'd timed it just right, he was pleased to note; the coffee was cool enough to drink and the Egg McMuffins were still warm.

When he was done eating he went to the restroom, and on his way back he finally remembered to buy a paper. *USA Today* was seventy-five cents, and he fed in three quarters before he noticed that the coin box right next to it held that morning's *New York Times*. He pressed the coin return, got his three quarters back, added a fourth quarter and bought the *Times.* On the way back to the car he was already planning his approach to the paper. First the local and national news, then the sports, and finally the crossword puzzle. What day was it, anyway? Thursday? The puzzles increased daily in difficulty, from Monday, not much of a challenge to a bright ten-year-old, to Saturday, which often left Keller feeling slightly retarded. Thursday was usually just about right. He could generally fill in a Thursday puzzle, all right, but it took some thought.

He settled in behind the wheel, made himself comfortable, and started in on the paper. He never did get to the crossword puzzle.

16

The paper Keller bought every morning came in four sections, but the edition the *Times* distributed outside of the immediate New York metropolitan area fit into just two. There was an assassination story on the front page, dealing primarily with its evolving political implications, and another story further on about the hunt for the killer, which seemed to have trailed off in several directions, none of which had thus far panned out. There was nothing about Miller Remsen, which came as no surprise to Keller; even if they'd found the body, which seemed unlikely at this stage, the only way it would interest anybody outside of Indiana would be if he'd scrawled *Catch me before I kill more governors* in lipstick on the mirror.

He almost missed the real story.

It was on the third page of the second section. "Arson, Murder Found in White Plains Fire," the headline announced, and it was White Plains that caught his eye. If it had been less specific and said Westchester instead he might have skipped right past it, but he'd been to White Plains countless times, first to see the old man and then to see Dot. He'd catch the train at Grand Central and a cab from the station, and he'd sit drinking iced tea on the wraparound front porch of the big old house on Taunton Place, or in the cozy kitchen. So he read about the fire in White Plains, and knew shortly that he wouldn't be going there again, because there was no more house, no more porch, no more kitchen. No more Dot.

Evidently there had been a story in yesterday's paper, which of course he hadn't seen. But earlier—Monday, he thought, though it could have been Sunday, it wasn't all that clear—earlier, he read, a fire had broken out in the early morning hours, raging out of control before firefighters could arrive on the scene, and consuming virtually all of the century-old house right down to its foundation.

The fire had begun in the kitchen, which was where they'd found the charred body of the householder and sole resident, identified by neighbors as Dorothea Harbison. Investigators had suspected arson immediately, attributing the all-consuming fury of the blaze to the liberal use of an accelerant throughout the residence. Initially it seemed at least possible that Ms. Harbison had set the fire herself; neighbors described her as quiet and reclusive and thought she'd shown signs of depression in recent months.

Keller wanted to argue with them, whoever they were. Reclusive? She didn't suffer fools or share her personal business with the world, but that didn't make her some goddam cat lady, wearing the same old flannel nightgown until it fell apart. Signs of depression? What signs of depression? She didn't go around giggling, but he'd never known her to be genuinely depressed, and she was about as suicidal as Mary Fucking Poppins.

But there was no longer a question of suicide, the story continued, because a medical examination revealed that the woman had been shot twice in the head with a small-caliber handgun. The wounds were not consistent with suicide—no kidding, thought Keller—nor was the handgun found at the scene, which led investigators to conclude that the woman had been shot to death and the fire set to conceal the crime.

"But it didn't work, did it?" Keller said out loud. "Fucking idiots."

He forced himself to read the rest of it. The motive for the murder was obscure, according to the *Times*, although police were not ready to rule out robbery. An unnamed police source was able to identify Dorothea Harbison as the former companion and caretaker of the late Giuseppe Ragone, aka Joe the Dragon, during the long years of his retirement from the world of organized crime.

As far as Keller knew, no one outside of the tabloid press had ever called the old man *Joe the Dragon*. There were people who referred to him, though never to his face, as Joey Rags, or the Ragman, because of the coincidence of his surname combined with his one-time involvement with a Garment District trucking local. Keller himself never thought of him or referred to him as anything other than the old man.

And the old man had never retired. He'd let go of a lot of his interests toward the end, but he was still brokering jobs and sending Keller out to take care of them right up to the very end.

"As Joe the Dragon's live-in companion and presumed confidante," the unnamed source went on, "Harbison would have been privy to a lot of O.C. information. Maybe someone was afraid she'd tell what she knew. Ragone's been gone a long time, but what is it they say? Sooner or later the chickens come home to roost."

It was as pointless as anything he might have done, but he couldn't help himself. He dropped coins in a pay phone and dialed Dot's number.

Coo-wheeeet!

Not a working number. Well, that was the truth, wasn't it? Burn a house to the ground and you had to expect an interruption in telephone service.

He got his quarters back and used them to call his own phone number, half expecting the same *coo-wheeeet* and the same recording. Instead he got a ring. His machine was set to pick up after two rings if he had messages and after four if he didn't, so that he could retrieve them from a distance while avoiding the toll if there were none to retrieve. He was surprised when it rang a third time, he'd expected messages after this long an absence, and he was even more surprised when the phone went on to ring a fourth and a fifth and a sixth time, and might have gone on ringing forever if he hadn't ended the connection.

Why would it do that? He didn't have call-waiting, so it couldn't be that the machine was already handling a call. If that happened he'd just get a busy signal.

He wondered why he was even bothering to dig his quarters out of the coin return chute. Who would he ever have occasion to call?

It was over, he saw now. That's what he'd been on the verge of realizing, that was the nasty little thought he'd kept at bay. And the pipe dream that had sustained him all the way back from Iowa, the mad fantasy that everything would be peaches and cream the minute he got back to his own apartment, was now so clearly impossible he wondered how he'd ever been dim enough to entertain it, let alone take it as gospel.

He'd somehow managed to regard New York as a haven, safe and sacrosanct. For years he'd made it a rule never to accept assignments in the city, and while he'd had to break the rule on a couple of occasions, most of the time he'd adhered to it. The rest of the country, and he'd covered a great deal of it at one time or another, was where he went to do his work. New York, his home, was where he came when the work was done.

But, however much people both in and out of the city might prefer to think otherwise, New York was part of America. New Yorkers watched the same newscasts and read the same newspaper stories. They might be better than most people at minding their own business, and it was not uncommon for an apartment dweller to be unable to identify people in his own building by name, but that hardly meant they turned a deaf ear and a blind eye to everything around them.

His picture had been all over TV and in every newspaper with the possible exception of *Linn's Stamp News*. (And it might even turn up there, if James McCue had managed to figure out just who it was who'd bought those Swedish reprints from him.) How many people lived within a block or two of Keller? How many knew him from the building, or had run into him at the deli, or at the gym, or anywhere in that unassuming life he'd been idealizing just minutes ago?

That life to which he could never return.

He went through the paper again, more carefully this time, and in a story he'd skimmed earlier he found evidence that at least one of Keller's neighbors had noticed his resemblance to the furtive chap in the photograph. Commenting on the multiple sightings of the fugitive, the journalist alluded to an unnamed Turtle Bay resident who'd become a person of interest to the police "only because of some apparent uncertainty as to the nature of his occupation, and his frequent trips out of town."

That would be enough to warrant a visit. Would they turn up anything incriminating in his apartment?

He couldn't think of anything. They'd find his laptop computer, and they'd turn his hard drive inside and out, but back when he bought the thing he'd known that email had a half-life longer than uranium's, and that a couple of sentences wafting through the ether would leave a trail that could outlive the sender. He and Dot had never sent each other an email, and vowed they never would.

Well, that would be an easy promise to keep, wouldn't it?

He'd used his computer mostly in connection with his hobby—corresponding with dealers, surfing for information, buying stamps on eBay, bidding in auctions. He'd checked airline websites before his flight to Des Moines, but he hadn't bought his ticket online because he was going to be flying as Holden Blankenship. So he'd made the reservation over the phone, and there wouldn't be any record of it on his computer.

Could they tell what sites he'd visited, and when? He wasn't sure, but figured the guiding principle—that when it came to technology, anybody could do anything—probably applied. One thing he was pretty sure they could do was pull up his phone records and establish that he'd called an airline a day or two before Blankenship flew to Des Moines, but at this point it didn't matter, at this point none of it mattered, because he'd finally managed to attract their attention, and that was all it took. He'd come as far as he had in life by staying out of the spotlight, and now he was in it, and that was the end of it.

The end of John Paul Keller. If he stayed alive, which seemed very iffy indeed, it would have to be somewhere else, and under some other name. He wouldn't miss the first two names; hardly anyone had ever used them, and he'd been called Keller by just about everybody since boyhood. That was who he was, and when he filled something out with his initials he sometimes thought they stood for Just Plain Keller.

He couldn't be Keller anymore. Keller was over and done with—and, when he thought about it, he realized that everything in Keller's life was already gone, so what difference could it make if the name vanished along with it?

The money, for one thing. He'd had, at last report, something in excess of two and a half million dollars in stocks and bonds, all of it in an Ameritrade online account set up and managed by Dot. The money would still be there, it wouldn't vanish with her death, but it might as well be gone for all the good it would do him. He had no idea what name she'd used on the account or how a person might go about accessing it.

Of course he had bank accounts, savings and checking. Maybe as much as fifteen thousand in his savings account, plus a thousand or so in checking. By now they'd have frozen his accounts, and they'd be just waiting for him to get his picture taken trying to use his ATM card. He couldn't use it now, anyway, because he hadn't brought it with him, so they'd probably confiscated it by now.

No money, then. And no apartment, either. He'd lived for years in an apartment on First Avenue that he'd bought at the very reasonable insider's price back when the Art Deco building went co-op, and the monthly maintenance charges didn't come to much, and he'd known he'd spend the rest of his days there until they carried him out feet first. It had always been his refuge, and now he didn't even dare go back there. It was out of his reach forever, along with his big-screen TV with TiVo and his comfortable chair and his bathroom with the pulsing showerhead and the desk he worked at and—

Oh, God. His stamps.

17

Keller crossed the Hudson on the lower level of the George Washington Bridge, took the Harlem River Drive to the FDR, and got off it a few blocks from his apartment. He'd spent the afternoon in a movie theater at a shopping mall outside of East Stroudsburg, Pennsylvania. It called itself a quadruplex, which sounded to Keller like someone who'd stepped on a landmine and lived to tell the tale, but only meant it could show four movies at once. Keller saw two of them, but only paid for one; rather than call attention to himself by going out and buying another ticket, he went from one theater to the men's room, then slipped into another theater to watch the second movie.

And if the usher had spotted him? What was he going to do, shoot his way out of it? Not likely, he'd stashed the SIG automatic in the glove compartment, and he was surprised to discover how vulnerable he felt without it. He'd only been carrying a gun for a few days, and it would be hard to imagine a less perilous venue than a darkened movie house on a weekday afternoon, with fewer than two dozen people in attendance and their median age somewhere around seventy-seven. He should have felt reasonably secure in such a setting, but it was beginning to dawn on him that he was never going to feel secure again, no matter where he went.

When the second feature ended, it was time to go. Head down, Homer Simpson leading the way, he returned to his car, and the first thing he did, before he fastened his seat belt or put the key in the ignition, was restore the gun to its place beneath his waistband. The pressure in the small of his back, he'd discovered, had become comforting.

It was dark when he left the movie theater, which had been pretty much the point of the visit. It was close to midnight by the time he was circling the blocks in his own neighborhood, trying to figure out what to do with the car. While his fantasy was still functioning, before the *Times* had come along to kick holes in it, he'd known just how to dispose of the Sentra. He'd drive it to some still-disreputable part of Brooklyn or the Bronx, and there he'd park it with the doors unlocked and the key in the ignition. He'd take the license plates off first, but he didn't think their absence would dissuade some neighborhood youth from taking the car out for a spin. Where it wound up after that, in the NYPD impound lot or some chop shop in Bensonhurst, was of no concern to Keller. He'd be back home, living the good life, and taking a cab for any distance too far to walk.

Right.

Now that New York had become about as safe for him as Des Moines, he was going to need a car to get out of it. So he'd have to stow this car, and he'd have to put it where it wouldn't get towed. That probably meant a parking lot, which in turn meant giving one more person a look at his face, and would probably entail passing a security camera or two. But it was hell finding a legal spot in his neighborhood, and even the illegal parking spaces were hard to come by. The U.N. Building was just a couple of blocks away, and cars immunized by their DPL plates against towing and ticketing slouched arrogantly alongside each bus stop and fire hydrant.

He passed one, a gleaming Lincoln Town Car, three times. It was blocking a hydrant, and it was doing all it could to block traffic at the same time, because the diplomat who'd parked it had been undiplomatic enough to leave it a full three feet from the curb. The third time around, Keller double-parked next to it, opened his trunk, rummaged around in his tool kit, and found what he needed.

Minutes later he was rounding the corner, and on the next block he found a space that left the Sentra sticking far enough into a bus stop to warrant a ticket, or possibly a tow. But it wouldn't get either, not with the DPL tags covering his own plates.

Bring the suitcase along? No, what for?

He left it and started walking toward his building. And, with a little luck, his stamp collection.

Keller and his stamps had a complicated history.

He'd collected as a boy, which was hardly remarkable. Many boys of his generation had childhood stamp collections, especially quiet introspective types like Keller. A neighbor whose business involved a lot of correspondence with firms in Latin America had brought him a batch to get him started, and Keller had learned to soak them from their paper backing, dry them between sheets of paper towel, and mount them with hinges in the album his mother had bought him at Lamston's. He'd eventually found other sources of stamps, buying mixtures and packets at Gimbel's stamp department, and getting inexpensive stamps on approval from a dealer halfway across the country, picking out what he wanted, returning the rest along with his payment, and waiting for the dealer to send the next selection. He'd kept this up for a few years, never spending more than a dollar or two a week, and sometimes forgetting to return the approvals for weeks on end because other pursuits intruded. Eventually he lost interest in the collection, and eventually his mother sold it, or gave it away, as there wasn't enough there to interest a dealer.

He was dismayed when he eventually found out it was gone, but not devastated, and he forgot about it and went on to other things, some of them more suspenseful than stamp collecting, though less socially acceptable. And time passed and the world changed. Keller's mother was long gone, and so were Gimbel's and Lamston's.

For decades, he rarely thought of his stamp collection unless his memory was triggered by some bit of knowledge he owed to those childhood hours with tongs and hinges. There were times when it seemed to him that the greater portion of the information stored in his head had got there as a direct result of his hobby. He could, without any great difficulty, name all of the presidents of the United States in order, and he owed this ability to the series of presidential stamps issued in 1938, with each president's head on the stamp with a value corresponding to his place in the procession. Washington was on the one-cent stamp, and Lincoln on the sixteen-cent stamp. He remembered this, even as he remembered that the one-cent stamp was green and the sixteen-cent stamp black, while the twenty-one-cent stamp, picturing New York's own Chester Alan Arthur, was a dull blue.

He knew that Idaho had been admitted to the union in 1890, because the fiftieth anniversary had been commemorated by a stamp in 1940. He knew that a group of Swedes and Finns had settled at Wilmington, Delaware, in 1638, and that General Tadeusz Kosciuszko, the Polish general who served in the American Revolution, had been granted American citizenship in 1783. He might not know how to pronounce the man's name, let alone spell it, but he knew what he did about him because of a blue five-cent stamp issued in 1933.

Occasionally a memory might turn him wistful, wishing he still had that essentially worthless collection that had filled so much of his time and turned his head into such a wonderland of trivia. But it never occurred to him to try to recapture those days. They were part of his youth, and they were gone.

Then, when the old man started slipping mentally, and when it was becoming clear that he was beginning to lose it big-time, Keller found himself contemplating retirement. He had some money saved up, and while it had amounted to less than 10 percent of what he'd eventually have in Dot's online account, he'd managed to sell himself on the notion that it was enough.

But what would he do with his time? Play golf? Take up needlepoint? Start hanging out at the senior center? Dot pointed out that he would need a hobby, and a bunch of childhood memories popped into his head, and the first thing he did was buy a worldwide collection, 1840-to-1940, just to get himself started, and before he knew it he had a shelf full of albums and a subscription to *Linn's* and dealers all over the country sending him price lists and approvals. And he'd also spent a surprisingly substantial portion of his retirement fund, so it was just as well when the old man was out of the picture entirely and he could go on working directly with Dot.

When he thought objectively about his stamps, he couldn't avoid concluding that the whole enterprise was nuts. He was spending the greater portion of his discretionary income on little pieces of paper that were worth nothing except what he and other like-minded screwballs were willing to pay for them. And he was devoting the greater portion of his free time to acquiring those pieces of paper, and, having done so, to mounting them neatly and systematically in albums created for that purpose. He put a lot of effort into getting them to look just right on the page, this in spite of the fact that he never intended for any eyes but his to see them. He didn't want to display his stamps at a show, or invite another collector over to have a look at them. He wanted them right there on the shelves in his apartment, where he and only he could look at them.

All of which, he had to admit, was at the very least irrational.

On the other hand, when he was working with his stamps, he was always entirely absorbed in what he was doing. He was expending considerable concentration on what was essentially an unimportant task, and that seemed to be something his spirit required. When he was in a bad mood, his stamps got him out of it. When he was anxious or irritable, his stamps took him to another realm where the anxiety or irritation ceased to matter. When the world seemed mad and out of control, his stamps provided a more orderly sphere where serenity ruled and logic prevailed.

If he wasn't in the mood, the stamps could wait; if he was called out of town, he knew they'd be there when he got back. They weren't pets that had to be fed and walked on a regular schedule, or plants that needed to be watered. They demanded his entire and absolute attention, but only when he had it to give.

He wondered sometimes if he was spending too much money on his collection, and perhaps he was, but his bills were always paid and he wasn't carrying any debt, and he'd somehow managed to accumulate two and a half million dollars in investments, so why shouldn't he spend what he wanted to on stamps?

Besides, decent philatelic material always increased in value over time. You couldn't buy it one day and sell it the next and expect to come out ahead, but after you'd owned it awhile it would have appreciated enough to cover the dealer's markup. And what other pastime worked that way? If you owned a boat, if you raced cars, if you went on safari, how much of what you spent could you expect to get back? What, for that matter, was your net return on bottles of Cristal and lines of cocaine?

And so he'd returned to New York for his stamps. There was nothing else to come back for, and ample reason to stay away. If he was a person of interest to the police, in addition to entering his apartment and sealing his bank accounts, they might very well have posted somebody to watch the place on the slim chance that he'd be fool enough to return.

If the cops weren't waiting for him, what about Call-Me-Al? The people who'd pulled the strings in Des Moines weren't willing to sit back and let nature take its course. They'd proved that in White Plains, because it wasn't the old man's chickens that had come home to roost, it was the turkeys on Al's team who'd shot Dot dead and burned the place down around her.

They might have already known his name, and where he lived. If not, they'd have asked Dot, and he could only hope she'd answered right away, and that two quick bullets in the brain were all the punishment she'd been forced to endure. Because she'd have talked sooner or later, anyone would, and in this case sooner was better than later.

But maybe nobody had the place staked out, not the cops and not Al's boys, either. Maybe all he had to do was figure out a way in and out without being spotted by the doorman.

It would probably take more than one trip, though. His collection was housed in ten good-sized albums, and the best plan he could come up with, sitting in the movie house in East Stroudsburg with his eyes on the screen, was to load up the oversize wheeled duffel that he'd bought on QVC a few years ago. He had never used it, it held far more stuff than he ever wanted to drag on any trip, business or pleasure, but the pitchman on the shopping channel had caught him at just the right moment, and before he knew what was happening he'd picked up the phone and bought the damn thing.

You could get four albums in it for sure, and possibly five, and the handle and wheels would enable him to get it to the car. Dump the albums in the trunk, go back for another load—two trips might do it, or three at the most.

There was some cash in the house, too, unless someone had found it by now. Not a fortune, just an emergency fund of somewhere between one and two thousand dollars. If this didn't constitute an emergency he didn't know what did, and he could definitely use the cash, but it wouldn't have been enough to draw him back to the city, not if it had been ten or twenty times as much as it was.

The stamp collection was something else. He'd lost his first collection all those years ago. He didn't want to lose this one.

18

If anyone was watching the place, Keller couldn't spot him. He spent a full half-hour looking and never saw anybody suspicious. Nor could he find any route into his building that didn't lead past the doorman. The closest thing to a possibility would involve finding a six-foot ladder somewhere and using it to reach the fire escape in the rear, from which he might be able to break into one of his fellow tenants' apartments. He'd have to be awfully lucky to pick an empty apartment, and even if he did, how was he going to get back down the fire escape with a king-size suitcase loaded with stamp albums?

The hell with it. The first thing he did was take off the Homer Simpson cap, which was all wrong for what he had in mind. He might need Homer soon enough, so he didn't just toss the cap but folded it as best he could and put it in his pocket. Then he crossed the street, shoulders back, arms swinging slightly at his sides, and walked right up to the doorman and into the lobby.

"Evening, Neil," he said as he entered.

"Evening, Mr. Keller," the doorman said, and Keller saw his blue eyes widen.

He gave the fellow a quick smile. "Neil," he said, "I bet I've had a few visitors, haven't I?"

"Uh—"

"Nothing to worry about," Keller assured him. "Nothing that won't get itself straightened out in a day or two, but right now it adds up to a lot of aggravation for me and a batch of other people." He dipped a hand into his breast pocket, where he'd put aside Miller Remsen's two fifties. "I have to see to a few things," he said, palming the folded bills into Neil's hand, "and nobody needs to know I was here, if you follow me."

There was nothing like the air of self-assurance, especially when it was coupled with a hundred dollars. "Sure, and I never saw you, sir," said Neil, with that slight Irish lilt to his speech that was rarely present outside of moments like this one.

He rode up in the elevator, wondering if there'd be one of those seals on his door, proclaiming it a crime scene. But there was nothing like that, not even a paper band assuring him that the apartment had been sanitized for his protection. Nor had anyone changed the locks; he used his key and the door opened. Things were not as he'd left them, he saw that right away, but he didn't waste time on any of the unimportant stuff. He went straight to the bookcase where he kept his stamps.

19

Gone, all of them.

It wasn't as though it took him entirely by surprise. He'd known there was a good possibility he'd come home to find his stamps missing, carried away by one or another of his visitors. The cops might very well have confiscated the stamps, but he thought it was more likely that Al, or whoever Al dispatched, had spotted the albums and knew enough about the market in collectibles to recognize their value. Whoever took them would be lucky to realize ten cents on the dollar, but even so he might regard it as worth risking a hernia to haul the ten big books out of there and find a stamp dealer who wasn't too scrupulous to pass up a bargain.

If the latter was what happened, they were gone forever. If the cops had them, they were still gone, for all the good it would do him. They might spend the next twenty years in an evidence locker somewhere, while heat and humidity and vermin and air pollution did their work, and the chances that they'd ever find their way back into Keller's possession, even if by some miracle somebody in Des Moines broke down and confessed to everything, including having framed Keller—even if all of that happened, in spite of the fact that he knew it never would or could, he'd still never see the stamps again.

They were gone. Well, all right. So was Dot. That had been entirely unexpected, he'd expected to have her as a friend for the rest of his life. So it had stunned and saddened him, and he was still sad about it, and would very likely feel that way for a long time. But he hadn't responded to her death by curling up in a ball. He'd gone on, because that was what you did, what you had to do. You had to go on.

The stamps didn't constitute a death, but they were certainly a loss, and having allowed for the possibility didn't do anything to lessen its impact. But they were gone, period, end of report. He wasn't going to be able to get them back, any more than he was going to be able to revive Dot. Dead was dead, when all was said and done, and gone was gone.

Now what?

His computer was gone, too. The cops would have taken that without having to think twice, and even now some technicians were sure to be poring over his hard drive, trying to coax out of it information it did not in fact possess. It was a laptop, a MacBook, quick and responsive and user-friendly, but as far as he could make out there was nothing incriminating on it, and all it would take to replace it was money.

His telephone answering machine was in pieces on the floor, which explained why it hadn't answered his phone. He wondered what it had done to upset anyone. Maybe someone had started to steal it, decided it wasn't worth the trouble, and bounced it off the wall in anger. Well, so what? He wouldn't have to replace it, because he didn't have a phone for it to answer, or anyone who'd want to leave him a message.

The answering machine wasn't the only thing on the floor. They'd been through his drawers and closets, and the contents of several dresser drawers had been dumped out, but as far as he could make out his clothes were all there. He picked out a few things, shirts and socks and underwear, a pair of sneakers, things he might find a use for on the way to wherever he would go next. Now, he thought, stamps or no stamps, he'd finally find a use for that fucking duffel bag, and he went to the closet where he kept it and the damn thing was gone.

Well, of course, he thought. The bastards had needed something to hold the stamp albums, and they wouldn't have known to bring anything because they'd only have found out about the stamp collection when they saw it. So they kept hunting until they found the duffel.

He'd have been unable to fill it, anyway. A shopping bag held what little he felt like taking.

He set the bag down and found a small screwdriver in the hardware drawer in the kitchen, used it to remove the switch plate on the bedroom wall. Years ago, before Keller moved into the apartment, there must have been a ceiling fixture in the bedroom, but a previous tenant had remodeled it out of existence. The wall switch remained, but didn't do anything, a fact Keller demonstrated repeatedly early on by forgetting and flicking the thing to no purpose.

When he bought the apartment and became a property owner instead of a tenant, it seemed to him that some sort of home improvement was in order to mark the occasion, and he took the switch plate off, intending to stuff the cavity with steel wool, spackle over it, and paint it to match the surrounding wall. But once he opened it up he recognized it for the ideal hiding place it was, and it had held his emergency cash fund ever since.

The money was still there, just over twelve hundred dollars. He replaced the switch plate, wondering why he was wasting time on it. He would never be coming back to this apartment.

He didn't waste further time replacing the dresser drawers, or straightening the mess his visitors had left. Nor did he wipe away his fingerprints. It was his apartment, he'd lived in it for years, and his prints were all over it, and what difference did it make? What difference did anything make?

When Keller got to the lobby, Neil was standing on the sidewalk to the left of the entrance, his hands clasped behind his back, his eyes aimed somewhere around the seventh floor of the building across the street. Keller looked, and the only lighted windows had their shades drawn, so it was hard to guess what was over there to hold such interest for the doorman. Keller decided it wasn't what he was seeing, it was what he was taking care not to look at, which in this case was Keller.

Sure, Officer, and I never set eyes on the man.

The man's stance didn't invite speech, so Keller passed him without a word, carrying his shopping bag in one hand, feeling the pressure of the SIG Sauer in the small of his back. He walked to the corner and put on his Homer Simpson cap even as he disappeared forever from Neil's field of vision.

On the next block, he stopped for a moment to watch a tow truck's two-man crew making their preparations for the removal of the Lincoln Town Car. No longer shielded by its DPL plates, or any plates at all, and being at once too far from the curb and right in front of a hydrant, it was an outstanding candidate for a tow, and would soon be on its way to the impound lot.

The sight of this gladdened Keller beyond all reason. There was, he knew, a German word—*Schadenfreude*—for what he was feeling; it meant experiencing joy through the pain of another, and Keller didn't suppose it was the noblest of emotions.

But he found himself smiling broadly all the way to his car, and just minutes ago he would have deemed it unlikely that he'd ever have occasion to smile again. *Schadenfreude*, he could only conclude, was better than no *Freude* at all.

The bridge and tunnel tolls were only collected from cars entering Manhattan. It cost you six dollars to come in and nothing to leave. That halved the number of agents required to collect the money, but Keller had always figured there was a further underpinning of logic to the scheme. After a visit to the big bad city, how many tourists still had enough money left to buy their way out?

What it meant to him was one less person who'd get a look at his face. He left the city via the Lincoln Tunnel and stopped at the first convenient place on the Jersey side to unfasten the DPL tags, which could draw unwelcome attention outside of the city. He didn't foresee any further use for them, but it seemed a waste to toss them, and he put them in the trunk, next to the spare tire.

He wondered if the Lincoln's owner would ever be reunited with his car, and if its disappearance might touch off an international incident. Maybe there'd be something about it in the papers.

He drove at first with no destination in mind, and when he finally asked himself where he was going, all he could think of was the Gujarati motel in Pennsylvania where he'd spent the previous night. "Me again," he'd say, and the slim dark girl in the parochial school getup would check him in with as little interest as she'd shown the first time. But could he even find the place? It was off Route 80, he knew that much, and he might recognize the exit when he got to it, but—

But it was a bad idea, he realized.

It was familiarity that made it attractive. He'd stayed there once, without incident, and that led him to regard it as safe. But suppose the girl who'd paid so little attention to him at the time had seen the inescapable photograph once more since his departure, and suppose it had rung a little bell, barely more audible than the rustle of that beaded curtain. She wouldn't bother to call the authorities, after all the man had checked out by then, and maybe she only fancied his resemblance to the man in the photograph. She might mention it to her parents, but that's as far as it would go.

Unless he was sufficiently brain-dead to show up again, giving her the chance for a good long look this time around, one that would confirm her suspicions. And the recognition might show on her face, the legendary inscrutability of Asians notwithstanding, in which case he'd have to do something about it. Or it wouldn't, and she'd check him in, wish him a pleasant evening, and pick up the phone the minute he was out of the office.

Besides, it was already two in the morning, and it would be another four hours or more before he reached the motel. Guests did drive all night and check in at daybreak, but not too many of them, because they'd run up against the motel's checkout time, which was generally noon at the latest. So anyone who showed up at six or seven in the morning was inviting more than the usual amount of attention, along with a time-wasting conversation about checkout time and the need to pay for a second night, and—

Never mind. It was a bad idea, and it was out of the question even if it had been a good idea, and the only appealing thing about it, its familiarity, was actually not so good after all.

Should he just grab the first right-looking motel he came to? It was late, and it had been a long day, and he might think more clearly after a night's sleep.

Still, he was awfully close to New York. Earlier, heading east, he'd felt safer the closer he got to New York. Now New York felt perilous, and he felt safer the more distance he put between himself and the city.

Should he eat something? Grab a cup of coffee?

He hadn't eaten anything since the movie house popcorn, but he wasn't hungry. Didn't much want coffee, either. And, while he was tired and his nerves frayed, he wasn't what you would call sleepy.

A rest area loomed ahead, and he pulled off and parked. The little building was locked up for the night, but the whole area was empty, and he peed in the bushes and went back to his car. He made himself comfortable behind the wheel and closed his eyes, and within seconds the lids popped right back up again. Another attempt yielded the same results. He gave up, turned the key, pulled out of the rest area and drove on.

20

Ten days later he made a tub of popcorn last all the way through a film in which a team of teenage computer nerds flimflammed a mob of Mafia tough guys and made off with several million dollars; the hero, who was a shade less geekier than his buddies, wound up with the girl, too. The film was obviously designed to appeal to a youthful audience, and the oldsters who bought their half-price tickets for weekday afternoons had given this one the wide berth it clearly deserved.

Keller would have passed, too, but it was the only show on offer that he hadn't already seen. There were eight screens at that theater, screening a total of six films—the two most popular pictures got two screens apiece, so that you never had more than an hour's wait for either of them. Keller had seen them both, and three of the other four, and now he'd seen the geek picture, too. He checked his watch, and it was early enough so that he could have slipped into one of the other rooms and taken a second shot at one of the other films, but most of them hadn't been that much fun the first time, and he didn't suppose a repeat viewing would uncover subtleties he'd missed the first time around.

The theater was part of a mall on the edge of Jackson, Mississippi. He'd spent the previous night in another of what he'd taken to thinking of as the Patel Motels, as if they constituted a vast chain of independents. This one was not far from Grenada, Mississippi, its official location a wide place in the road with the improbable name of Tie Plant. He'd weighed his options during the movie, but he hadn't quite decided whether he'd drive a little farther or start looking for a motel on the way out of Jackson. Decisions of that sort, like where to go next or what to do when he got there, tended to make themselves.

He left the theater, walked to his car. He was wearing the Homer Simpson cap, as always, but a few days ago he'd expanded his wardrobe with the addition of a denim jacket that someone had conveniently abandoned in another movie house somewhere in Tennessee. It had been a warm evening, so the jacket's owner could have gotten all the way home before he missed it, and when he came back in a day or two and failed to recover it, he could walk around scratching his head and wondering why anyone would walk off with such a ratty old thing, its cuffs and collar frayed and some of its seams starting to come undone.

Keller liked the garment well enough. It smelled a little of its former owner, just as his own blazer smelled a little of him, but it wasn't rank enough to put him off. It made a change, and an appropriate one in his current surroundings. A blue blazer, as *Playboy* and *GQ* assured their readers a couple of times a year, was the keystone of a man's wardrobe, perfectly acceptable at every sartorial situation short of a black-tie dinner or a wet T-shirt contest. That seemed to be true, and Keller had appreciated the garment's versatility ever since he left Des Moines, but in the rural South it had a harder time passing in a crowd. Keller wasn't whooping and slapping his knee at truck-pulling contests or handling serpents at Baptist jamborees, but all the same he felt less conspicuous in some good old boy's denim jacket.

■ ■ ■

There were two impulses that seemed to come naturally to a fugitive, or at least to the sort of fugitive Keller seemed to have become. The first was to run hard and fast, and the second was to go to ground somewhere, to get in bed and hide under the covers.

Obviously, you couldn't do both. But what Keller had come to see was that you couldn't do either one, not if you wanted to remain safe.

If you holed up, if you found one place and stayed there, you would keep running into the same people over and over. Sooner or later one of them would take a good long look at you, and the next thing he'd do was pick up a phone.

And if you ran for the border, there you'd be, going through post-9/11 security with no passport and no driver's license and a face every cop in the country was looking for. And if some miracle got you across the border, you'd be in some Mexican border town crawling with cops and informants, all on the lookout for gringo fugitives. Not exactly where he wanted to be.

So the trick, as far as he could make out, was to steer a course between the two extremes, to keep forever on the move without ever moving too far or too fast. One hundred miles a day, two hundred tops, and pick safe places to sleep and safe ways to get through the days.

You couldn't beat daytime movies. The theaters were virtually empty, and the employees bored out of their skulls. And at night you couldn't do better than a motel room, with the door locked and the TV on, but the sound turned down so nobody would complain.

He hadn't risked a motel every night. In Virginia, off I-81, he'd walked up to the door of a typical independent motel only to pick up some sort of vibe that stopped him in his tracks and sent him straight back to his car. Just nerves, he told himself, but whatever had prompted the impulse, he felt he had to honor it. He wound up spending that night in a rest area, and woke up with a big truck parked close on one side and what looked like the entire Partridge family having a picnic on the other. He was sure someone must have seen him, he was right there in plain sight and the sun was shining away, but he'd slept sitting up with his head tilted forward and the cap hiding his face, and he got out of there without incident.

Two nights ago, in Tennessee, he'd left it too long, and he came to three motels in a row with their NO VACANCY signs lit. He spotted a sign, FARM FOR SALE, and drove half a mile on a dirt road until he came to the property in question. There were no lights in the farmhouse, no vehicles to be seen except for an old Ford with its wheels removed. He thought of breaking into the house, if an actual break-in was even required; it seemed altogether possible the doors had been left unlocked.

And if someone showed up at daybreak to show the house? Or if some neighbor with a place farther along on the dirt road noticed his car as he drove by?

He drove instead to the barn, and parked his car where it wouldn't be seen. He shared the barn with an owl, who made more noise than he did, and some unidentifiable rodents, who made as little noise as possible, as intent on avoiding the owl as he was on avoiding human beings. The place smelled of animals and hay mold and other less definable barn odors, but he figured he was a long ways away from the nearest human, and that was worth something. He spread some straw around, smoothed it out, and stretched out on it, and he wound up getting a good night's sleep for his troubles.

On his way out the next morning he went and had a look at the Ford. The wheels were off, as he'd noted earlier, and somebody had pulled the engine, but the old car still sported a pair of license plates. TENNESSEE / THE VOLUNTEER STATE, he read, and there didn't seem to be anything on the plate to indicate the year. Rust made one of the bolts hard to turn, but he kept at it, and when he drove out of there the Sentra had Tennessee tags, and his Iowa plates were tucked out of sight under some straw in a corner of the barn.

The motel he found outside of Jackson had a sign on the counter indicating that one Sanjit Patel was its proprietor, but evidently this particular Patel had raised himself to that level of the American dream where he could hire people outside his family, and even outside his tribe. The young man behind the counter was a light-skinned African-American whose name tag identified him as Aaron Wheldon. He had a long oval face and short hair, wore glasses with heavy black rims, and beamed at Keller's approach, showing a lot of teeth. "Bart Simpson! My main man!"

Keller smiled in return, asked the price of a room, learned it was $49. He put three twenties on the counter and pushed the proffered registration card an inch or so toward the young man. "Maybe you could fill this out for me," he said. After a pause he added, "I wouldn't need a receipt."

Wheldon's eyes were thoughtful behind the thick lenses. Then he smiled broadly again and handed over a room key and a ten-dollar bill. With tax the room ought to come to something like $53, Keller knew, but ten dollars change struck him as a good compromise, because the state of Mississippi wouldn't see the tax, anymore than Sanjit Patel would see any of the fifty dollars.

"And I misspoke," Wheldon said, "saying Bart Simpson when anybody can see that's his daddy Homer on your cap. Y'all have a nice evening, Mr. Simpson."

Sure, and I never saw you, sir.

In the room, he turned on the TV and switched channels until he found CNN, and as usual he watched half an hour's worth of news before checking to see what else was available. And in the morning he found a coin box and bought a newspaper.

On his way south through Pennsylvania, he'd been able to pick up the *New York Times*, and he read a second story about the White Plains fire, this one informing him that the identification of charred remains as the body of Dorothea Harbison had been confirmed through dental records. That ended a hope he'd barely allowed himself to entertain, that somehow the body could have been that of someone else.

As the days passed, Keller kept buying the paper—*USA Today* on weekdays, whatever else he could find on the weekend. The coverage of the assassination and its aftermath seemed to fade and shrink right in front of him. Years ago Keller had developed a mental mechanism for coping with the reality of his work, picturing his victim, then leaching the color out of the image in his mind, turning it to a black-and-white picture. A series of further steps softened its focus and backed away from it, making it look smaller and smaller until it was nothing but a gray dot that winked and was gone. The technique was effective but not permanent—years later, a person he'd worked hard to forget might suddenly pop up in his mind, life-size and in color—but it had got him through some potentially difficult times, and now he saw that all he'd done was anticipate reality. Because time, unassisted by human will, did much the same thing on its own, as stories bloomed and faded from the news, their visibility diminished by some new outrage that burst out alongside them and replaced them entirely as objects of human interest.

It happened in the media, and when he thought about it he realized it happened much the same way in one's own consciousness, without effort and even in spite of effort. Things faded, blurred, lost their focus—or simply came to mind less frequently, and with less force.

He didn't have to search for an example. Some years ago he'd owned a dog, a fine Australian cattle dog named Nelson, and he'd arranged for a young woman named Andria to walk it for him. One thing had led to another, until he and Andria had come to share far more than Nelson's leash. He'd cared for her, and bought her a great many pairs of earrings, and then one day she left, and took the dog with her.

It was the sort of thing you had to accept, and so he'd accepted it, but it had wounded him profoundly, and there was never a day that he didn't think about Nelson, and about Andria.

Until one day he didn't.

And it was not as though it was suddenly over forever, and that neither the girl nor the dog ever came to mind again. Of course they did, both of them, and when they did he felt the same emotions he'd felt that first day, and had felt even more acutely a day later when the shock wore off. But the thoughts came less and less frequently, and the emotional charge that accompanied them grew less and less powerful, until the day came when those twin losses, while never forgotten, were just a part of his own long and curious history.

But why dig them up now as an example? He didn't have to look that far in the past. Just over a week ago he'd suffered the two greatest losses of his life in the course of a single day. His best friend was killed and his stamp collection was stolen, and he thought about them all the time, and yet already he could see that the thoughts were coming less frequently, and that each day they lost a little of their immediacy and began to find their way into the past. They still filled him with pain and regret, they still burned like acid, but each day he lived with them he got a little further away from them.

So it turned out you didn't have to forget things, not really. You just relaxed your grip on them and they floated off all by themselves.

21

Driving around New Orleans, looking for evidence of the devastation caused by Hurricane Katrina, he felt like one of the tourists walking around New York in the aftermath of 9/11, asking passersby how to get to Ground Zero. He'd seen the news coverage, knew how the winds and flooding had kicked the crap out of the city, but he didn't know his way around the place and couldn't tell what he was looking at. There were whole neighborhoods ruined, parts of the city that would never be the same, but he was uncertain where they were and unwilling to ask directions.

Besides, why look at blight? He'd been to Ground Zero as a volunteer, dishing out food to rescue workers, but he hadn't felt the need to return since then to stare at a hole in the ground. He wasn't about to pick up a hammer and help rebuild New Orleans, and wouldn't even be staying long enough to watch others rebuild it, so why stand around slack-jawed, gawking at the wreckage?

He drove around, found a neighborhood that looked interesting, and parked the car right on the street. There were no signs saying you couldn't, and no meters to feed. He tried to decide between the blazer and the denim jacket. It was too warm out for either, so he tugged his T-shirt out of his pants and arranged it to conceal the gun. It didn't really work, it was too snug and he was sure a person could see the gun's outline through it, and did he really need to walk around packing a pistol? He stashed the gun in the glove compartment, locked the car, and went off to see New Orleans.

Was it a good idea?

Probably not, he had to admit. The safest course of action would consist of doing what he'd been doing, keeping human contact to a bare minimum, spending his afternoons in darkened movie houses and his nights in motel rooms, getting his food from drive-up windows at fast-food outlets, and letting time pass with as little risk as possible. He knew how to do all of that, and there was no reason why he couldn't go on doing it indefinitely.

Well, that was a stretch. He was still using Miller Remsen's credit card to fill the Sentra's gas tank, and any day now that might stop being a good idea. He wasn't using much gas, because he wasn't putting in any high-mileage days behind the wheel, and he still had most of a tank of gas left from the last fill-up, not long after he'd crossed from Tennessee into Mississippi. And maybe he ought to make that the last tank of gas the late Mr. Remsen bought for him.

It was hard to say, because for all he knew Remsen was still lying undiscovered behind his counter, while all his neighbors filled their gas tanks at his expense. Each issue of *USA Today* had a page of news from all over, including one item each day from each of the fifty states. The stories were presumably of local interest, so that if you were from Montana, say, on a business trip to Maryland, with no access to the Missoula *Misery* or the Kalispell *Cat Box Liner,* good old *USA Today* would keep you connected to all the news back home.

It didn't really work for New York; anything halfway important that happened there was considered national news, but maybe it worked for Indiana. Keller had been checking every day, and had read brief items from all over the state, few of them remotely interesting, and none of them having to do with a man found dead in his ramshackle gas station. But that didn't mean they hadn't found him yet. Even by the standards of the news-from-all-over page, Keller had to admit it wasn't much of a story.

Whether or not they'd found the body, Keller knew the safe way to play it was to ditch Remsen's credit card. He could probably risk buying gas for cash, now that he wasn't using too much of it, and who was to say another credit card wouldn't come his way, as unexpectedly as Remsen's had?

But the Sentra had plenty of gas in its tank for now, and it wasn't burning any of it at the moment, and wouldn't as long as it stayed parked. The more immediate question was whether he was running a risk by walking around New Orleans, and that was one he didn't much want to ask himself because he knew he wasn't going to like the answer.

Yes, it was a risk.

On the other hand, could he really drive all the way to New Orleans, then turn around and drive out again, only to sustain himself with prefabricated burgers and fries from yet another soul-deadening fast-food joint? That hadn't been so bad in Tie Plant, Mississippi, or White Pine, Tennessee, where one's choices were limited, but Keller had been in New Orleans a few times over the years, and he could still remember the beignets and chicory coffee at Café du Monde. And that was just the tip of the Tabasco bottle—could he really leave this city without a bowl of gumbo, or a plate of red beans and rice, or an oyster po'boy sandwich, or jambalaya, or crawfish étouffée, or any of the spectacular dishes you could get virtually anywhere in New Orleans, and nowhere else in the world?

Of course he could. He could walk away from all of it—or drive away, actually—but he wasn't sure it would be a good idea.

Over the years, when he was working for the old man, he'd been dispatched on several occasions to deal with men who'd gone into hiding, generally as part of the government's Witness Protection Program. Furnished with new identities and set up in a new environment, all these individuals had needed to do was keep a low profile and stay out of the limelight.

One of them was the man Keller had pursued to Roseburg, Oregon, and up until then he was a Witness Protection Program success story, a client who had adapted readily to his new life in the Pacific Northwest. He'd been an accountant originally, with no criminal background, and had wound up knowing too much and, when the feds leaned on him, telling what he knew. But he remained a mild-mannered accountant at heart, and he'd done just fine in Roseburg, running a quick-print franchise and mowing his front lawn every Saturday morning, and could have gone on that way forever if someone hadn't happened to recognize him on an ill-advised family outing in San Francisco. But someone did, and Keller came calling, and that was that.

The others, however, weren't constitutionally capable of settling forever into the quiet life the federal agents arranged for them. One couldn't stay away from the racetrack, and another became inexplicably homesick for Elizabeth, New Jersey. Another got drunk periodically and told his business to strangers, and it didn't take too long for him to pick the wrong stranger. And then there was the paragon who'd turned federal witness to get out from under a child molestation charge; spirited away to Hays, Kansas, he'd been picked up for loitering outside a school playground in Topeka. The feds managed to get the charges dropped, but not before the word got back east, and Keller was scouting around, looking for the guy, when he got arrested right there in Hays for willful abduction and unnatural sexual conduct with a minor. The old man shook his head and said something about doing the world a favor; then he called Keller back to New York, having arranged for a fellow prisoner to strangle the pervert in his cell.

Boredom was the enemy, and if the new life you created for yourself was unendurably monotonous, how could you stay with it?

So he'd treat himself to a day in New Orleans. A few hours, anyway. He wouldn't get drunk and run his mouth, wouldn't throw his money around at the racetrack or Harrah's casino, wouldn't haunt schoolyards or carouse on Bourbon Street. A couple of meals, a walk through streets shaded by live oaks. Then back in the car and back to the highway, and New Orleans, like everything else, could slip from the present into the past.

Knowing it couldn't last, knowing one afternoon was all he'd have in New Orleans, Keller made the most of it. He walked down streets at random, taking in the older homes, some of them virtual mansions, others quite modest. They all looked good to him, and he did something he hadn't done in years, let himself imagine what it would be like to live here, what sort of life he might lead if he bought one of these houses and spent the rest of his days in and around it. It wasn't a terribly exotic fantasy, and a month ago he could have achieved it readily enough. But a month ago all he'd wanted to do was live out his days in New York, and that was out of the question, and so was this. His net worth was now limited to the cash in his pocket and five Swedish stamps he couldn't sell, and he could no more afford to buy one of these houses than he could risk giving up the highway and settling down.

Still, it was something for his mind to play with while he walked these streets and looked at these houses. He'd want one with an upstairs porch, he decided. He could easily picture himself sitting in a white wooden rocking chair on just such a porch, looking out over the street, maybe sipping at a glass of—what?

Iced tea?

He pushed aside thoughts of Dot—her porch, her iced tea—and walked on. On St. Charles Avenue, where the streetcar used to run in the days before Katrina, he stopped at one small restaurant for a cup of coffee and a bowl of seafood gumbo. He sat in a booth, and the waitress who brought him his meal commented cheerfully on his Homer Simpson cap. After she'd left his table he took the cap off and set it on the seat beside him. He was tiring of Homer, and wondered if the cap had outlived its usefulness. Keller's picture had stopped showing up on the newscasts, and the papers had tired of running it, so maybe his face was less likely now to set off alarms in people's head. But they still noticed Homer, you couldn't help noticing Homer, and after they'd noticed the vivid yellow embroidery, maybe their eyes would be drawn to a face they'd otherwise glide right past.

The gumbo was terrific, the coffee a substantial cut above what they handed out through the drive-up windows. He'd almost forgotten that food could be a pleasure, but New Orleans, a city that was about food as surely as New York was about real estate and Washington about politics, had refreshed his memory.

He had just about made up his mind to leave the Homer cap behind, but it was on his head when he walked out of the café. He was still wearing it an hour later when he felt hungry enough to eat again, and stopped at a hole in the wall, just a counter and stools opposite a grill. There were hooks in the wall behind the row of stools, and people hung their jackets and such on them, and he took off his cap and hung it up. He had a magnificent plate of red beans and rice and smoked sausage, and another cup of good coffee, and when he'd finished and was ready to go he found that another patron had walked off with his Homer cap and left a New Orleans Saints cap in its place.

Interesting, he thought, how decisions had a way of making themselves if you just got out of their way. The Saints cap was adjustable, of course, as just about all ball caps seemed to be nowadays, but he didn't need to adjust it. It fit perfectly just the way it was, and he settled it in place, gave the brim a tug, and walked on.

There was a twenty-four-hour drugstore on St. Charles, and it even came equipped with a drive-up window. He didn't need it to be open all night, and he couldn't see the use of a drive-up window for a drugstore unless you were picking up a prescription. But he'd been showing his face to all of New Orleans already today, so why not push his luck and see what they had that he needed?

Specifically, he was looking for something that might help him deal with his hair. He wasn't quite ready to risk visiting a barber, who could hardly be expected to cut his hair without taking a long hard look at him, and would only look longer and harder when Keller asked for a change in hair color.

What he really wanted was something to make him look older. If he could dye his hair gray, well, that would be ideal. The photo, taken during his visit to Albuquerque, showed a man with dark hair and a younger face than the one he wore now. With a little gray in his hair, and the hair trimmed into more of an older man's cut, he'd look less like his picture, and less threatening as well.

He found a kit containing an electric clipper and a couple of different interchangeable blades, all of which according to the hype on the package could be used to "create easily at home all of the latest hairstyles available from the world's most exclusive barbers." That sounded a little optimistic to Keller, who was prepared to settle for less from the contraption.

There was a bewildering selection of products to color the hair, some specifically for men, others marketed to women. Keller wondered how the dye was supposed to know the sex of the person using it, or why it would care.

Every possible hue was represented, including blue and green, but the one thing he couldn't find was gray. If you already had gray hair, every manufacturer had ways for you to deal with it. If your gray hair had a yellowish cast to it, you could try this product; if you wanted to bring out its hidden blue highlights, whatever they were, you could try that one. Or you could get rid of the gray and restore your hair's natural color, two mealy-mouthed ways of describing the process of dyeing your gray hair some color it could no longer manage to be on its own.

He couldn't understand why they wouldn't let you dye your hair gray, although he was beginning to believe that he was the only person alive that wanted to. He wound up picking up a packet of a product for men promising to get rid of the gray and restore the natural color to a head of light brown hair. But would it do anything if you applied it to hair as dark as his own? He was dubious, but figured he'd buy it, anyway.

And he bought the clippers, too. If all else failed, he could use them to take his hair right down to the scalp. Then all he'd have to do was keep his cap on, and at the end of ten days or two weeks he'd have a nice short buzz cut.

Walking along, aiming himself in the general direction of where he'd parked the car, he wondered if he'd actually taken the cap of the fellow who'd walked off with Homer. Suppose his cap had been swiped by someone who'd walked in bareheaded, and Keller had turned around and stolen some other fellow's cap in return, essentially robbing Peter to get even with Paul.

That was something he could live with, something that didn't figure to weigh too heavily on any celestial balance sheet, but what if the cap's rightful owner spotted him walking down the street?

Well, he was on his way out of New Orleans, so that became

less of a likelihood with every passing moment. Besides, the article in question was a Saints cap, and half of the city seemed to be similarly attired. The team had had a good year, had done far better than anybody expected them to do, and the whole country had elected to see in their performance the resurgence and regeneration of the city itself. If the Saints could make the playoffs, the reasoning seemed to hold, then certainly New Orleans could get over a dinky little thing like a hurricane.

Homer Simpson had set him apart, even while it made his face less recognizable. The Saints cap did every bit as much to conceal his face, but did so by bonding him with the people among whom he walked.

He grinned, gave the brim a tug.

The street he was on was called Euterpe. The first time he saw the street sign he'd been unsure how to pronounce it, though he could have narrowed it down to a couple of likely choices. Then he encountered other parallel streets with names like Terpsichore and Melpomene and Polymnia, and they didn't quite do it, but then Erato and Calliope turned up and he worked it out. He knew from crossword puzzles that Erato was one of the nine muses, and it seemed to him that Calliope, in addition to being a steam instrument you might encounter on a carnival midway, was another. And that was why Euterpe had been faintly familiar, because she'd turned up in a crossword puzzle once or twice herself, and that meant you pronounced it You-Tour-Pee, with that long *e* on the end of the word, as in all those Greek names, Nike and Aphrodite and Persephone and, well, Calliope.

Imagine naming streets after the nine muses. Where else would it ever occur to them to do that? Well, Athens, maybe, but where else?

He walked along Euterpe and came to Prytania, who as far as he knew wasn't a muse at all. *Rule, Prytania, Prytania rules the waves . . .* He crossed Prytania and walked another block to a street called Coliseum, which was Roman, not Greek, and which bordered a small park that might have been two football fields laid end to end. Except Coliseum, which had been laid out either by a drunk or by someone imaginative enough to name streets after the muses, or both, meandered like the mighty Mississippi itself, making the resultant park wider than a football field in some parts and narrower in others.

Which was just as well, Keller thought, because in order to play football there you'd have to cut down a couple dozen live oak trees, and anyone who'd do that ought to be hanged from one of them instead. They were magnificent trees, and while it might not be the best route back to his car, it was worth a few minutes just to walk on the greensward among these majestic oaks, with the light fading and the day drawing to a close and—

A woman screamed.

22

“Stop! Oh, God! *Somebody help me!”*

His first thought was that someone had screamed at the sight of him, recognized him as the Des Moines Assassin and cried out in terror. But the thought was gone before the scream had ceased to echo in the still air. It had come from fifty yards away, off to the left and halfway across the little park. Keller saw movement, screened partly by a tree trunk, and heard another cry, less distinct this time, and cut short.

A woman was being attacked.

Not your problem, he told himself, immediately and unequivocally. He was the object of a nationwide manhunt, and the last thing he was going to do was get involved in somebody else’s problem. And it was probably just a domestic quarrel, anyway, one of Nature’s noblemen kicking the crap out of his slattern of a wife, and if the cops came she’d decide not to press charges, and might even take her husband’s side and go after the cops then and there, which was why cops hated responding to calls of that sort.

And he wasn’t a cop, and didn’t have a dog in this fight, as they would put it in the states he’d been spending time in lately. So what he would do now was turn around and leave the park and walk back up Euterpe—pronounced You-Tour-Pee—and figure out a route that would get him back to his car, and then find his way out of this town as quickly as he possibly could.

That was the only course of action that made the slightest bit of sense.

But what he was doing, even as he was working all of this out in his mind, was racing full speed toward the source of the screams.

No question what was going on. There was nothing remotely ambiguous about the scene that confronted Keller. Even in the dim light, it was unmistakable.

The woman, dark-haired, slender, was sprawled out on the grass, one hand braced against the ground, the other held up to ward off her attacker. And the guy was your stereotypical mad rapist from central casting, his hair a ragged dirty-blond mop, his broad flat mug sporting a week's growth of patchy beard, and a teardrop jailhouse tattoo on one cheekbone to let you know he wasn't just another pretty face. He was crouched over her, tearing at her clothes.

"Hey!"

The man whirled at the sound, bared his teeth at Keller as if they were weapons. He came up out of his crouch, light glinting off the blade of his knife.

"Drop it," Keller said.

But he didn't drop the knife. He moved it from side to side as if trying to hypnotize a subject, and Keller looked not at the knife but at the man's eyes, and reached behind his own back for the gun in his waistband. But of course it wasn't there, it was tucked away in the glove compartment of a locked car, damn it all, and he'd be lucky if he ever saw it again. He was facing a man with a knife, and all he had was a plastic bag from Walgreen's. What was he going to do, give the guy a haircut?

The woman was trying to tell him that the man had a knife,

but he knew that. He didn't listen to her but focused on the man, focused on his eyes. He couldn't tell their color, not in that light, but he could see a keen manic energy in them, and he let go of his shopping bag and balanced his weight on the balls of his feet and tried to remember something useful from the various bits and pieces of martial arts training he'd had over the years.

He'd had classes and one-on-one instruction in kung fu and judo and tae kwon do, along with some Western-style hand-to-hand combat training, though he'd never trained in any disciplined fashion, never stayed with any of it for any length of time. But every trainer he'd ever known had offered the same instruction when you were unarmed and the other guy had a knife. The thing to do, they all would tell you, was turn around and run like hell.

The chances were considerable, they'd all agreed, that he wouldn't chase you. And Keller was sure that was true with this drooling blond madman. He wouldn't run after Keller, he'd stay right where he was and get back to raping the woman.

Keller watched his eyes, and when the man moved, Keller moved. He sprang to the side, kicked high in the air, and caught the wrist of the hand that held the knife. He was wearing sneakers and wished they could have been steel-toed work shoes, but his aim and his timing almost made up for whatever the sneakers lacked, and the knife went flying even as the man roared in pain.

"Okay," he said, stepping back, rubbing at his wrist. "Okay, you win. I'm going."

And he started to back away.

"I don't think so," Keller said, and went after him. The guy turned, ready to fight, and swung a roundhouse right that Keller ducked underneath. He straightened up and butted the guy in the chin, and when the guy's head snapped back Keller reached out and grabbed hold of it, one hand closing on a fistful of greasy yellow hair, the other cupping the bristly chin.

Keller didn't have to think about what came next. His hands knew what to do, and they did it.

He let go of the man, allowed the body to slip to the ground. A few feet away, the woman was staring, her mouth open, her shoulders heaving.

Time to go, he thought. Time to turn around and slip off into the night. By the time she pulled herself together he'd be gone. *Who was that masked man? Why, I don't know, but he left this silver bullet. . .*

He walked over to the woman, held out a hand. She took it and he drew her to her feet.

"My God," she said. "You just saved my life."

If there was a response to that, Keller didn't know what it might be. The only ones that came to mind started with *Aw, shucks.* He stood there with what definitely felt like an *Aw shucks* look on his face, and she stepped back, took a look at him, and then lowered her eyes to look down on the man at her feet.

"We have to call the police," she said.

"I'm not sure that's such a good idea."

"But don't you know who he is? This has to be the man who killed the nurse three nights ago in Audubon Park, raped her and stabbed her ten, twenty times. He fits the description. And that's not the first woman he attacked. He was going to kill me!"

"But you're safe now," he told her.

"Yes, and thank God for that, but that doesn't mean we can let him walk away."

"I don't think there's much chance of that."

"What do you mean?" She took a closer look. "What did you do to him? Is he . . ."

"I'm afraid so, yes."

"But how can that be? He had a knife, you saw it, it must have been a foot long."

"Not quite."

"Close enough." She was getting her composure back, he noticed, and more quickly than he would have expected. "And you had your bare hands."

"It's too warm for gloves."

"I don't know what that means."

"It was sort of a joke," Keller said. "You said I had bare hands, and I said it was too warm to be wearing gloves."

"Oh."

"It wasn't all that great a joke," he admitted, "and explaining it doesn't do a lot to improve it."

"No, please, I'm sorry, I'm just a little slow at the moment. What I meant, of course, is that you didn't have anything *in* your hands."

"I had a shopping bag," he said, and found it and picked it up. "But that's not what you meant."

"I meant like, you know, a gun or a knife, something like that."

"No."

"And he's dead? You actually killed him?"

She was hard to read. Was she impressed? Horrified? He couldn't tell.

"And you just turned up from out of nowhere. If I were some kind of religious crank I'd probably figure you were an angel. Well?"

"Well what?"

"Well, are you an angel?"

"Not even close."

"I didn't just offend you, did I? Using the term 'religious crank'?"

"No."

"So I guess that means you're not a religious crank yourself, or you'd be offended. Well, thank God for that. That was a joke."

"I thought it might be."

"It's not very funny," she said, "but it's the best I can do right now, with just my bare hands. Ha! That got a smile out of you, didn't it?"

"It did."

She took a breath. "You know," she said, "even if he's dead, we're still supposed to call the police, aren't we? We can't just leave him here for the Sanitation Department to pick up. I've got my phone in my purse, I'll just call 911."

"Please don't."

"Why? Isn't that what they're for? They may not prevent crime or catch criminals, but afterwards you call them and they come in and take care of stuff. Why don't you want me to—"

She broke off the words on her own, and she looked at him, and he saw her take in the visual information, saw it all register. She put her hand to her mouth and stared at him.

Hell.

23

"You're safe," he told her.

"I am?"

"Yes."

"But—"

"Look," he said, "I didn't save your life so that I could kill you myself. You don't have to be afraid of me."

She looked at him, thought it over, nodded. She was older than he'd thought at first, well up in her thirties. A pretty woman, with dark hair that fell to her shoulders.

"I'm not afraid," she said. "But you're—"

"Yes."

"And you're here in New Orleans."

"Just for today."

"And then—"

"Then I'll go somewhere else." In the distance he heard the wail of a siren, but where it was headed and whether it was an ambulance or a police car was impossible to say. "We can't just hang around here," he said.

"No, of course not."

"I'll walk you to your car," he said, "and then I'll get out of your life, and out of your city. I can't tell you what to do, but if you could just forget you ever saw me—"

"That might be difficult. But I won't say anything, if that's what you mean."

That was what he meant.

They left the park, walked along Camp Street. The siren—ambulance, police, whatever it was—had faded out somewhere in the distance. At length she broke the silence to ask where he would go next, and before he could think how to respond she said, "No, don't tell me. I don't even know why I asked."

"I couldn't tell you if I wanted to."

"Why not? Oh, because you don't know. I guess you have to wait until they tell you where to go next. You're smiling, did I say something ridiculous?"

He shook his head. "I'm out here all by myself," he said. "There's nobody to tell me what to do next."

"I thought you were part of a conspiracy."

"The way a pawn's part of a chess tournament."

"I don't understand."

"No, how could you? I'm not sure there's anything to follow. Where's your car parked?"

"In my garage," she said. "I got restless, I went out for a walk. I live a few blocks over that way."

"Oh."

"And you don't have to walk me home, really. I'll be all right." She laughed sharply, broke it off. "I was just about to say this is a safe neighborhood, and it is, really. You're probably in a hurry to get . . . well, wherever it is you're going."

"I ought to be."

"But you're not?"

"No," he said. It was true, he wasn't in a hurry, and he wondered why. They fell silent, walked past another large two-story frame house with porches on both floors. A rocking chair, he thought, and a glass of iced tea, and someone to talk with.

Without planning to, he said, "Not that you'd have any reason to believe me, and not that it matters, but I didn't kill that man in Iowa."

She let his words hang there, and he wondered why he'd felt the need to say them. Then, softly, she said, "I believe you."

"Why would you believe me?"

"I don't know. Why did you just now fight that man and kill him and save my life? The police are looking for you everywhere. Why would you run such a risk?"

"I've been wondering that myself. From the standpoint of self-preservation, it was a pretty stupid thing to do. And I knew that, too, but that didn't help. I just . . . reacted."

"I'm glad you did."

"So am I."

"Are you?"

What he said, instead of answering her question, was, "Ever since the assassination in Des Moines, ever since I saw a picture of myself on CNN, I've been running. Driving around, sleeping in my car, sleeping in cheap motels, sleeping in movie theaters. The only person I ever really cared about is dead and the only possession I treasured is gone. All my life I've always figured things would work out and I'd get by, and for years they did, and I did, and it feels as though the string's pretty much played out. Sooner or later I'll slip up, or sooner or later they'll get lucky, and they'll catch up with me. And the only good thing about that is I'll get to stop running."

He drew a breath. "I didn't mean to say all that," he said. "I don't know where it came from."

"What difference does it make?" She stopped walking, turned to face him. "I said I believed you. That you didn't do it."

"And I think I said it didn't matter. Not that you believe me, that does matter, though I don't know why it should. But whether I did it or not, *that* doesn't matter."

"Of course it does! If they framed an innocent man—"

"They framed me, all right. But it's a hell of a stretch to call me innocent."

"That man in the park just now. He wasn't the first man you ever killed, was he?"

"No."

She nodded. "You were awfully proficient at it," she said. "It looked like something you might have done before."

"I left New Orleans years ago. That's unusual, most people who start out here never leave. The city gets a hold on a person."

"I can understand that."

"But I had to get out," she said, "and I left. And then after Katrina, when half the city left, that's when I came back. Trust me to get everything backwards."

"What brought you back?"

"My father. He's dying."

"I'm sorry."

"So's he. He didn't want to go to a hospice. This is a man who wouldn't let them evacuate him during the hurricane, and he said he'd be damned if he'd leave his house now. 'I was born in this house, *chère,* and I shall damn well die in it.' As a matter of fact he was born in a hospital, like most people, but I guess you're allowed to exaggerate when you're being eaten alive by cancer. And I tried to think what I had to do in my life that was more important than nursing him and letting him die at home, and I couldn't think of a thing."

"You're not married."

"Not anymore. You?"

He shook his head. "Never."

"Mine lasted a year and a half. No children. All I had was a job and an apartment, and they were nothing I couldn't walk away from. Now I do substitute teaching a couple of days a week, and hire a woman to tend to Daddy when I'm working. What I make doesn't do much more than cover what I have to pay her, but it makes a change."

Chère, he thought. Like the singer? Or was it short for Sharon or Sherry or Cheryl, something like that?

Like it mattered.

"That's my house on the next block. With the azaleas and rhododendrons in front, so overgrown they're hiding the downstairs porch. They ought to be trimmed, but I wouldn't know where to start."

"It looks nice. A little lush and untamed, but nice all the same."

"The ground-floor sitting room's got his bed in it, so he doesn't have to bother with the stairs, and I made up a bed for myself in the den for the same reason. The whole second floor's empty, and I can't remember the last time anyone had occasion to go up there."

"Just the two of you in that big house?"

"There'll be three tonight," she said, "and you'll have the entire second floor all to yourself."

He waited in the hallway while she saw to her father. "I've brought a man home, Daddy," he heard her say.

"Well, aren't you the little hellion."

"Not like that," she said. "You're an old man with a dirty mind. This gentleman's a friend of Pearl O'Byrne's, he needs a place to stay. He'll be upstairs, and if it works out he might rent that front room."

"Just be more work for you, *chère*. Not saying the money won't come in handy."

He felt like an eavesdropper, and walked out of earshot. He was looking at a framed print of a horse jumping a fence when she emerged and led him to the kitchen.

She made a pot of coffee, and when it had dripped through she filled two large mugs and set them on the kitchen table, along with a sugar bowl and a little pitcher of cream. He said he preferred his coffee black, and she said so did she, and returned the cream to the refrigerator. They talked while they drank their coffee, and then she said he must be hungry and insisted on making him a sandwich.

Once, years ago, starved for a sounding board, he'd bought a stuffed animal, a little plush dog, and carried it around with him for a week or two just so he'd have someone to talk to. The dog had been a good listener, never interrupting, just taking everything in, but he'd been no better in the role than this woman was now. He talked until they'd finished the pot of coffee, and didn't object when she made a second pot, and talked some more.

"I was wondering what was in the bag," she said, when he'd told about wanting to change his appearance. He showed her the clippers and the packet of hair dye. The clippers would probably work okay, she said, although it would be hard for a person to use them on his own head. As for the hair dye, she thought he'd be taking an awful chance. It might work to turn gray or white hair the promised shade of light brown, but apply it to hair as dark as his own and you might wind up with something more in the tangerine family.

And you couldn't really dye dark hair gray, she told him. What you could do, say for a costume ball or a theatrical role, was spray what was essentially a gray paint onto your hair. It would wash out, though, so you would have to renew it after every shampoo, or even after getting caught in the rain, and a wig would be simpler and more effective.

He said he'd thought about a wig, and ruled it out, and she agreed, saying you could always spot a man wearing a hairpiece. But could you? If it fooled you, you'd never know you'd been fooled.

"I dye my hair," she said suddenly. "Could you tell?"

"Are you serious?"

She nodded. "I started six, seven years ago, when the first gray hairs showed up. All the women in my family go gray early, they have this magnificent silver hair and everyone says how they look like queens. I said the hell with that, and I went looking for Miss Clairol. I've never let it grow out, so I don't know how gray I'd be by now if I did, and with luck I'll never find out. You really can't tell?"

"No," he said, "and I'm still having trouble believing you."

She fluffed her hair. "Well, I just touched it up last week, so it shouldn't show, but if you look closely maybe you can see the roots."

She leaned toward him, and he looked down into her hair. Was there some gray showing at the roots? He couldn't really tell, it was hard to put the image into focus at that range, but what he did notice was the smell of her hair, all fresh and clean.

She straightened up, and her face looked a little flushed. All that coffee, he thought. She said, "You want to keep from being recognized, right? I have some ideas. Let me think about it, and tomorrow we'll see what we can do."

"All right."

"Do you want any more coffee? Because I've already had more than I should."

"I feel the same way."

"I'll show you to your room," she said. "It's a nice room. I think you'll like it."

24

In the morning he showered in the upstairs bathroom, then put on the same clothes and went downstairs. She had breakfast on the table, grapefruit halves and French toast with syrup, and after a second cup of coffee she got her Ford Taurus out of the garage and gave him a ride to where he'd parked the Sentra. There was a ticket on it, as she'd said there might be, but what would they do if it went unpaid? Send a summons to a broken-down farm in eastern Tennessee?

He followed her back home, and parked in her garage as instructed, while she left the Taurus in the driveway. "You're going to stay here for a while," she'd told him over breakfast, and he said he bet she was good at getting little kids to mind what she said. She said if she was being bossy that was just too bad. "I didn't object when you saved my life," she said. "So don't give me grief when I return the favor, you hear?"

"Yes, ma'am."

"That's better," she said. "It sounds funny, though. 'Yes, ma'am.'"

"Whatever you say, *chère*. That better?"

"Now when did you turn into an Orleanean?"

"Huh?"

"Calling me *chère*."

"That's your name, isn't it? It's not? It's what your father calls you."

"It's what everybody calls everybody," she said. "In New Orleans. It's French for *dear.* You order a po'boy for lunch, the old girl who brings it is apt to call you *chère*."

"The waitress in the place I go in New York calls everybody *hon.*"

"Same idea," she said.

But she didn't say what her name was. Nor did he ask.

He sat at the round kitchen table in one of the oak captain's chairs while she played barber. His shirt was off and she'd draped a bedsheet over his shoulders. She was wearing faded jeans and a man's white dress shirt with the sleeves rolled up, and she looked a little like Rosie the Riveter in a patriotic World War II poster, only her rivet gun was the electric clippers from Walgreen's.

Back in New York, Keller had gone to the same barber for almost fifteen years. The man's name was Andy and he owned his own three-chair barbershop, and once a year he flew back to São Paulo to visit his relatives. That was all Keller knew about him, along with the fact that he was a heavy user of breath mints, and he didn't suppose Andy knew very much about him, either, because his monthly visits were relatively silent affairs, and Keller almost always fell asleep in the chair and didn't wake up until Andy cleared his throat and tapped the arm of the chair.

He didn't expect to doze off now, but the next thing he knew she was telling him he could open his eyes. He did, and she steered him down the hall to the bathroom, where he looked long and hard at his reflection in the mirror. The face that gazed back at him was his face, that much was evident, but it looked very different from anything he'd ever seen in a mirror before.

His hair had been shaggy and now it was short, but not crew-cut short. It was just long enough to lie flat, and she'd shaped it in what had once been called an Ivy League style, or a Princeton. Add a tweed sport coat and a knit tie and a pipe and he might look almost professorial.

But she hadn't just cut his hair, he realized. His forehead was higher, and his hairline indented at the temples. She'd used the clippers to create the illusion of a decade's worth of male-pattern baldness, and added a good ten years to his appearance in the process. He tried different expressions, smiling and frowning, even glaring, and the effect was interesting. It seemed to him that he looked a good deal less dangerous, less like a man who could assassinate a governor and more like the trusted assistant who wrote his speeches.

He went back to the kitchen, where she was running a vacuum cleaner. She switched it off when she saw him and he told her he felt like Rip Van Winkle. "When I woke up," he said, "I was ten years older. I looked like somebody's lovable old uncle."

"I wasn't sure you'd like it. I have some ideas about the color, too, but what I'd like to do is wait a day or two so both of us can get used to it the way it is now, and then it'll be easier to figure out what else to do."

"That makes sense. But—"

"But it means staying here, is that what you were going to say? Last night you talked about how tired you were of running."

"That's true."

"Don't you think maybe it's time to stop running, now that you've finally got a good chance? Your car's parked off the street. No one can see it, but it's there whenever you need it. You can have the room upstairs for as long as you want. No one else has any use for it and you're not getting in anybody's way up there. It's no trouble at all cooking for one extra person, and if you start to feel guilty about imposing I'll let you take me out for dinner every once in a while. I bet I know a restaurant or two you might like."

"I could get new ID," he said. "A driver's license, even a passport. It's trickier than it used to be, they've tightened up security in the past few years, but you can still do it. It takes time, though."

"What exactly have y'all got," she said, "besides time?"

She cleaned out the dresser and closet in his bedroom, filling two Hefty bags with clothes she swore no one had worn in twenty years. "All of this should have gone to the Goodwill ages ago," she said. "You'll have enough room for your things, won't you?"

His things, everything he owned in the world, filled a small suitcase and a shopping bag. He had almost enough room to give every garment its own dresser drawer.

Later, she had to go out, and wondered if he could stay downstairs where he could hear her father if he called out. "He sleeps most of the time," she said, "and when he's awake he doesn't do much but talk back to the television set. He can get to the bathroom by himself, and he doesn't like to be helped, but if he should fall down—"

He sat in the kitchen and read the paper, and when he'd finished it he went upstairs for a book in the hall bookcase that had caught his eye earlier. It was a Loren Estleman western, about an itinerant hangman, and he sat in the kitchen reading it and drinking coffee until the old man called out.

He went in and found the man sitting up in bed, his pajama top unbuttoned, a cigarette smoldering between two fingers of his right hand. You could see the illness in his face. Keller wondered what kind of cancer the man had, and if it was smoking-related, and if he should be smoking now. Then he asked himself what difference it could possibly make at this stage.

"It's liver cancer," the man said, reading his mind. "Smoking's got nothing to do with it. Well, next to nothing. You believe doctors, smoking's to blame for every damn thing. Acid rain, global warming, you name it. My daughter around?"

"She stepped out."

"Stepped out? You got a nice way of putting things. Not teaching her brats, is she? She usually gets this colored girl to look after me when she does."

"I think she had some shopping to do."

"Step over this way so I can get a better look at you. Man gets old and sick, he gets to order people around. I call that inadequate compensation, myself. You think much about dying?"

"Sometimes."

"A man your age? I swear I never once gave it a moment's thought, and now here I am doing it. I'll say this, I don't think much of it. You sleeping with her?"

"Sir?"

"Can't be the hardest question anybody ever asked you. My daughter. Are you sleeping with her?"

"No."

"You're not? Y'all aren't queer, are you?"

"No."

"You don't look it, but in my experience you can't always tell. There's people who swear they can, but I don't believe them. You like it here?"

"It's a beautiful city."

"Well, it's New Orleans, isn't it? We get used to it, you see. I meant this house. You like it?"

"It's very comfortable."

"You be staying with us for a while?"

"I believe so," he said. "Yes, I think I will."

"I'm tired. I think I'll get some sleep."

"I'll let you be."

He was on his way out the door when the old man's voice stopped him in midstep.

"You get the chance," he said, "you sleep with her. Or one day you'll be too old to do it anymore. And what you'll do is hate yourself for every chance you let get away from you."

The following day they were at an optometrist's shop on Rampart Street. She'd vetoed his plan to get reading glasses, insisting they wouldn't look right, and when he said he didn't need regular glasses, she told him he'd be surprised. "And if your vision is almost perfect," she said, "he'll give you lenses with almost no correction."

It turned out that he needed one prescription for distance and another for reading. "Two birds with one stone," the optometrist said. "In other words, bifocals."

Jesus, bifocals. He tried on frames, and the one he liked was of heavy black plastic. She looked at him, laughed, said something about Buddy Holly, and steered him to a less assertive metal frame, with rounded rectangular lens openings. He tried it on, and had to admit she was right.

There were shops where they made your glasses in an hour, but this wasn't one of them. "About this time tomorrow," the fellow said, and they stopped at Café du Monde for café au lait and beignets, and paused on their way through Jackson Square to watch a woman feeding the pigeons as if her life depended on it.

She said, "Did you see the paper? The DNA test came back. He was definitely the man who raped and killed that nurse in Audubon Park."

"No surprise there."

"No, but wait'll you hear what they think happened. You know how the live oaks will have branches that come almost to the ground?"

"They're the only tree I know that's like that."

"Well, see, it makes them real easy to climb. And that's what they believe he did, climbed up into one of the trees to wait for a victim to pass by."

"I think I can see where this is going."

"And then, because he had a something-point-something blood alcohol level, he lost his balance and fell, and he landed on his head and broke his neck and died."

"The world is a dangerous place."

"But a little less so," she said, "now that he's not in it anymore."

Her name was Julia Emilie Roussard. She'd written it on the flyleaf of one of the books he picked up.

It took him two days to use it. For all the conversations they had, there was somehow never an occasion where he could fit her name into one of his sentences.

He took her out to lunch after they picked up his eyeglasses (with a complimentary leather case bearing the optometrist's name and address, and an impregnated strip of cloth for cleaning the lenses). On the way home she reminded him that he'd talked about two losses, his best friend and his most prized possession. Who was the friend, she wondered, and what was the possession?

He answered the second part first. His stamp collection, gone when he got into his apartment.

"You're a stamp collector? Seriously?"

"Well, it was a hobby, but I was pretty serious about it. I gave it a lot of my time, and put quite a bit of money into it." He told her a little about his collection, and how the childhood hobby had drawn him back in as an adult.

"And the friend?"

"It was a woman," he said.

"Your wife? No, you said you've never been married."

"Not a wife, not a girlfriend. It was never physical, it wasn't that kind of a relationship. I suppose you could say she was a business associate, but we were very close."

"When you say business associate . . ."

He nodded. "She was killed by the same people who set me up. They tried to make it look as though she'd burned herself up in a fire, but they didn't try too hard. They set a fire any rookie investigator would spot right away as arson, and they left her with two bullets in her head." He shrugged. "They probably didn't care what the cops called it. It's not like anybody could do anything about it."

"Do you miss her?"

"All the time. That's probably the reason I talk so much. I wouldn't ordinarily, not on such short acquaintance. There's two reasons, actually, and one is that you're very easy to talk to, but the other is that I'm used to talking to Dot, and she's gone."

"That was her name? Dot?"

"Dorothea, actually. I always thought it was Dorothy, and either I got it wrong or the papers did, because Dorothea was the way it appeared in the press coverage of the fire. But all anyone ever called her was Dot."

"I never had a nickname."

"People always call you Julia?" There!

"Except for the kids, who have to call me Miss Roussard. That's the first time you've ever used my name, do you realize that?"

"You never told me what it was."

"I didn't?"

"I figured there'd be papers in the house, but I didn't want to snoop around. You'd tell me when you wanted to."

"I thought you knew. I just took it for granted we had that conversation. You saved my life and I got to watch you break a man's neck and then you walked me home and we drank coffee in the kitchen. How could you not know my name?"

"I opened a book," he said, "and there it was. Oh, for God's sake."

"What?"

"Well, how did I even know it was you? Maybe you bought the book secondhand, or maybe it came down in the family."

"No, it's me."

"Julia Emilie Roussard."

"Oui, monsieur. C'est moi."

"French?"

"On my daddy's side, Irish on my mama's. I told you she died young, didn't I?"

"You told me she went gray early."

"And died early, too. Thirty-six years old, and she left the table one night and went straight to bed because she felt a little feverish, and the next morning she was dead."

"My God."

"Viral meningitis. She was healthy one day and dead the next, and I don't think my daddy ever did understand what happened to him. To her of course, but also to him. And to me, and I was eleven at the time." She looked at him. "I'm thirty-eight now. I'm two years older than she was when she died."

"And you don't have a single gray hair, either."

She laughed, delighted. He said he was several years older than that, and she told him he looked it. "With your new haircut," she said. "I think what we'll do is bleach it, and then dye it a nice medium brown. If you're not happy with the way it turns out, we can always dye it back to the way it is now."

■ ■ ■

But it turned out fine. *Mousy brown,* Julia called it, and said that women supplied by nature with hair that color were often moved to do something about it. "Because it's kind of blah, you know? It doesn't attract attention."

Perfect.

If her father even noticed the difference, he didn't see fit to comment on it. Keller, checking the mirror, decided the lighter color went with the professorial effect, which the bifocals had reinforced big-time. The glasses, now that he was getting used to them, were a revelation. He hadn't exactly needed them, he'd been getting along fine without them, but there was no question they improved his distance vision. Out walking on St. Charles Avenue, he could make out street signs he'd have squinted at previously.

He went for that walk on a day when Julia was teaching, and a plump brown dumpling of a woman named Lucille came to see to Mr. Roussard. When Julia got home he was waiting for her on the front stoop. "It's all arranged," he said. "Lucille's agreed to stay late, so let's you and I go to an early movie and a nice dinner."

The movie was a romantic comedy, with Hugh Grant in the Cary Grant role. Dinner was in the French Quarter, served in a high-ceilinged room by waiters who looked almost old enough to be playing Dixieland jazz at Preservation Hall. Keller ordered a bottle of wine with dinner, and they each had a glass and agreed it was very nice, but they left the rest of the bottle unfinished.

They'd taken her car, and when it came time to drive home she handed him her keys. It was a mild night, and the air had a tropical feel to it. Sultry, he thought. That was the word for it.

Neither of them spoke on the way home. Lucille lived nearby, and wouldn't accept a ride, and just shook her head when Keller offered to walk her home.

He waited in the kitchen while Julia checked on her father. He couldn't sit still and walked around, opening doors, peering into cupboards. Everything's close to perfect, he thought, and now you're about to screw it up.

It seemed to him that she was taking forever, but then she came up behind him and stood looking over his shoulder. "All these sets of dishes," she said. "Things accumulate when a family lives in the same place forever. There'll be some yard sale here one of these days."

"It's nice, living in a place with a history."

"I suppose."

He turned toward her and smelled her perfume. She hadn't been wearing scent earlier.

He drew her close, kissed her.

25

"You know what I was worried about? I was afraid I wouldn't remember how to do it."

"I guess it all came back to you," he said. "Been a while, has it?"

"Ages."

"Same for me."

"Oh, come on," she said. "You, running around the country, having adventures everywhere?"

"The running around I've been doing lately, the only women who spoke to me were asking me did I want to supersize that order of fries. Imagine if they asked you that at a good restaurant. 'Sir, would you care to supersize that coq au vin?'"

"But before Des Moines," she said. "I'll bet you had a girl in every port."

"Hardly. I'm trying to remember the last time I was . . . with anybody. All I can tell you is it's been a long time."

"My daddy asked me if we were sleeping together."

"Just now?"

"No, he never even stirred. I think Lucille let him get at the Maker's Mark. The doctor doesn't want him drinking, but he doesn't want him smoking, either, and I say what difference can it possibly make? No, this was a couple of days ago. 'You an' that fine-looking young man sleeping together, *chère*?' You're still a young man to Daddy, even the way I got your hair fixed."

"He asked me, too."

"He didn't!"

"That first time you left me alone with him. He came right out and asked me if I was sleeping with you."

"I don't know why I should be surprised. It's just like him. What did you say?"

"That I wasn't, of course. What's so funny?"

"Well, that's not what I told him."

He propped himself up on an elbow, stared at her. "Why on earth would you—"

"Because I didn't want to tell him one thing and then have to go back and tell him another. Oh, come on, don't tell me you didn't know this was going to happen."

"Well, I had hopes."

"'Well, I had hopes.' You must have known when you asked me out to dinner."

"By that time," he said, "they were high hopes."

"I was afraid you'd make a move that first night. Inviting you to stay here, and after I did it struck me that you might think that was more of an invitation than I had in mind. And that would have been the last thing I wanted just then."

"After what happened in the park? It was the last thing I would have suggested."

"All I wanted," she said, "was to do a favor for someone who had saved my life. Except—"

"Except what?"

"Well, I wasn't thinking this consciously at the time. But looking back, I might not have dragged you home if you didn't look real cute."

"Cute?"

"With your full head of shaggy dark hair. Don't worry, you're even cuter now." She reached to stroke his hair. "There's only one thing. I don't know what to call you."

"Oh."

"I know your name, or at least the names they put in the paper. But I haven't called you by name, or asked what to call you, because I don't want to say the wrong thing sometime with other people around. And you were talking about getting a new set of ID."

"Yes, I want to get started on that."

"Well, you don't know what name it'll be, do you? So I want to wait until you do and start out calling you by your new name."

"That makes sense."

"But it would be nice to have something to call you at intimate moments," she said. "There was a moment before when you said my name, and I have to say it gave me a little tingle."

"Julia," he said.

"It works better in context. Anyway, I don't know what to call you at moments like that. I could try *cher*, I suppose, but it seems sort of generic."

"Keller," he said. "You could call me Keller."

In the morning he backed his car out of the garage and visited cemeteries until a tombstone inscription provided him with the name of a male child who'd died in infancy forty-five years ago. He copied down the name and date of birth, and the next day he headed downtown and asked around until he found the Bureau of Records.

"Got to replace everything," he told the clerk. "I had this little house in St. Bernard's Parish, so do I have to tell you what happened?"

"I'd say you lost everything," the woman said.

"I went to Galveston first," he said, "and then I headed up north and stayed with my sister in Altoona. That's in Pennsylvania."

"Seems to me I've heard of Altoona. Is it nice?"

"Well, I guess it's okay," he said, "but it's good to be home."

"Always good to be home," she agreed. "Now if you could just let me have your name and date of birth—oh, you've got it all written down, haven't you? That saves asking you how to spell it, not that Nicholas Edwards presents all that much of a challenge."

He went home with a copy of Nicholas Edwards's birth certificate, and by the end of the week he had passed a driving test and been rewarded with a Louisiana driver's license. He counted up his cash and used half of what he had left to open a bank account, showing his new driver's license as ID. A clerk at the main post office had passport application forms, and he filled one out and sent it, along with a money order and the requisite pair of photos, to the office in Washington.

"Nick," Julia said, looking from his face to the photo on his license, then back at him again. "Or do you prefer Nicholas?"

"My friends call me Mr. Edwards."

"I think I'll introduce you as Nick," she said, "because that's what people are going to call you anyway. But I'll be the one person that calls you Nicholas."

"If you say so."

"I say so," she said, and took hold of his arm. "But when we're upstairs," she said, "I'll go right on calling you Keller."

She came upstairs with him every evening, then returned to her bed in the first-floor den in case her father needed her during the night. Both professed regret at the enforced separation, but on reflection Keller realized he was just as happy to wake up alone. He had a hunch Julia probably felt the same way.

One night, after they'd finished their lovemaking but before she slipped out of his bed, he mentioned something that had been on his mind a while. "I'm running out of money," he said. "I'm not spending much, but there's none coming in, and what's left won't last too much longer."

She said she had a little money, and he said that wasn't really the point. He'd always paid his own way, and wasn't comfortable otherwise. She asked if that was why he'd mowed the front lawn the day before.

"No, I was getting something from the car"—the gun, still in the glove compartment, which he'd finally gotten around to relocating to his dresser drawer—"and I saw the mower, and earlier I'd noticed the grass needed cutting, so I went and did it. An old man with one of those aluminum walkers watched me for a few minutes and asked me what kind of money I got for a job like that. I told him they didn't pay me a dime, but I got to sleep with the lady of the house."

"You didn't tell him that. Did you? You just made that whole thing up."

"Well, not all of it. I really did mow the lawn."

"And did Mr. Leonidas stop and watch you?"

"No, but I've seen him around, so I put him in the story."

"Well, he was the perfect choice, because he'd have told his wife, and his wife would have broadcast it to half the city before you'd put the mower back in the garage. What am I going to do with you, Keller?"

"Oh, you'll think of something," he said.

And in the morning she poured his coffee and said, "I was thinking. I guess what you have to do is get a job."

"I don't know how to do that."

"You don't know how to get a job?"

"I've never actually had one."

"You've never—"

"I take that back. When I was in high school I worked for this older guy, he'd get jobs cleaning out people's attics and basements, and he'd make his real money selling what he got paid to haul away. I was his helper."

"And since then?"

"Since then, the kind of work I've done and the people I've worked for, you don't need a Social Security card. Nick Edwards applied for one, incidentally. It should turn up in the mail any day now."

She thought for a moment. "There's a lot of work in the city these days," she said. "Could you do construction?"

"You mean like building houses?"

"Maybe something a little less ambitious. Working with a crew, renovating and remodeling. Putting up Sheetrock, spackling and painting, sanding floors."

"Maybe," he said. "I don't suppose you need a graduate degree in engineering for that sort of thing, but it probably helps if you know what you're doing."

"You haven't been doing it in a while, so your skills are a little rusty."

"That sounds good."

"And they did it a little differently where you come from."

"That too. You're not too bad at making up stories yourself, Miss Julia."

"If I do a good job," she said, "they'll let me sleep with the gardener. I think it's time for me to make a couple of phone calls."

26

The next day he showed up at the job site, on a narrow side street off Napoleon Avenue. A longtime tenant had died, leaving the upstairs flat vacant and in need of a gut rehab. "Owner says turn it into a loft, one big room with an open kitchen," said the contractor, a rawboned blond named Donny. "You missed the fun part, ripping them walls out. Let me tell you, it gives you a feeling."

Now they had half the place Sheetrocked, and the next step would be painting, walls and ceiling, and when that was done they'd work on the floors. How was he with a roller, and how did he feel about ladders? He was fine with ladders, he said, and he'd be okay with a roller, though he might be a little rusty at first. "You just take your time," Donny said. "Be no time at all before it all comes back to you. I just hope ten bucks an hour is all right with you 'cause that's what I'm paying."

He started with the ceiling, he knew enough to do that, and he'd used a paint roller before, painting his own apartment in New York. Donny had a look from time to time, and gave him a tip now and then, mostly about how to position the ladder so he wouldn't have to move it as often. But evidently he was doing okay, and when he took the occasional break he managed to watch the others nailing sections of Sheetrock in place and covering the seams with joint compound. It didn't look all that tricky, not once you knew what it was you were supposed to do.

He worked seven hours that first day and left with seventy dollars more than he'd started with, and an invitation to show up at eight the next morning. His legs ached a little, from all that climbing up and down the ladder, but it was a good ache, like you'd get from a decent workout at the gym.

He stopped to pick up flowers on the way home.

"That was Patsy," Julia told him, after hanging up the phone. Patsy Morrill, he remembered, was a high school classmate of Julia's; her name had been Patsy Wallings before she got married, and Donny Wallings was her kid brother. Patsy had called, Julia told him, to say that Donny had called her to thank her for sending Nick his way.

"He says you don't say much," she reported, "but you don't miss much, either. 'He's not a guy that you have to tell him something twice.' His very words, according to Patsy."

"I didn't know what the hell I was doing," he said, "but by the time we were done for the day, I guess I pretty much got the hang of it."

The next day he did some more painting, finishing the rest of the ceiling and starting in on the walls, and the day after that there were three of them, all painting, and Donny had switched him to a brush and put him to work on the wood trim. "On account of you got a steadier hand than Luis," he explained privately, "and you're not in such a damn rush."

When the paint job was finished, he showed up as instructed at eight, and there were just the two of them, him and Donny. He wouldn't be using Luis for the next couple of days, Donny confided, because the man didn't know dick about sanding floors.

"Actually," Keller said, "neither do I."

That was okay with Donny. "Least I can explain it to you in English," he said, "and y'all'll pick it up a damn sight faster'n Luis would."

The whole job lasted fifteen days, and when it was done the place looked beautiful, with a new open-plan kitchen installed and a new tile floor in the bathroom. The only part he didn't care for was sanding the wood floors, because you had to wear a mask to keep from breathing the dust, and it got in your hair and your clothes and your mouth. He wouldn't have wanted to do it day in and day out, but a couple of days' worth now and then was no big deal. Laying ceramic tile in the bathroom, on the other hand, was a genuine pleasure, and he was sorry when that part of the job was over, and proud of how it looked.

The owner had shown up a couple of times to see how the job was going, and when it was finished she inspected everything and pronounced herself highly satisfied. She gave him and Luis each a hundred-dollar bonus, and she told Donny she'd have another job for him to look at in a week or so.

"Donny says she'll be able to ask fifteen hundred a month for the place," he told Julia. "The way we've got it fixed up."

"She can ask it. She might have to take a little less, but I don't know. Rents are funny now. She might get fifteen hundred at that."

"In New York," he said, "you'd get five or six thousand for a space like that. And they wouldn't expect ceramic tile in the bathroom, either."

"I hope you didn't mention that to Donny."

And of course he hadn't, because the story they'd gone with was that he was Julia's boyfriend, which was true enough, and that he'd followed her down from Wichita, which wasn't. Sooner or later, he thought, someone familiar with the place would ask him a question about life in Wichita, and by then he hoped he'd know something about the city beyond the fact that it was somewhere in Kansas.

A friend of Donny's called a day or two later. He had a paint job coming up, just walls, as the ceiling was okay. Three days for sure, maybe four, and he could pay the same ten bucks an hour. Could Nick use the work?

They wrapped it up in three days, and he had the weekend and two more days free before Donny rang up to say that he'd bid on that job and got it, and could Nick come by first thing the next morning? Keller wrote down the address and said he'd be there.

"I'll tell you," he said to Julia, "I'm beginning to believe I can make a living this way."

"I don't know why not. If I can make a living teaching fourth grade—"

"But you've got qualifications."

"What, a teaching certificate? You've got qualifications, too. You're sober, you show up on time, you do what you're told, you speak English, and you don't think you're too good for the job. I'm proud of you, Nicholas."

He was used to Donny and the others calling him Nick, and he was getting used to being called Nicholas by Julia. She still called him Keller in bed, but he could sense that would change, and that was okay. He'd been lucky, he realized, in that the name he'd found in St. Patrick's Cemetery was one he could live with. That hadn't been a consideration when he was squinting at weathered headstones, all he'd cared about was that the dates worked, but he saw now that he could have been saddled with a far less acceptable name than Nick Edwards.

He'd taken to giving her half his pay for his share of the rent and household expenses. She'd protested at first that it was too much, but he insisted, and she didn't fight too hard. And what did he need money for, aside from buying gas for the car? (Although it might not be a bad idea to save up for a new car, or at least a new used car, because he was fine until somebody asked to see his registration.)

After dinner, they took their coffee out on the front porch. It was pleasant out there, watching people walk by, watching the day fade into twilight. He saw what she meant about the shrubbery, though. It had been allowed to grow a little too tall, and cut off a little too much of the light and the view.

He could probably work out how to trim it. As soon as he had a day off, he'd see what he could do.

One night, after they had made love, she broke the silence to point out that she'd called him Nicholas. What was really interesting was that he hadn't even noticed. It seemed appropriate for her to call him that, in bed as well as out of it, because that seemed to be his name.

That was what it said on his Social Security card and his passport, both of which had turned up in the mail. The same day's mail that brought the passport also contained an invitation to apply for a credit card. He'd been preapproved, he was told, and he wondered just what criteria had been used to preapprove him. He had a mailing address and a pulse, and evidently that was all they required of him.

Now, under the slow-moving blades of the ceiling fan, he said, "I guess I might not have to sell those stamps after all."

"What are you talking about?"

She seemed alarmed, and he couldn't imagine why.

"I thought you lost them," she said. "I thought you said your whole collection was stolen."

"It was, but I bought five rare stamps in Des Moines, before everything went to hell. They'd be tough to unload, but they're still the closest thing I've got to a negotiable asset. The car's worth more and there's a bigger market for it, but you have to have clear title, and I don't."

"You bought the stamps in Des Moines?"

He got the stamps from his top dresser drawer, managed to find his tongs, and switched on the bedside lamp to show her the five little squares of paper. She asked a few questions—how old were they, what were they worth—and he wound up telling her all about them, and the circumstances of their purchase.

"I would have had plenty of cash for the trip back to New York," he said, "if I hadn't shelled out six hundred dollars for these. That left me with less than two hundred. But at the time that looked like more than enough, because I'd be charging everything, including my flight home. I had the stamps all paid for when the announcement came over the radio."

"You mean you hadn't heard about the assassination?"

"Nobody had, not when I was talking myself into buying the stamps. The best I can make out, Longford was eating rubber chicken with the Rotarians right around the time I was parking my car in Mr. McCue's driveway. I didn't grasp the significance right away, I thought it was coincidence, me being in Des Moines the same time a major political figure was assassinated. I had a completely different job to do, at least I thought I did, and, well—what's the matter?"

"Don't you see?"

"See what?"

"You didn't kill the man. Governor Longford. You didn't kill him."

"Well, no kidding. It seems to me I told you that a long time ago."

"No, you don't get it. You know you didn't do it, and *I* know you didn't do it, but what you and I know is not enough to stop all those policemen from looking for you."

"Right."

"But if you were sitting in some stamp shop in—where did you say?"

"Urbandale."

"Some stamp shop in Urbandale, Iowa. If you were sitting there at the very moment the governor was shot, and if Mr. McWhatsit was sitting across from you—"

"McCue."

"Whatever."

"His name used to be McWhatsit," he said, "but his girlfriend said she wouldn't marry him unless he changed it."

"Shut up, for God's sake, and let me get this out. This is important. If you were there and he was there, and he'll remember because of the announcement on the radio, then doesn't that prove you weren't downtown shooting the governor? It doesn't? Why not?"

"They went on making that announcement all day," he said. "McCue will remember the sale, and he might even remember that it happened right around the time he heard about the assassination. But he won't be able to swear exactly when that was, and even if he did a prosecutor could make him look like an idiot on the witness stand."

"And a good defense attorney—"

But she stopped when she saw the way he was shaking his head. "No," he said gently. "There's something you don't understand. Let's say I could prove my innocence. Let's say McCue could offer testimony that would absolutely get me off the hook, and while we're at it let's say that some other witness, some rock-solid pillar of the community, could come along to corroborate his testimony. It doesn't matter."

27

"It doesn't matter. The case would never come to trial. I wouldn't live that long."

"The police would kill you?"

"Not the police. The cops, the FBI, they're all the least of it. The police never caught up with Dot, they never even knew she existed, and look what happened to her."

"Who then? Oh."

"Right."

"You told me his name. Al?"

"Call-Me-Al. Which only means that's *not* his name, but it'll do if we need something to call him. I wonder if he even knew what he was going to use me for when he first began setting me up. Well, that's something else that doesn't matter. Longford's dead and I'm the guy everybody's looking for, but if I turn up, I'm the fly in Al's ointment. If he finds me, I'm dead. If the cops find me first, I'm still dead."

"He would be able to make that happen?"

He nodded. "Nothing to it. He's pretty resourceful, that's clear enough. And it's not all that difficult to arrange for something to happen to someone in custody."

"It doesn't seem—"

"Fair?"

"That's what I was going to say. But who ever said life was fair?"

"Somebody must have," he said. "At one time or another. But it wasn't me."

A little later she said, "Suppose . . . no, it's silly."

"What?"

"Oh, it's straight out of TV. A man's framed and the only way out is to solve the crime."

"Like O.J.," he said, "searching all the golf courses in Florida for the real killer."

"I told you it was silly. Would you even know where to start?"

"Maybe a graveyard."

"You think he's dead?"

"I think Al's a believer in playing it safe, and that would be the safest way to play it. He used me as the fall guy, because he knew there was no trail that could lead back from me to him. But the actual shooter would know somebody, Al or somebody who worked for Al, so there'd be some linkage there."

"But no one would be looking for it because everybody would think you were the real shooter."

"Right. And meanwhile, just to guard against the possibility of anybody finding out what really happened, or the chance the shooter would brag about what he'd done, because he was drunk or to increase his chances of getting laid—"

"Would that work?"

"I suppose it might, with a certain sort of woman. The point is, once the governor was dead, the shooter made the jump from asset to liability. If I had to guess, I'd say he took his last breath within forty-eight hours of the assassination."

"So he's not playing golf with O.J."

"Not a chance. But he might be sharing peanut butter and banana sandwiches with Elvis."

■ ■ ■

That Thursday they ran into a plumbing problem at work. It demanded a higher level of expertise than Donny's, so they knocked off early and left the field to a master plumber from Metairie. Keller came straight home so he could tell Lucille to take the rest of the day off, but found Julia on the front porch. He could tell she'd been crying.

The first thing she said was that there was coffee in the kitchen, and he went there and filled two cups to give her a minute to compose herself. He brought them to the porch, and by then she'd freshened up a little.

"He almost died this morning," she said. "Lucille's not an RN but she's had some training. His heart stopped, and either it started up again on its own or she got it going. She called the school where I was working and I came home, and by then she'd called the doctor, and he was here when I got here."

"You said almost died. He's all right?"

"He's alive. Is that what you meant?"

"I guess so."

"He had a small stroke. It affected his speech, but it's not too bad. He's just a little harder to understand, but he made himself very clear when the doctor wanted to take him to a hospital."

"He didn't want that?"

"He said he'd rather die first, and the doctor's a crusty old bastard himself, and said that's what it would probably come to. Daddy shot back that he was going to die anyway, and so was the damn doctor, and what was so bad about dying? Then the doctor gave him a shot so he could get some rest, but I think maybe it was just to shut him up, and then he told me that the thing to do now was get him to the hospital."

"What did you say?"

"That my father was a grown man who had the right to decide

what bed he was going to die in. Oh, he didn't want to hear that from me, and he laid such a good guilt trip on me that he could teach a course on the subject, if they were to add it to the med school curriculum. Assuming it's not already there."

"You held your ground?"

"I did," she said, "and it may have been the hardest thing I've ever done, and do you know what was the hardest part?"

"Questioning your own judgment?"

"Yes! Standing firm and arguing, and all the while a little voice in my own head is yammering away. Where do I come off thinking I know more than the doctors, and am I just doing this because I want him to die, and am I being brave with the doctor because I haven't got the courage to stand up to my own father? There was a whole committee holding a meeting in my head, all of them pounding the table and hollering."

"He's resting now?"

"Asleep, last I looked. Are you going in there? If he's awake, he may not know you. The doctor told me to expect some gaps in his memory."

"I won't take it personally."

"And there'll be more strokes, he told me that, too. They'd have him on blood thinners if it wasn't for the cancer. Of course, if he was in the damn hospital they could monitor the blood thinners, balancing the level every hour so he wouldn't bleed out *or* stroke out, and—Nicholas, did I do the right thing?"

"You honored the man's wishes," he said. "What's more important than that?"

He went into the sitting room, and the sickroom smell was worse than usual, or maybe it was his imagination. At first he couldn't detect the old man's breathing, and thought the end had come, but then the breathing resumed. He stood there, wondering how to feel, what to think.

The old man's eyes opened, fixed on Keller. "Oh, it's you," he said, his voice thickened but otherwise clear as a bell. Then his eyes closed and he was gone again.

When Keller got to work the next morning, he took Donny aside and handed him a ten-dollar bill. "You gave me too much yesterday," he said. "Sixty dollars, and we only worked five hours."

Donny pushed the bill back at him. "Gave you a raise," he said. "Twelve dollars an hour. I didn't want to say anything in front of the others." Meaning Luis and a fourth man, Dwayne. "You're worth it, buddy. Don't want you looking for the grass to be greener somewhere else." He winked. "Nice to know you're an honest man, though."

He waited until after dinner to tell Julia, and accepted her congratulations. "But I'm not surprised," she said. "Patsy's mother didn't have any stupid children. He's right about that, you're worth it, and he's smart not to chance losing you."

"Next thing I know," he said, "you'll be telling me I've got a future in this business."

"It may not look like it. I don't suppose the pay amounts to much, compared to what you used to get."

"I used to spend most of my time waiting for the phone to ring. When I worked I got paid okay, but you can't compare it. It was a different life."

"I can imagine. Or maybe I can't. Do you miss it?"

"God, no. Why would I?"

"I don't know. I just thought this might be boring, after the life you were used to."

He thought about it. "What was interesting," he said, "and not all the time, but sometimes, was the aspect of having a problem and solving it. You rip out a dropped ceiling and you'll find all the problems any man can ask for, and you can solve them without anybody getting hurt."

She was silent for a long moment, and then she said, "I think we'd better see about getting you a new car. What's so funny?"

"Dot used to complain that I'd go off on tangents. Master of the Non Sequitur, she called me."

"So you want to know how I got there?"

"It's not important. It just struck me funny, that's all."

"How I got there," she said, "is I was thinking it sounds as if you might want to hang around for a while. And the one thing that could screw things up is that car of yours. The license tags may be a dead end, but if you got pulled over and they asked to see the registration—"

"I'd have the papers that were in the glove box when I switched plates at the airport. I thought of doctoring them, substituting my name and address for what's on there."

"Would that work?"

"It might get past a quick glance, but not a long hard look. And it's an Iowa registration for a car with Tennessee tags being driven by a damn fool with a Louisiana license. So no, I'd have to say it wouldn't work. That's why I haven't bothered to try."

"You could stay under the speed limit," she said, "and obey every traffic regulation, and never even risk another parking ticket. And then some drunk rear-ends you, and the next thing you know you've got cops asking questions."

"Or some cop could come back from a vacation at Graceland and wonder why my Tennessee plate doesn't look much like the ones he saw up there. I know, there are all kinds of things that could go wrong. I'm putting money aside, and when I've got enough saved—"

"I'll give you the money."

"I don't want you to do that."

"You can pay me back. It won't take long, you're making an extra two dollars an hour."

"Let me think about it."

"I'm all for that," she said. "Think all you want, Nicholas. Saturday morning we'll go car shopping."

There wasn't much shopping involved. The next time he saw Donny, he mentioned he was going to be looking for a car. You get yourself a truck, Donny said, and you'll never be happy with a plain old car again. Donny knew somebody with a Chevy half-ton pickup, not much on looks but mechanically sound. It would have to be all cash, Donny said, but he could probably find somebody to take the Sentra off Nick's hands. Keller said he already had somebody lined up.

The truck's owner was an older woman who looked like a librarian, and it turned out that's just what she was, at what she described as the big branch library in Jefferson Parish. Keller couldn't guess how she'd wound up owning the truck, and her air suggested she was somewhat baffled herself. But the papers looked okay, and when he asked the price she sighed and said she'd been hoping to get five thousand dollars, which made it pretty clear she didn't expect to. Keller offered four, figuring to meet her somewhere in the middle, and felt almost guilty when she sighed again and nodded her agreement.

Julia had driven him to the woman's house in the Taurus, and he followed her back and parked out in front on the street. He told her how he'd wanted to raise his own bid when the woman said yes to four thousand, and she told him not to be silly. "It's not her truck," she said.

"Not anymore. It's ours."

"It was never hers. Some man owned it, her son or her boyfriend or I don't know who, and one way or another she wound up with it, and believe me, the truck's not the saddest part of the story. What?"

"I was just thinking," he said. "You realize you're not more than a handful of notes away from a country song?"

The Sentra wound up in the Mississippi. If he'd felt guilty lowballing the librarian, he felt worse deep-sixing a car that had given him trouble-free performance for months. He'd eaten in it, he'd slept in it, he'd driven it all over the country, and now he was showing his gratitude by dumping it in the river.

But nothing else he could come up with struck him as one hundred percent safe. If he left it to be stolen, he'd sever his own connection with it. But it would provoke official attention sooner or later, and when it did it would still be the vehicle Governor Longford's assassin had rented in Des Moines, and whoever ran the engine serial number would learn that much readily enough. And anyone with a strong interest in finding him would have a reason to start looking in New Orleans.

It was a good bet to stay in the river forever, he told Julia, and if it ever did get hauled out, nobody was going to bother looking for the serial number.

Back in the city, he took her for a ride in his truck.

28

Her father seemed at first to be recovering from his stroke. Then he must have had another one, because when Julia went in there one morning he had taken a sharp turn for the worse. His speech was impossible to make out, and he didn't seem able to move his legs. Earlier, he'd had to use a bed pan; now Keller found himself called to help when Julia changed her father's diapers.

The doctor came and hooked up an IV. "Otherwise he'll starve," he told Julia, "and even so we can't monitor him the way we should. He can't change his mind now, you know, so it's up to you to let us hospitalize him."

Later she said, "I don't know what to do. Whatever I decide is going to be wrong. I just wish—"

"You wish what?"

"Never mind," she said. "I don't want to say it."

It was pretty clear how she'd have finished the sentence. She wished the man would die and get it over with.

Keller went in and watched the old man sleep and wondered how anyone could wish otherwise. Left to his own devices, Roussard would likely turn his face to the wall, refuse food and drink, and be gone in a day or two. But through a miracle of medical science he'd been hooked up to an IV, and Julia had been instructed how to replenish the liquids that dripped into his body, and so he'd go on, until another of his failing systems found a way to shut down.

Keller stood by his bedside and thought of another old man, Giuseppe Ragone or Joey Rags or, God help us, Joe the Dragon. Keller had never thought of him as anything but the old man, and had never actually called him anything to his face. Or had he called him *Sir* early on? It was possible. He couldn't remember.

That old man was in decent shape physically until right up to the end, but it was always something, wasn't it, and in his case it was the mind that didn't hold up. He started making mistakes and losing track of details, and one time he sent Keller to St. Louis to take care of business, and the business was in a particular hotel room, the number of which the old man wrote down for Keller. Except he didn't write down the room number, he wrote down 3-1-4, which was nothing like the room number, and all Keller could figure out later was that it was the area code for St. Louis. Keller, sent to the wrong room, did what he was supposed to do, but not to the person he was supposed to do it to. There was a woman in the room, too, so two people died for no reason at all, and what kind of a way was that to run a business?

There were other incidents, enough of them to cut through Dot's denial, and the capper was when the old man recruited some kid from the high school newspaper to help him write his memoirs. Dot managed to nip that in the bud, and told Keller to take a trip. He was collecting stamps by then, preparing for his retirement, and she urged him to go to a stamp show and register under his own name and use his own credit card for everything.

In other words, be someplace else when it happened.

She'd put a sedative in the old man's bedtime cup of cocoa, so he'd be sound asleep when she held a pillow over his face. And that was that. Sweet dreams, and a gentler exit than the old man had provided for no end of people over the years.

"I can't say it's what he'd have wanted," Dot told him later, "because he never said, but I'll tell you this much. It's what I'd want. So if I ever get like that, Keller, and you're around, I hope you'll know what to do."

He agreed, and she'd rolled her eyes. "Easy to say now," she said, "but when the time comes, you'll say to yourself, 'Let's see now, wasn't there something I was supposed to do for Dot? I can't seem to remember what the hell it was.'"

"I was looking in on your father," he told Julia. "You know, if there's anything you want to say to him while you've got the chance, this might be a good time."

"You don't think—"

"It's nothing I can put my finger on," he said, "but for some reason I don't think it's going to be more than another day or two."

She nodded, got to her feet, and went to the sickroom.

Later that night she went upstairs with him. They didn't make love, but lay together in the dark. She talked about when she was a girl, along with family history that went back before she was born. He didn't say much but mostly just listened, and thought his own thoughts.

When she went downstairs he got up and went out onto the upstairs porch. It was overcast, with no moon or stars. He thought about the faithful old Sentra, rusting away at the bottom of the Mississippi, and he thought about Dot and his stamps and his mother and the father he'd never known. Funny how there'd be things you wouldn't think of for ages, and then they'd just pop into your head.

He stayed on the porch for an hour or so, long enough for her to get to sleep, and he was careful on the stairs, avoiding the board that creaked.

Dot had used a pillow. Simple enough, and quick, and the only problem was that it would leave petechial hemorrhages, most noticeably on the eyes. That hadn't mattered, because the family physician Dot called signed off with barely a look at the deceased. When an elderly person dies of apparent natural causes, you don't usually have to worry about an autopsy.

Nor would there be an autopsy in this house, for a man who'd suffered two strokes that they knew about and was on the way out with liver cancer. But the doctor might take a more careful look than the old man's physician in White Plains, and if he saw red pinpoint dots on Clement Roussard's eyeballs, he'd think Julia had given him a helping hand into the next world. He might not disapprove, he might think it was the final loving act of a dutiful daughter, but why should he get to have an opinion one way or the other?

If they'd been allowed to hospitalize him, and were thus able to monitor him closely, they might have put him on a blood thinner to make further strokes less likely. But with his compromised liver, Coumadin, the blood thinner of choice, could easily make him hemorrhage and bleed out internally. Since that might happen anyway, even without Coumadin, there'd be nothing in such a death to raise suspicions.

Coumadin was a prescription drug, and Keller didn't have access to it. But before Coumadin was prescribed to prevent clotting in humans, it was called warfarin and used to poison rats; it thinned their blood, and they bled to death.

You didn't need a prescription for warfarin, but he hadn't even needed to buy it. He'd come across an old packet of the stuff in the garage, with the gardening supplies. He couldn't find a sell-by date on it, but thought it would probably still work. Why should the passage of time render it less toxic? And it was very likely not pharmaceutical grade, so you would be well advised not to use it on a human being for therapeutic purposes, as you might with Coumadin. But this wasn't a case where he had to worry about impurities or side effects, was it?

He added powdered warfarin to the bag holding the IV drip, stood at the man's bedside while it dripped into his vein. He wondered how it would work, and if it would work.

After a few minutes he went to the kitchen. There was coffee in the pot and he heated a cup in the microwave. If she woke up and came in he'd just say he'd been unable to sleep. But she didn't wake up and he finished his coffee and rinsed his cup in the sink and went back to the old man's side.

The doctor barely examined the patient beyond feeling for a pulse. Keller didn't think he'd have noticed petechial hemorrhages, or even a gunshot wound in the temple. He signed the death certificate, and Julia called the funeral director her family used, and fifteen or twenty people, family or friends, attended the service. Donny Wallings and his wife were there, and he met Patsy and Edgar Morrill, and both couples returned to the house after the service. The body was cremated, which Keller thought was a good idea, all things considered, so there was no cemetery visit, no second service at graveside.

The two couples didn't stay long, and when they were alone Julia said, "Well, now I can go back to Wichita. God, the look on your face!"

"Well, for a moment there—"

"When I first moved back I had to keep telling myself I'd only be staying as long as he needed me. In other words, until he died. But I think I knew right away I was never going to leave again. It's home, you know?"

"It's hard to imagine you anyplace but New Orleans. Anyplace but this house, really."

"There was nothing wrong with Wichita," she said, "and I had a life there. My yoga class, my book group. It was a place to live, but it isn't a place to return to."

He knew what she meant.

"I could go someplace else, and in a couple of months I could re-create my life in Wichita. Maybe it would be Pilates instead of yoga, maybe I'd take up bridge instead of trying to puzzle out what Barbara Taylor Bradford really meant. But it would be the same life, and my new friends would be the same as my Wichita friends, and just as replaceable when I moved somewhere else a few years down the line."

"And now?"

"Now I'll have to go through his things, and figure out what to give away and where it should go. Will you help me with that?"

"Of course."

"And we'll have to clean out that room. All the smells, the cigarette smoke and the sickness. I don't know what I'm going to do with his ashes."

"Don't people bury them?"

"I guess, but doesn't that sort of defeat the whole purpose? Like you wind up with a grave after all? I know what I'd want."

"What?"

"The same treatment your car got, but not the river. Just scatter my ashes in the Gulf. Will you take care of that, if you should ever have the chance?"

"Odds are you'll be the one who has to figure out what to do with me. And that sounds as good as anything, by the way. The Gulf of Mexico's as good a place as any."

"Not Long Island Sound? You wouldn't want to go home?"

"No, I like it here."

"I think I'm going to cry." She did, and he held her. Then she said, "Not too soon, okay? The Gulf's not going anywhere. You stick around for a while, okay?"

Donny knew someone with a boat who was willing to take the two of them out on the Gulf. They were on the water for less than an hour, and when they docked, the ashes were scattered. The boat's owner wouldn't even take money for gas.

The rental firm picked up the hospital bed, and two young men in a white van came for the IV equipment. Keller had filled a trash bag with the bed linen and towels that had seen service in the sickroom, along with the pajamas and such that her father had worn there. Cancer wasn't contagious, the clothes and linen could have been laundered, but he bagged it all and put it at the curb.

A friend of Patsy Morrill's came to smudge the sickroom. Keller didn't have a clue what that meant, but found out when the woman produced a bundle of what she said was dried sage, lit one end of it with a wooden match, and walked around the room, sending plumes of smoke here and there. Her lips were moving throughout, but it was impossible to tell what she was saying, or even if she was producing a sound. She did whatever it was she was doing for one of the longer quarter hours in Keller's experience, and when she was done Julia thanked her carefully and asked if she would take money for her services.

"Oh, no," the woman said. "But I would just about kill for a cup of coffee."

She was an odd creature, elfin in stature, and both her age and her ethnic background were hard to guess. She praised the coffee effusively, then left her cup two-thirds full. On her way out, she told the two of them that they had a wonderful energy.

"What an odd creature," Julia said, after they'd watched her drive away. "I wonder where Patsy found her."

"I wonder what the hell she did." He followed Julia into the sitting room and frowned. "Whatever it was," he said, "I think it may have worked, unless it's just a matter of substituting one smell for another."

"It's more than that. She changed the energy in here. And please don't ask me what that means."

It was a whole new experience for Keller. He hadn't actually done anything he hadn't done before. But this was the first time he'd stuck around to clean up after.

29

One evening after dinner the phone rang, and it was Donny. He read out an address across the river in Gretna. Keller copied it down, and the next morning he got out a map and figured out how to get there.

Donny's truck was parked in the driveway of a one-story frame structure of the type Keller recognized as a shotgun house, long and narrow, with no hallways; the rooms were arranged one behind the other, and the name was supposed to come from the observation that you could stand at the front door with a shotgun and clear out the whole house with a single round. The style had originated in New Orleans shortly after the War Between the States (which is what Keller had lately learned to call the Civil War) and spread throughout the South.

This particular specimen was in sad shape. The exterior needed painting, there were slates missing from the roof, and the lawn was a wasteland of weeds and gravel. The inside was worse, the floor littered with debris, the kitchen filthy.

Keller said, "Gee, there's nothing left for us to do, is there?"

"She's a real beauty, isn't she?"

"Was that a SOLD sign I saw out in front? Got to be one hell of an optimist who bought this place."

"Well, hell," Donny said, "I guess I been called a lot worse'n that." He grinned, delighted with Keller's openmouthed reaction. "Closed on her yesterday," he said. "You ever see that cable show, *Flip This House*? That's my plan. A little love's all it should take to turn this shithole into the prettiest house on the block."

"Might take a little work," Keller said, "mixed in with the love."

"And a few dollars in the bargain. Here's what I got in mind." And he walked Keller through the old house, outlining his plans for its transformation. He had some interesting ideas, including adding a second floor onto the back half of the house, converting it into what was known locally as a camelback shotgun. That last, he conceded, was on the ambitious side, but it could make a big difference in the home's resale value.

"So here's what I'm getting at," Donny said.

"The down payment took most of his cash," Keller told Julia, "and the rest will go for materials and the other men, because he can't expect guys like Dwayne and Luis to work on spec. But he figured maybe I'd be willing to roll the dice, and when it's done and he sells it, I'd be in for a third of the net profit."

"Which probably translates into a good deal more than twelve dollars an hour."

"If the job doesn't take too long, so the carrying charges don't mount up too high. And if we get a buyer who'll close in a hurry and pay a decent price."

"I'd say you made your decision already."

"How can you tell?"

"'If *we* get a buyer.' And what could you possibly say but yes?"

"That's what I thought. The only downside is I won't be bringing home any money for a while."

"That's all right."

"No payments on the loan for the truck, and no contributions to the household budget."

"It's a hell of a situation," she agreed. "If it wasn't for sex, you'd be no use to me at all."

It wasn't until her father's ashes were scattered and the sickroom emptied and smudged that Julia moved upstairs, to the bedroom she'd occupied as a child. Keller kept his own room, kept his things in the drawers and closet, but spent nights in hers.

The job in Gretna ran behind schedule and over budget, which didn't really surprise anybody. Both men put in long hours, working seven-day weeks, starting at daybreak and keeping at it until they lost the light. Donny's cash didn't last as long as he'd hoped, and after he'd maxed out his credit cards he had to obtain a $5,000 loan from his father-in-law. "The old bastard asked me what I could put up for collateral, and I said, 'How about your daughter's happiness?' You can guess how that went over, but hell, I got the money, didn't I?"

The work was satisfying, especially when Donny decided to go the whole route, and they designed and built the second-floor addition. "It felt like building a house," Keller told Julia. "Constructing one, you know? Not just remodeling."

When the last of the work was done, with the lawn sodded and new shrubbery in place, he brought Julia to see it. She'd been there earlier, with the work barely under way, and said it was hard to believe it was the same house. Outside of the beams and rafters, he said, it barely was.

They went to the Quarter for a celebration dinner, although the real celebration would come when they landed a buyer. They chose the same high-ceilinged restaurant they'd gone to before, ordered essentially the same meal, and didn't finish their wine this time, either. They talked about the job, and its satisfactions, and the likelihood of Donny's getting the price he was going to ask for it.

If the profit was all Donny anticipated, he told her, they'd do this again, and next time Keller would be a partner. She said he was that already, wasn't he? A full partner, he explained, putting up half the purchase price, paying half the expenses, and netting half the profits. Donny was already looking for their next property, and had several under consideration.

"Well, he's a Wallings," she said. "They're enterprising."

First, though, Donny had two cash jobs lined up, a condo paint job on Melpomene and some post-Katrina rehab for a house in Metairie. A Wallings was practical, Julia said, in addition to being enterprising. And before they undertook either of those jobs, Keller said, they were going to have a few days off.

"Well, of course," she said. "He's an Orleanean, isn't he?"

When they got home she asked him what had gone wrong.

"Because your whole mood changed between when we left the restaurant and when we got to the car. The weather was fine so that couldn't be it. Did I say something? No? Then what was it?"

"I didn't think it showed."

"Tell me."

He didn't want to, but neither did he care to keep things from her. "For a minute there," he said, "I thought someone was looking at me."

"Well, why not? You're a nice-looking fellow and . . . oh my God."

"It was a false alarm," he said. "He was looking past me, waiting for the valet to bring his car around. But I remembered a man I heard about who got in trouble because he went to San Francisco, where somebody who just happened to be there saw him and recognized him."

She was quick, if you gave her the first sentence she got the whole page. "We should probably stay out of the Quarter," she said.

"That's what I was thinking."

"And other places tourists tend to go, but it's really mostly the Quarter. No more Café du Monde, no more Acme Oyster House. For oysters, Felix's has a place uptown on Prytania that's just as good, and they don't get as crowded."

"During Mardi Gras—"

"During Carnival," she said, "we'll stay home altogether, but we'd do that anyway. Poor baby, no wonder your mood changed."

"What bothered me," he said, "wasn't getting a scare, because it didn't last long enough to amount to all that much. By the time I knew to be afraid I could tell there was nothing to be afraid of. But I've got a whole new life, and it fits me like a glove, and I cut every tie to the past when we shoved that car into the river."

"And you thought that whole part of your life was over."

"And it is," he said, "but what I also thought was that nothing from the past could find me, and that's not exactly true. Because there's always the possibility of an accident. Some sharp-eyed son of a bitch from New York or L.A. or Vegas or Chicago—"

"Or Des Moines?"

"Or anywhere. And he happens to come here on vacation, because it's a popular spot."

"Not so many tourists since the hurricane," she said, "but they're starting to come back."

"And all it takes is one, who happens to be in the same restaurant, or on the street when we come out of the restaurant, or any damn thing. Look, it's not very likely. We don't exactly live the high life here, we keep a low profile by nature. Most of the time we're home alone, and when we see somebody it's Edgar and Patsy or Donny and Claudia. We always have a good time, but nobody's putting our pictures in the *Times-Picayune.*"

"They might," she said, "when you and Donny emerge as the hottest outfit in post-Katrina reconstruction."

"Don't hold your breath. Neither of us is that ambitious. You know what appeals to Donny about flipping houses? As much as the opportunity for profit? The chance to quit bidding on jobs. He hates that part, everything you have to take into consideration to come up with a price that's low enough to get you the job but high enough so you come out ahead doing it. Of course he has to do all the same calculations when he's the owner himself, but he says it doesn't give him the same kind of headache."

That changed the subject, and it stayed changed, but in bed that night, after a long shared silence, she asked if there was any way to get himself all the way off the hook.

He said, "You mean as far as Al is concerned, since the police are only a problem if I get arrested and somebody runs my prints. With Al, well, time's a healer. The more time passes, the less he's going to care whether I'm alive or dead. As far as taking action to get him off my back . . ."

"Yes?"

"Well, the only way I can see is to find some way to learn who he is and where to get hold of him. And then go there, wherever it is, and, uh, deal with him."

"Kill him, you mean. You can say the word, it's not going to bother me."

"That's what it would take. You couldn't sign a mutual nonaggression pact with him, settle the deal with a handshake."

"Anyway," she said, "he ought to be dead. What's so amusing?"

"Who knew you'd turn out to be such a tough guy?"

"Hard as nails. Is there any way to find him? You must have thought about it."

"Long and hard. And no, I don't think there is, and if there is I sure can't figure it out. I wouldn't even know where to start."

30

Donny got an offer on the house right away. It was less than he was asking but still well above his costs, and he decided not to hold out for more. "The sooner we're out of one deal, the sooner we can get into the next," he told Keller, and after the deal closed Keller's one-third share of the net was just over eleven thousand dollars. He hadn't been keeping track of his hours, but knew his profit amounted to a good deal more than twelve dollars an hour.

He came home with the news, and you'd have thought Julia already heard. The table was set with the good china, and there were flowers in a vase. "I guess someone told you," he said, but no one had, and she congratulated him and kissed him and said the flowers and all were because she had news of her own. They'd offered her a full-time teaching position for the coming year.

"A *permanent* position," she said, "and I wanted to tell them that nothing's permanent in an uncertain world, but I decided to keep my mouth shut."

"Probably wise."

"That means more money, of course, but it also means benefits. And it means not having to make the acquaintance of a new batch of brats every month or so. Instead I'll get one batch of brats and be stuck with them for the whole year."

"That's great."

"On the downside, it also means working five days a week for forty weeks a year, not just when some teacher gets sick or decides to move to I don't know where."

"Wichita?"

"It ties a person down, but would it keep us from doing anything we really wanted to do? What's great is having the summers off, and if you ever want to get away from New Orleans, summer's the time when you want to do it. I think I should tell them yes."

"You mean you haven't already?"

"Well, I wanted to discuss it with you. You think I should go for it?"

He did, and said so, and she served a dish she'd adapted from a New Orleans cookbook, a rich and savory stew of meat and okra served over rice, with a green salad, and lemon pie for dessert. The pie was from a little bakery on Magazine Street, and while he was tucking into a second piece she told him she'd bought him a present.

"I thought the pie was the present," he said.

"It's good, isn't it? No, but this was also from Magazine Street, just two doors up from the bakery. I wonder if you ever noticed it."

"Noticed what?"

"The shop. I don't know, maybe I made a mistake. Maybe you won't like it, maybe it'll just be a case of throwing salt in old wounds."

"You know," he said, "I don't have a clue what you're talking about. Do I get a present or don't I?"

"It's not exactly a present. I mean, I didn't wrap it. It's not the kind of present you would wrap."

"That's good, because it'll save the time it would take to unwrap it, and we can use that time having this conversation."

"Am I being nuts? 'Yes, Julia, you're being nuts.' Don't go anywhere."

"Where would I go?"

She came back with a flat paper bag, so in a sense the present was wrapped after all, if informally. "I just hope I didn't do the wrong thing," she said, handing it to him, and he reached into the bag and drew out a copy of *Linn's Stamp News*.

"There's this shop, it's not much more than a hole in the wall. Stamps and coins and political campaign buttons. And other hobby items, but mostly those three. Do you know the shop I'm talking about?"

He didn't.

"And I walked in, and I didn't want to buy you stamps, because I thought that probably wouldn't have been a good idea—"

"You were right about that."

"But I saw this paper, and didn't you mention it once? I think you did."

"I may have."

"You used to read it, didn't you?"

"I was a subscriber."

"And I thought should I get it for him or not? Because I know your stamps are gone, and how much they meant to you, and this might only make you feel the loss more. But then I thought maybe you'd enjoy reading the articles, and who knows, you might even want to, I don't know, start another collection, although that might be impossible after having lost everything. Then I thought, oh, for God's sake, Julia, give the little man two dollars and fifty cents and go home. So I did."

"So you did."

"Now if it was a really terrible idea," she said, "just put it back in the bag it came in and hand it to me, and I'll guarantee you never have to look at it again, and we can both pretend this never happened."

"You're wonderful," he said. "Have I ever told you that?"

"You have, but we've always been upstairs. This is the first time you've told me on the ground floor."

"Well, you are."

"The present's okay?"

"Yes, and the future's promising."

"I meant—"

"I know what you meant. The present, *this* present, is more than okay. I don't know if I'll find the articles interesting, I don't know if I'll even want to look at the ads, much less do anything about them. But all of that is something I ought to find out."

"I live another day," she said. "Why don't I pour you another cup of coffee, and why don't you take *Linn's* into the den?"

He looked at the front page and wondered why he was wasting his time. The lead article was about the high prices realized at an auction in Lucerne of an exceptional collection of stamps and postal history from Imperial Russia, before the 1917 revolution. Less prominent was coverage of the discovery of an error, a recent U.S. coil stamp with one color missing, and an article about reactions in the hobby to the post office's announcement of new stamps planned for the coming year.

The same stories, he thought, week after week and year after year. The details changed, the numbers changed, but the more it all changed, the more it remained the same. He had to check the date of the paper to reassure himself it wasn't an issue he'd already seen, months or years before.

The same dim-witted letters to the editor, too, the outpourings of the same self-involved malcontents, this one whining at the cost of keeping up with the huge crop of new issues, the next furious because the idiots at the post office insisted on ruining stamps on his mail by defacing them with heavy cancellations, and others joining in the endless debate on how to interest young boys and girls in the hobby. The only way you could do that, Keller figured, was to find a way to make philately more exciting than video games, and there was no way that would work, not even if you came out with a series of stamps that exploded.

Keller turned next to "Kitchen Table Philately," which he'd heard was the paper's most popular feature. This had always struck Keller as unfathomable, yet he had to admit he found it irresistible himself. Each week, one of two pseudonymous reviewers—interchangeable, as far as Keller could determine—analyzed in excruciating detail a mixture of stamps he'd bought for a small sum, often as little as a dollar, from a *Linn's* advertiser. This week was typical, with Mr. Anonymous grumpy beyond belief because his two-buck assortment of stamps had taken a whole two weeks to reach his mailbox, and unhappy as well because fully 11 percent of the mixture's contents were small definitive stamps rather than the large commemoratives promised. Christ, he thought, give it a rest, will you? If you can't actually manage to get a life, can't you at least *pretend* you've got one?

And then something curious happened. He read another article, and got caught up in what he was reading. The next thing he knew he was looking at one of the ads, a listing of Latin American issues offered by a worldwide dealer in Escondido with whom Keller had done business over the years. Like most listings, this one consisted of nothing but catalog numbers, indicators of condition, and prices, so it wasn't really something a person could read, but Keller's eyes were drawn to it, and from there he found his way to another ad, and after that he put down the paper and went upstairs for a minute. He came down with his Scott catalog and returned to the den, picked up *Linn's,* and resumed where he'd left off.

"Nicholas?"

He looked up, yanked out of his reverie.

"I just wanted to let you know I'm going upstairs. You'll turn off the lights when you come up?"

He closed the catalog, set the paper aside. "I'll come up now."

"If you're having fun—"

"I've got an early day tomorrow," he said. "And that's all the fun I can stand for one night."

He showered and brushed his teeth, and she was in bed waiting for him. They made love, and afterward he lay with his eyes open and said, "That was very sweet."

"For me, too."

"Well, just now, sure. I meant bringing me the paper. That was very thoughtful of you."

"I'm just glad it turned out all right. I'm assuming that it did?"

"I got caught up in it," he said. "But do you want to hear something really pathetic? I found an ad with what looked like some interesting material, and I actually went upstairs to get my catalog."

"To check the value?"

"No, that's not why I wanted it. I may have told you that I used the catalog as a checklist. So I brought it downstairs in order to be able to tell whether or not a given stamp was one I needed for my collection."

"That makes sense," she said. "I don't see what's so pathetic about it."

"What's pathetic," he said, "is I need *all* the stamps for my collection, everything ever made except for Sweden one through five. Because, outside of those five stamps I had no business buying, I don't *have* a collection."

"Oh."

"And here's the best part. There was a point when I realized it was pathetic—or ridiculous, or whatever you want to call it. But that didn't stop me. I went on working out just what stamps I would buy to help fill in the collection I no longer own."

He almost missed it.

He worked late the following day, and by the time he got home all he was up for was dinner and an hour of TV before they went up to bed. The day after that he was off, and spent the morning doing a tentative preliminary pruning of the shrubbery, trying to find a line of compromise between the plants' desire to grow tall and his and Julia's preference for a little more light and visibility on the front porch. He stopped a little after noon, wondering if he'd lopped off too much or too little.

Late in the afternoon they took her car and drove to a seafood shack on the Gulf just across the state line in Mississippi. Donny and Claudia had enthused over it, and it was all right, but on the way home they agreed it wasn't worth the time it took to get there and back. They went inside, and she had a couple of loads of wash she'd been meaning to do, and Keller caught sight of *Linn's* on the chair in the den and picked it up so he could toss it out. Because he'd read most of the articles, and he didn't collect stamps anymore, so why keep the thing around?

But instead he sat down with it and found himself leafing through it, and he tried to figure out a way to collect without a collection. One possibility, he thought, was to continue his collection as if he still owned it, buying only stamps he hadn't already owned, and keeping them not in an album (because he already had albums, or *had* had them) but in a box or stockbook. The premise would be that they were awaiting eventual placement in his albums when they found their way back to him, which of course would never happen, which meant he'd never have to mount the stamps but could concentrate exclusively upon obtaining them.

In a sense, he'd be collecting stamps the way an ornithologist collected birds. Each new bird, once it had been spotted and identified, would go on the birder's life list; he didn't need physical possession of the creature in order to claim it as his own. By the same token, the stamps Keller had owned, the stamps that had been taken from him, were still his. They were on his life list.

He'd still use the Scott catalog as his checklist. When he bought a new stamp, he'd circle its number in his catalog so he wouldn't make a mistake and buy it again. The new acquisitions, he thought, could be circled in another color, blue or green, so he'd be able to tell at a glance whether his acquisition came before or after the date the collection disappeared, and whether he owned a particular stamp in fact or in theory.

It was deeply weird, he knew, but was it that much stranger than collecting stamps in the first place?

He turned the pages of the newspaper, too much involved in his own thoughts to pay much attention to what passed before his eyes. So he'd probably looked at and looked away from the small ad before it ever registered.

Toward the back of the paper, but before you got to the classifieds, *Linn's* gave over the better part of a page to small-space ads, one or two inches tall and a column wide, that amounted essentially to dealer's announcements. One might proclaim oneself a specialist in France and its colonies, or in the British Empire before 1960. There was one chap who'd had the same ad running for all the years Keller had subscribed, offering AMG issues, the stamps produced by the Allied Military Government for use in occupied Germany and Austria after the end of the Second World War. There he was, Keller noted, still at it, word for precious word, and—

Two columns over, he saw this:

JUST PLAIN KLASSICS
Satisfaction Guaranteed
www.jpktoxicwaste.com

Keller stared at the ad. He blinked several times, but it was still there when he looked at it again. It was impossible, but unless he'd dozed off and was dreaming, the ad was really there, and it couldn't be, because it was impossible.

There had been times in his life when he'd been dreaming, realized it was a dream, and willed himself out of it—but remained in the dream, even though he thought he'd returned to waking consciousness. Was this like that? He got up, walked around, and sat down again, wondering whether he was really walking around or had just incorporated the walking into his dream. He picked up the paper, and he read some of the other ads, to see if they were the usual thing or the sort of gibberish dreams were apt to produce.

As far as he could tell, they were okay. And the ad from Just Plain Klassics was still there, and still impossible.

Because the only person who could possibly have placed that ad was dead, shot twice in the head and burned up in a fire in White Plains.

31

It took him a few blocks out of his way, but Keller drove along Magazine Street to get a look at the stamp shop. He spotted it, but only because he knew where to look for it. The signage was minimal, and that explained why he'd never noticed it before.

He thought of stopping in, to see if they had any other issues of *Linn's* around. That way he could find out if the ad had run before, but why bother? What difference did it make?

Ten minutes later he was parked across the street from an Internet café, where a kid who looked more like a college wrestler than your prototypical geek pointed him to a computer. He hadn't sat in front of one since he was bidding for stamps on eBay, back before the flight to Iowa. His laptop had been gone by the time he returned to his New York apartment, and he'd never even considered replacing it. What for?

Julia, who'd sold her own computer before moving back from Wichita, had talked about getting another, but with about the same sense of urgency as she talked about cleaning out the attic. It might happen, possibly even in their lifetime, but you couldn't call it a high-priority item.

Even if she'd had a computer, he wouldn't have used it for this. A public machine in a public setting, far from his own neighborhood, was what the situation called for.

He settled in, booted up Explorer, and typed in www.jpktoxic waste.com. And clicked on Go.

The headline could have been a coincidence. A dealer specializing in the classic issues from philately's first century, 1840 to 1940, might chance upon Just Plain Classics as a name for his business venture, and might decide to distort the spelling as an homage, say, to Krispy Kreme doughnuts.

If so, he'd managed to hit on a name that resonated with Keller. Not so much because those were the stamps Keller collected, since he was hardly unique in this respect, but because the initials were his. JPK = John Paul Keller—or, as Dot was apt to point out, Just Plain Keller.

The owner of Just Plain Klassics hadn't troubled to include his name, but he wasn't unique in that respect. He hadn't included a postal address, either, or a phone or fax number, but limited himself to the URL of his website. A lot of philatelic business was conducted on the Web these days, and plenty of classified ads limited their contact information to an email address, but this was unusual in a display ad.

But what nailed it was the URL itself. www.jpktoxicwaste.com.

Years ago, back when the old man was still running things, he and Dot had been troubled by the fact that their boss was turning down job after job for no apparent reason. Accordingly they went proactive before either of them had become familiar with the term, and Dot placed an ad in a *Soldier of Fortune* imitator called *Mercenary Times.* Odd jobs wanted, removals a specialty—something along those lines, with the firm's name given as Toxic Waste, and a post office box in Hastings or Yonkers, someplace like that.

JPK. Toxic Waste.

Coincidence? It had about as much chance of being coincidental as his trip to Des Moines. But if it wasn't a coincidence, then it was a visitation from the dead, because no one but Dot could possibly have placed that ad.

The website, when the computer found its way there through the ether, was anticlimactic. Just the initials at the top, JPK in plain boldface capitals. Nothing about stamps, nothing about toxic waste. Nothing, in fact, but a very brief notice announcing that the site was under construction, along with a mathematical formula that made no sense to him:

19 △ = 28 x 24 + 37 - 34 ÷ 6

Huh?

He got on Google, tried various permutations. JPK, just plain klassics, JPK Stamps. Nothing. If you were going to replace the first *c* in *classics* with a *k*, why not do the same with the last one? He tried JPK klassiks, and JPK classics, and got nowhere. Google returned no end of hits for toxic waste, none of which he found himself eager to pursue, and when he tried to type in the formula, or equation, or whatever it was, he couldn't figure out how to reproduce some of the symbols. He did the best he could, and Google was quick to tell him that his search did not match any documents. He gave up and went back to the original URL, jpktoxicwaste.com, and got the same page all over again, advising him once more that the site was under construction, and providing him with the same formula. This time he copied it off the site, then returned to Google and pasted it in, and didn't get any hits.

Do the math, Keller.

He worked it out with pencil and paper. It looked algebraic, and the algebra he'd studied in high school was long gone, but maybe he could get somewhere with simple arithmetic. 28 times 24 was 672, plus 37 was 709, minus 34 was 675 (though why you would add 37 only to subtract 34 a moment later was beyond him).

Divide all that by 6 and it came to 112.5. So 19 little triangles was equal to 112.5, which meant one of them was what? The answer wouldn't come out even, and by the time he'd worked it out to nine decimal places—5.921052631—he decided that couldn't be right.

Easy as pi, he thought. Maybe it was just Internet flotsam, stray debris floating in cyberspace and preying on the unwary.

You'd think a place that called itself a café, Internet or otherwise, would have coffee available. Keller asked, and the wrestler shook his head and pointed at a machine prepared to dispense Coca-Cola and a variety of energy drinks.

Keller found a Starbucks on the next block and splurged on a latte. He took it to a table along with his work sheets, looked at the original equation. Drop the symbols, he thought, and what did you get?

19 triangles equals 282437346.

He dug out his wallet, found his Social Security card, examined it, and added hyphens accordingly.

282-43-7346.

Where did the 19 triangles come in? And what good was a Social Security number, anyway?

Oh.

Forget the triangles, and use all eleven digits, and move the hyphens around a little. . .

1-928-243-7346.

Oh.

Northern Arizona. 928 was the area code for northern Arizona.

He didn't know anybody in northern Arizona. He didn't know

anybody anywhere in Arizona, not that he could think of. The last time he could remember being anywhere in the state was a while ago, and he'd gone to Tucson on business. The person he was seeking had lived in a gated community surrounding a members-only golf course. Tucson was in southern Arizona, and its area code was 520.

As far as he could see, there were three possibilities.

First, it was all coincidence. That was impossible, because even the long arm of coincidence had a limited reach. It was too complicated a coincidence, of the sort it would take for a monkey at a typewriter to produce *Hamlet.* Even if he started out okay, sooner or later you'd get a line that read, "To be or not to be, that is the gezorgenplatz."

Second, the message was from Dot. True, she was dead, but she'd found a way to communicate from beyond the grave. She'd ruled out materializing in front of him, or whispering in his ear, because she'd figured it would spook him, so instead she'd come up with this brilliant idea of running a cryptic ad in *Linn's.* But that was impossible, too, because how could someone in the spirit world get an ad in a newspaper?

Third, the message was from the irrepressible Call-Me-Al. He'd know about Keller's hobby, because it was probably his bully boys who'd carted the collection away. He'd know Keller's initials, even if he didn't know that they stood for Just Plain Keller, and he could have hit on Just Plain Klassics by coincidence. But, even if that struck him as a reasonable way to continue the hunt for Keller, would he go so far as to disguise the phone number, counting on Keller to puzzle it out? I mean, why bother? He didn't have to worry that someone else would get wind of him. All he had to do was put the bait out there and wait for Keller to take the hook.

Anyway, it was flat-out impossible that he would have included the toxic-waste business. Dot and Keller were the only two people on the planet to whom that would make any sense. The case was an old one, and everybody connected with it was long dead, and the murder weapon, if you were hung up on coincidence, was at the bottom of the same river that received the Nissan Sentra, albeit hundreds of miles to the north. And Dot wouldn't have given up the phrase toxic waste, not even under torture, because it would never occur to her. *"Now, woman, give us something to draw him in, or we'll pull out your toenails." "Toxic waste, toxic waste!"* Yeah, right. Not a chance.

So there were three possibilities, and they were all impossible.

One more possibility. Dot, before she was killed, decided to make a run for it. First, though, she wanted to set things up so she could get a message to Keller when the time came. And how could she do that? Why, through an ad in *Linn's*, and a phone number left on a website, something he could access without leaving a trail.

You could set up a website and it would stay up unattended for a long time. You could place a *Linn's* ad, pay a whole year or more in advance, and just let it run until it ran out. And maybe the website *was* under construction, maybe she'd planned to make things a little clearer for Keller. Maybe she'd done this early on, setting up the site, ordering the ad, and then the bastards broke in and killed her, and the ad and the website were out there to no purpose. And, until Julia brought home the paper, to no effect.

Was all of this possible? He didn't know, and couldn't think about it anymore. Because no matter how much thought he gave it, when all was said and done there was really only one thing to do.

He found a place where he could buy a prepaid cell phone, and made sure it was set to block caller ID. The police might be capable of determining where the phone was when the call was placed, but it wasn't the police who had run the ad or set up the website, and if Al had such technological forces at his command, well, that was just a chance Keller would have to take.

Even so, he got on I-10 and drove halfway to Baton Rouge before pulling into a gas station and making the call.

He was expecting no answer at all, or maybe *coo-wheeeet!*, but on the third ring someone picked up. And then a voice he'd never expected to hear again said, "I just hope this isn't another damn telemarketer in Bangalore. Well? Whoever you are, say something."

32

"I know what you thought," she said, "because what else could you think? But now's not the time to go into it. I thought the same about you, as far as that goes. Where are you, and how long will it take you to get out here?"

"Flagstaff, Arizona?"

"How did—oh, the area code. Well, not Flagstaff, but that's close enough. Flagstaff's got an airport, but it might be easier to fly to Phoenix and drive up. Or for all I know you're close enough to drive the whole way. Where are you, anyway?"

In for a penny, in for a pound. "New Orleans," he said, "but as far as coming out there, it's not easy for me to get away."

"You're all right, aren't you? Not under lock and key, for God's sake."

"No, nothing like that, but it's complicated."

"Oh? In that case I'll come to you. The only thing to stop me is a hair appointment, and that shouldn't be too hard to get out of. Give me your number, I'll get right back to you . . . Keller? Where'd you go?"

"I'm here."

"So?"

"I just got this phone," he said, "and there's got to be a card somewhere with the number on it, but I don't know what happened to it."

"That's the last word in unlisted numbers," Dot said, "where even the owner himself can't track it down. But don't get too cocky, because somewhere in India there's a little guy who's going to call you on it and try to sell you Viagra. Here's what we'll do. You call me. Give me an hour, and by then I'll know when I'm getting in and where I'm staying. And don't worry if you can't find my number. Just press the Redial button and that clever little phone of yours will do the rest."

An hour later he learned that she wouldn't be coming for three days, and he thought he'd wait a day or two to figure out what to tell Julia. He drove home and Julia met him in front of the house. She said the weather forecast was for rain but it didn't feel like rain, and what did he think? He said he couldn't really say one way or the other. She said neither could she, not really, and was there something on his mind?

"Dot's alive," he said.

The weather forecast turned out to be on the money. It started raining late that afternoon and kept raining on and off for the next three days. It never reached downpour proportions, but it never quite cleared up, either, and he had to use the windshield wipers driving downtown to Dot's hotel.

She had booked herself into the Intercontinental. He brought his new cell phone along and called her after he'd turned his truck over to the valet, and she met him in the lobby and took him up to her room. Two other guests shared the elevator with them, so they didn't say a word until they got off on her floor.

"Not that those two would have noticed," she said. "What do you figure, cheaters or honeymooners?"

"I wasn't paying attention."

"Neither were they, Keller, which was my point. It doesn't matter. My God, look at you. You look different, but I can't put my finger on it."

"My hair."

"There you go. The whole shape of your face is different. What did you do?"

"Cut it differently, raised the hairline. Lightened it a little."

"And glasses. Those aren't bifocals, are they?"

"They took a little getting used to."

"They're taking me a little getting used to, and you're the one who's wearing them. I like the effect, though. Very studious."

"I see better," he said. "But you, Dot, you look way different."

"Well, I'm older than I used to be, Keller. What do you expect?"

But she didn't look older, she looked younger. Her hair had been dark years ago, when they first met, and by the time he'd left for Des Moines there was far more salt than pepper in the mix. Now the salt was all gone—it was easier, as he well knew, to turn gray hair dark than to reverse the process—and along with the gray she'd lost twenty or thirty pounds. The pants suit she was wearing, a far cry from her usual at-home attire, showed off her new figure, and she was wearing lipstick and eye makeup for the first time he could recall.

"I've got a personal trainer," she said, "if you can get your mind around that one, plus a sweet little Vietnamese girl who does my hair once a week. I closed on my condo out there expecting to lie in the sun like a beached whale and sit up nights with a box of soft-center chocolates, and will you look what happened to me?"

"You look terrific, Dot."

"So do you. What did you do, take up golf or something? You never used to be so big in the shoulders."

"It's probably from swinging a hammer."

"A garrote's quieter," she said, "but I don't suppose it does as much in terms of muscular development." She called room service, told them to send up two big pitchers of iced tea and two glasses, then hung up the phone and looked at him. "We've got a lot of catching up to do, haven't we?"

He went first, starting with their last conversation in Des Moines and bringing her all the way to his new life in New Orleans. She listened carefully, interrupting now and then for amplification, and when he was done she sat there shaking her head. "You were going to retire," she said, "and here you are doing manual labor."

"I didn't know what I was doing at first," he said, "but it's not that hard to pick up."

"It shouldn't be. Look at all the morons who do just fine at it."

"And it's satisfying," he said. "Especially when what you're doing is taking something that's a real mess and straightening it out."

"You've been doing that for years, Keller. Though I can't recall you ever using a paint roller before. But tell me more about this lady friend of yours."

He shook his head. "Your turn," he said.

She said, "Once we knew what was going on, all I could do was disappear, and the sooner the better. I figured you might get away or you might not, but there was nothing I could do about it either way.

"So the first thing I did was go online and sell everything we owned, every last share, every bond, everything. The whole works, every lock, every stock, every barrel. And then I arranged a wire transfer and stashed every single dime of it in our account in the Caymans."

"We have an account in the Caymans?"

"Well, I do," she said, "the same as I had the Ameritrade account. I set it up as soon as the Ameritrade balance started to amount to something, just in case, and it was sitting there waiting when I needed it. I transferred the money, and then I took care of the house, and then I walked a few blocks and waited for the bus."

"You took care of the house. What does that mean?"

"You're a smart boy, Keller. What do you think it means?"

"You set it on fire."

"I got rid of anything that might point anywhere," she said, "and I pulled the hard drive out of the computer and treated it the same way you did the cell phone, and I put it back right where I found it, and then, yes, I set the house on fire."

"They found a body."

She made a face. "I was going to skip that part," she said. "You know, I was going to take my chances, and then this woman turned up, and all I could think was that God sent her."

"God sent her?"

"You remember how Abraham was about to sacrifice Isaac? And God sent a ram for him to sacrifice instead?"

"That story never made much sense to me," he said.

"Well, it's the Bible, Keller. What the hell do you want from it? All I know is I was scrambling, trying to decide where to pour gasoline, and the doorbell rang. And I went there, and there she was."

"Selling magazine subscriptions? Taking a survey?"

"She was a Jehovah's Witness," she said. "You know what you get when you cross a Jehovah's Witness with an agnostic?"

"What?"

"Someone who rings your doorbell for no apparent reason. You can figure out the rest, can't you? I invited her in and sat her down, and then I got the gun from the silverware drawer and shot her a couple of times, and she got to be the corpse they found in the kitchen. I poured enough gas on her hands so I wouldn't have to worry about fingerprints. Mine aren't on file anywhere, but how did I know hers weren't? People who turn up on your doorstep, you never know where they've been. Why are you frowning?"

"I read something about a positive identification based on dental records."

"Right."

"Well, how did you manage that?"

"That's why I have to figure God sent her, Keller. The little darling had false teeth."

"She had false teeth."

"Cheap ones, too. You could just about spot 'em before she opened her mouth. First thing I did, I yanked 'em out and popped mine in."

"Yours?"

"What's so remarkable about that?"

"I didn't know your teeth were false."

"You weren't supposed to know," she said. "That's why I paid ten or twenty times as much for them as Jehovah's little godchild paid for hers, so they'd look like the original equipment. I lost all my teeth before I was thirty, Keller, and I'll save that story for another day, if it's all the same to you. I switched the teeth and set the fire and got the hell out."

"I always thought—"

"That my teeth were real? See these?" She drew back her lips. "I have to say I like them even better than the ones I left in White Plains. They don't look perfect, that's the giveaway with so many of them, and yet they look really nice. Don't ask what they cost."

"I won't," he said, "and that's not what I was going to say. What

I always thought was that Jehovah's Witnesses always came around in pairs."

"Oh, right. Him."

"Him?"

"I shot him first," she said, "because he was bigger, and looked more like trouble, although I can't say either one of them struck me as a dangerous customer. I shot him, and then I shot her, and I put him in the trunk of my car and dumped him where nobody would find him for a while, and then I came back and switched the teeth and set the fire, di dah di dah di dah."

She left her car in the garage, so no one would go looking for it, and she took no more than would fit into a small overnight bag. She took a bus to the train station and a train to Albany and holed up there for six weeks in an apartment hotel catering mostly to people with political business in the state capital.

"State senators and assemblymen and the lobbyists who throw money at them," she said. "I had plenty of cash, and credit cards in my new name, and I bought a car and picked up a laptop and did a little research. I decided Sedona looked good."

"Sedona, Arizona."

"I know, it rhymes, just like New York, New York. And there the resemblance ends. It's small and upscale, and the climate's ideal and the setting's beautiful, and the town doubles its population every twenty minutes, so a person could drop in out of the blue without drawing attention, and after six months you'd be an old-timer. I figured I'd drive there and see some of the country on the way, and then I thought it through and decided the hell with seeing the country, so I sold the car and flew out to Phoenix and bought a new car and drove to Sedona. I picked out a two-bedroom penthouse condo for myself, and from one window I can see the golf course and from another I've got a great view of Bell Rock, and you probably don't even know what that is."

"A rock that chimes on the hour?"

"The hair's different," she said, "but it's still the same old Keller underneath it, isn't it? As soon as I was settled in, I tried to work out a way of getting in touch with you, assuming I could do that without holding a séance. I knew from the news coverage that you made it out of Des Moines, and the law never caught up with you, but if Al got to you first there wouldn't have been anything in the papers. And if you were alive, there was only one way I could think of to reach you without attracting anybody else's attention, so that's what I did."

"You placed an ad in *Linn's.*"

"I ran that damn advertisement every place I could find. Who would have guessed there were so many papers and magazines for stamp collectors? Besides *Linn's* there's *Global Stamp News,* and *Scott's Monthly Journal,* and the magazine the national stamp society sends its members—"

"The American Philatelic Society. It's a pretty good magazine."

"Well, that's a load off my mind. Good or bad, my ad's been in it, every goddamn month. Plus some others I can't think of. *McBeal's*?"

"Mekeel's."

"There you go. I've got run-until-canceled status with all of them, and every month all the charges show up on my Visa statement. And I was beginning to wonder how long I should go on running the ad, because I was starting to feel like that football team owner who always leaves a ticket at the front gate for Elvis, just in case he shows up. And he at least gets some free publicity out of it."

"It must have cost you quite a bit."

"Not really. Small ads at low rates, and they get even lower on a long-term basis. The real cost was emotional wear and tear, because every time I got my credit card statement that was one more month without word from you, and it was that much more likely that I'd never hear from you again. You at least had closure, Keller. You knew for sure that I was dead, but I had to sit around wondering."

"I wonder which was worse."

"You could probably make a good case either way," she said, "but either way we're both alive, so the hell with it. You saw the ad and called the number—"

"After I finally figured out that it was a number."

"Well, if I made it too obvious the phone would have been ringing off the hook. And I knew you'd work it out once you put your mind to it. But what I still can't understand is why it took you so long. Not to work it out but to pay attention to it in the first place. How many times do you suppose you saw that ad before it rang any kind of a bell?"

"Just once."

"Just once? How is that possible, Keller? I don't suppose you could have had the post office forward your mail, but that ad ran in all the places I mentioned and one or two I forgot. How hard is it to find a copy of *Linn's*? Or send in and get a new subscription?"

"Not hard at all," he said, "but why would I bother? What would be the point? Dot, I saw the ad because Julia picked up a copy of *Linn's* and brought it home with her. She wasn't sure she should give it to me, and I wasn't sure I wanted to look at it."

"But you did."

"Obviously."

"What's not obvious," she said, "is why you weren't sure you wanted to, and why you didn't have a subscription anymore. I'm missing something, Keller. Help me out."

"I don't have a subscription," he said, "because it's for stamp collectors, and it's hard to be a stamp collector when you don't have a collection."

She stared at him. "You don't know," she said.

"I don't know what?"

"Of course you don't. How could you? You sort of glossed over that part, going to your apartment, or maybe I wasn't paying attention, but—"

"I may not have mentioned it. It's one part I don't like to think about. I went to my apartment—"

"And the stamps were gone."

"Gone, all ten albums. I don't know who took them, the cops or Al's guys, but whoever it was—"

"Neither of them."

He looked at her.

"Oh, God," she said. "I should have told you right away. Somehow it never entered my mind that you didn't know, but how could you? Keller, it was me. I took your stamps."

The first thing she'd done in Albany, after she'd found a place to stay, was buy a car. And the first thing she did with the car was drive it to New York City.

"To get your stamps," she said. "Remember that time you got a case of the whim-whams and gave me elaborate instructions of what to do if you wound up dead? How I should go straight to your apartment and take your stamps home with me, and what dealers I should call and how to negotiate the best price for your collection?"

He remembered.

"Well, I wasn't going to sell them, not so long as there was a chance on earth you were alive. But as far as getting them out of your apartment, I took care of that as soon as I possibly could, because I didn't know how much of a window I had before the police came calling. I showed your doorman the letter I had authorizing me to act on your behalf and giving me full access to your apartment and its contents, and—"

"You know, I have absolutely no recollection of writing that letter."

"Well, don't go getting tested for Alzheimer's just yet, Keller. I wrote it out myself on a computer at Kinko's. I designed a nice letterhead for you, if I say so myself, and I didn't sweat the signature, because how familiar would your doorman be with your handwriting? He didn't have to let me in because I had the key you gave me."

"How'd you manage to get them all out of there? Those books are heavy."

"No kidding they're heavy. I found a bag in the closet that held six of them"—his wheeled duffel, he thought—"and I got the doorman to give me a hand, and he brought a luggage cart they keep in the basement, and between us we got everything into the trunk of my car. Oh, and I took your computer, too, but you're not getting that back. Unless you want to look for it at the bottom of the Hudson."

"Between the two of us," he said, "we're hard on rivers." He picked up his iced tea and took a long drink of it. "This is all tough for me to take in," he admitted. "Let me make sure I've got it straight. The stamps—"

"Are in a climate-controlled storage locker in Albany, New York. Well, actually, it's in Latham, but you probably don't know where that is."

"Albany's close enough. And everything's there? My whole stamp collection is intact, and I can go there and pick it up?"

"Anytime you want to. I probably should go with you, to make sure they don't give you a hard time. We could fly to Albany tomorrow, if that's what you decide you want to do."

"I get the feeling," he said, "that it wouldn't be your first choice."

"Well, I'd like to spend a few days and see New Orleans. But after that it's your call. You'll have your stamps back, and you'll have two and a half million dollars just in case the construction business goes sour. You can just sit back and enjoy yourself."

"Or?"

"Lord, did I finish that last glass of tea? I'm going to have some from your pitcher, if you don't mind."

"Go right ahead."

"I'll regret it, when I have to get up once an hour to pee, but if that's my greatest regret I'd say I'm in good shape. Keller, I think we're both pretty safe at this point. The cops seem to think you're dead or in Brazil or both, which is about what I thought until my phone rang the other day. And I don't know what our friend Al thinks, but at this point he probably has other matters that get the greater part of his attention. He knows I'm dead, and if you're still on his list you're way down toward the bottom of it. So there's nothing we absolutely have to do."

"But?"

She sighed. "Oh," she said, "I'm sure it's the sign of a defect of character, and there's probably a seminar I could take to address the issue, and if there is you can bet someone's offering it in Sedona. But what do you figure are the odds I'll ever take that seminar?"

"Slim."

"There you go. Keller, I can't help it. I really would like to get even with that son of a bitch."

"It was driving me crazy," he said, "that he was alive and you weren't."

"Same with me, that he was alive and *you* weren't. Now it turns out we're both alive, and we're both millionaires, and we should probably let it go at that, but—"

"You want to go after him."

"You bet I do. And you?"

He drew a breath. "I think I'd better go talk to Julia," he said.

33

"I'd like to meet her," Julia said, and insisted Keller ask Dot to join them for dinner. They tried to decide on a restaurant, and Julia said, "No, you know what let's do? Bring her over here, and I'll cook."

When he picked Dot up she wore a different suit, with a skirt instead of pants, and her hair was different. "I had to cancel my little Vietnamese girl in Sedona," she said, "so I asked the concierge, and wound up with a local product who couldn't stop talking. But I like what she did with my hair."

Keller brought her into the house and introduced her to Julia, and stepped aside and waited for something to go wrong. By the time they sat down to dinner, after Dot had had the grand tour of the house and said all the appropriate things, he realized nothing terrible was going to happen. Both women were too well brought up.

Julia served pie for dessert, pecan this time, from the little bakery on Magazine Street, and they all had coffee, which Dot chose over iced tea. Throughout the evening Julia had referred to him as Nicholas, and Dot hadn't called him anything at all, but as he was pouring her a second cup of coffee she called him Keller.

"I mean Nicholas," she said, and looked across at Julia. "It's a good thing I live a thousand miles from here, so you don't have to sit around on pins and needles waiting for me to drop a brick in front of company. Have you ever done that, Julia? Called him Keller?"

When he was driving her back to the Intercontinental, she said, "That's a real lady you found yourself, Keller. I'm sorry, I'll be a long time getting used to any other name for you. You've been just plain Keller to me for a long time now."

"Don't worry about it."

"But why did she blush when I asked if she ever called you Keller? Jesus, Keller, now you're the one blushing."

"The hell I am," he said. "Just forget it, okay?"

"Okay," she said. "Mea fucking culpa, and consider it forgotten."

"Do I ever forget and call you Keller? I turned red as a beet."

"I don't think she noticed."

"Oh? I doubt there's a great deal that goes unnoticed around your friend Dot. I like her. Though she's not quite what I expected."

"What did you expect?"

"Someone older. And, well, on the dowdy side."

"She used to be older."

"How's that?"

"Well, she seemed older, and dowdy too, I guess. She never wore makeup, and she sat around in housedresses. I think that's what you call them."

"Watching TV and drinking iced tea."

"Both of which she still does," he said, "but I guess she gets out more, and she's lost a lot of weight, and she buys nice clothes now, and gets her hair done. It's dyed."

"I'm shocked, darling. She's very flippant and sarcastic, but underneath it all she's very much the lady. When I was showing off the house, she kept pointing out things like the window seat that reminded her of her house in White Plains. She must have loved that house, and yet she was tough-minded and decisive enough to burn the place down."

"She didn't have much choice."

"I realize that, but it still couldn't have made it easy. I wonder if I could do that."

"If you had to."

"When all is said and done, it's just a house. And you could always build me a new one, couldn't you? With an open-plan kitchen and ceramic tile in the bath."

"And central air."

"My hero. Didn't you say they found a body in the wreckage?"

He was ready for this. "She left her false teeth behind," he said. "Which they could identify from dental records. I never even knew her teeth weren't her own, so the possibility never occurred to me."

"Oh, that explains it. Nicholas?" She put a hand on his arm. "I was afraid I'd be jealous, even if it was never that kind of relationship in the past. But her whole vibe with you is somewhere between big sister and Auntie Mame. You know what the elephant was?"

"The elephant in the living room?"

"That we walked around and didn't mention. What you're going to do now."

"I don't really have to do anything."

"I know. You've got your stamps, or at least you're going to have them, and you're going to have a lot of money, too. And we can just go on living this life, which is exactly the life I want to be living—"

"Me, too."

"—and not worry about money, and just be comfortable and happy."

"And?"

"And never really feel comfortable eating in the French Quarter. If you went after them, would you know where to look?"

"Not really."

"Des Moines?"

"I don't know if any of them live in Des Moines. It's a sure bet Al doesn't. I've got a Des Moines phone number, the one I called every day to find out if it was time to take out that poor mope who never did anything besides water his lawn. I wonder if he has any idea how close he came to getting his ticket punched."

"You don't think that phone number would lead anywhere?"

"No," he said, "or they wouldn't have given it to me. But as far as I can tell, it's all we've got."

"I wonder," she said.

In the morning she drove him and Dot to the airport. Keller had thought they would take a cab, but Julia wouldn't hear of it. Dot headed inside with her suitcase, to give them a moment, and Julia got out of the car to kiss him good-bye.

She said, "Be careful, you hear?"

"I will."

"I'll tell Donny you were called away. Family business, I'll tell him."

"Sure." He studied her. "Is there something else?"

"Not really."

"Oh?"

"It's nothing," she said. "It'll keep."

34

"The area code's five-one-five," Dot said, squinting at the slip of paper. "That's Des Moines? And you've been carrying this around for months and never dialed it?"

"Why would I dial it?"

"I see your point. If it's the number they gave you, it's not going to lead anywhere. Dial it anyway."

"Why?"

"So we can rule it out, and you'll have more room in your wallet for all the money you've got in the Caymans."

He took out his cell phone, opened it, closed it again. "If it's a live number, and I call it—"

"Is that the phone you called me on in Sedona? The one where not even you can say what the number is?"

"Well, yes, but—"

"Dial the number," she said, "and if the guy with the hair in his ears picks up, we'll throw the phone out the window."

Coo-wheeeet!

"That's what I thought," she said, "but now we know for sure. What else do we know? I talked to Al a couple of times on the phone. Not for very long, and he didn't say much, but I might recognize his voice. Enough to pick him out of an auditory lineup, if there was such a thing."

"I just wish we had a place to start."

"So do I. He called me out of the clear blue sky, you know. Never a word about how he heard of me, who gave him the number. But he had to have heard from somewhere, and he didn't just dial numbers at random. He knew my number and he knew my address. The first FedEx envelope full of money, he didn't have to ask me where to send it. He just sent it."

"So somebody who knows you also knows him."

"We don't know that, Keller. Somebody who knows me talked to somebody who knows him, and we don't know how many extra somebodies may have gotten into the act. And the old man was running that show a long time, and never changed his phone number once in all those years."

"So there are a lot of people out there who could have had the number."

"And there could be a long chain between the first one and Al, and all you'd need is one broken link along the way and you wouldn't get anywhere." She frowned. "Still, if I ask enough people, somebody might know something. You think it's a different name every time he picks up the phone? Call me Al, call me Bill, call me Carlos?"

"Or he's a creature of habit and never got past Al."

"That would make it easier for him to remember who he was supposed to be. One of the few things I brought along from White Plains was my phone book, and there are a lot of numbers I could call. The more people I talk to, the better the chance that one of them will know what I'm talking about. Of course that's only the half of it."

"The more people you talk to, the more likely it is he'll know somebody's looking for him."

"That's the other half, all right. And I'll have to talk to these people without letting them know who I am, because I died in a fire in White Plains, as you may recall."

"Now that you mention it, it seems to me I heard something along those lines."

"I don't know who else did. It would have been a pretty small story outside of the New York area. But I can't be alive with one person and dead with another. It's too small a world for that." She shrugged. "I'll figure something out. Maybe I'll use one of those gizmos you clamp on the phone and it changes your voice. If there was anyplace else to start . . ."

"Well, there might be."

"Oh?"

"They gave me a phone," he said. "The guy with the ears gave it to me when he took me to the motel they picked out for me."

"The Laurel Inn, or something like that."

"That was it. The Laurel Inn. Gave me this phone, told me to use it to call in. Well, I wasn't going to use that phone any more than I was going to stay in that room."

"You were suspicious from the jump."

"There are certain precautions that are automatic, and yes, it felt a little hinky, but it was my last job and it was going to feel that way no matter what. I wasn't going to stay at the Laurel Inn, and I wasn't going to make any calls on that phone, and I wasn't even going to carry it around with me, because I figured they could locate it whether or not it was turned on."

"They can do that?"

"My rule of thumb is anybody can do anything. So if they tried to locate the phone, all it would do was lead them to the Laurel Inn, because that's where I left it."

"In your room."

"Room two-oh-four."

"You remember the number. I'm impressed, Keller. It's almost as impressive as your trick with the presidents. Who was our fourteenth president, do you happen to remember?"

"Franklin Pierce."

"That's my boy. Now for the bonus round, what color stamp was he on?"

"Blue."

"Blue, Franklin Pierce, and room two-oh-four. That's some memory, but—"

"But so what? Dot, it's possible that they bought that phone the same way I bought this one, and never made a call with it before Hairy Ears handed it to me."

She was right on it. "But if not," she said, "you could press a button and get a list of the last eight or ten numbers called."

"Right."

"And you might even be able to trace it, find out who bought it and when."

"It's possible."

"Same question, Keller. So what? I never stayed at the Laurel Inn, and maybe the maids there aren't in the same league with your average Dutch housewife, but do you really think the phone's going to be there after all this time?"

"It might be."

"Seriously?"

"They gave me a room with a king-size bed," he said.

"Which is nice, I suppose, but since you were never going to sleep in it—"

"And when I left the phone, I didn't want anybody using it. So I lifted up the mattress and stuck the thing all the way in the middle of the bed."

"Can you imagine the way the cops must have tossed that room?"

"After a high-profile political assassination? Yes, I think I can."

"All they had to do was take the mattress completely off the bed."

"They might have done that."

"But maybe not?"

"Maybe not."

"Assuming it's still there, would it even work? Wouldn't the battery be dead by now?"

"Most likely."

"But I suppose they sell batteries."

"Even in the middle of Iowa," he said.

"The Laurel Inn. You wouldn't happen to remember their phone number, do you? No, of course not. They never put it on a stamp."

He went over to the window and looked out at the city while she used the phone and spoke first to an information operator, then to the reservations person at the Laurel Inn. She hung up and said, "Well, there's a woman who's convinced I'm completely out of my mind."

"But it worked."

"'We have to be on the second floor, because my husband can't bear to have footsteps overhead. And I don't want traffic noise, and I'm sensitive to light, and we both need to be near the stairs, but not right on top of the stairs, and I looked at a diagram on the Web and you know what room would suit us perfectly?'"

"It sounds nuts," he agreed, "but when you were talking to the clerk, you sounded perfectly reasonable."

"We've got two-oh-four for three nights starting tomorrow. What's the matter?"

"Oh, I don't know. That seems like a long time to share a room."

"One night would be a long time for the two of us to share a room, Keller. You're not going to be spending even one night at the Laurel Inn, and neither am I. The only reason to book us in there is so that we can get the key. You didn't happen to keep your key all these months, did you? Along with that phone number?"

"No, and it wouldn't be good anyway. They use key cards and they reset the system every time they turn the room over."

"You have to pity all the guys who spent years learning to pick locks, and woke up one morning in an electronic world. They must feel like linotype operators in the age of computerized typesetting, with these sophisticated skills that turned out to be completely useless. Why are you looking at me like that?"

"Like what?"

"Never mind. I had to book three nights because I couldn't go through all that song and dance about how only two-oh-four would do, not if I was only going to keep the room for a single night. I wonder if they've even got a diagram of the layout on their website."

"I wonder if they've even got a website."

"Everybody does, Keller. Even I have a website."

"It's under construction."

"And it may stay that way for quite a while. I'll book us a couple of tickets, or do you want to drive? How far is it?"

"It's got to be a thousand miles, or close to it."

"And our reservation's for tomorrow night, so I guess we fly. Do you still have a gun?"

"The SIG Sauer I picked up in Indiana. I can't take it on a plane."

"Not even in checked luggage?"

"There's probably a regulation against it, and even if there isn't, it's too good a way to draw attention. Some clown sees the outline of a gun in your bag and you're in for a long day."

"You want to drive? I'll fly up and pick up the room key and you can hit the road in your dusty pickup. Des Moines's north of here, right?"

"Like most of the country."

"But pretty much due north? Right there on the Mississippi, isn't it?"

He shook his head. "West of it."

"Weren't you in Iowa, that time the client did a number on us—"

"That *other* time a client did a number on us."

"The *Mercenary Times* case. Wasn't that Iowa, and didn't you throw something into the Mississippi?"

"That was Muscatine."

"*That's* the name of the damn place. I was trying to think of it earlier and I kept getting Muscatel, and I knew that wasn't it. Des Moines is west of there, *not* on the Mississippi?"

"Now you've got it."

"Unless I get on *Jeopardy!,* I don't know why I need to fill my head with all this crap. You want to do that, drive up while I fly?"

"Just so I can bring a gun? No, the hell with it. Anyway, I don't want to be there in a vehicle that somebody could trace back to New Orleans."

"I didn't even think of that. We'll both fly." She picked up her phone. "I'll book our flight. Tell me your name again, will you? I don't know why I can't remember it. What they need to do, Keller, is put your picture on a stamp."

35

They flew Delta to Des Moines, with a change of planes in Atlanta. Both legs of the flight were routine, except that they had to sit three rows apart from Atlanta to Des Moines, and Dot was sure the man next to her was an air marshal. "I kept telling myself not to do anything suspicious," she said. "It was nerve-racking and reassuring at the same time."

She'd booked her ticket in her new name, Wilma Ann Corder. She'd found the name years ago, the same way Keller had found Nicholas Edwards, and had assembled a whole identity kit, passport and driver's license and Social Security, along with half a dozen credit cards. She'd rented a post office box in that name and even subscribed to a needlepoint magazine, which she tossed every month when she checked her box. "Then for three years," she said, "they sent me these plaintive requests to renew my subscription. But what the hell do I care about needlepoint?"

As Wilma Ann Corder, she picked up a rental car in Des Moines. It wasn't from Hertz and it wasn't a Sentra, and Keller thought that was all to the good. On the way to the Laurel Inn she said, "You were lucky, Keller. Nick Edwards suits you, especially with the new haircut and glasses. And Edwards is common as dirt. Corder's pretty rare, but there are just enough of them around so that I keep getting asked if I'm related to this one or that one. I tell them it was my ex-husband's name and I don't know anything about his family. As for Wilma, don't get me started."

"You don't like it?"

"I can't stand it. I've got just about everybody trained out of calling me that."

"What do they call you?"

"Dot."

"How did Dot get to be short for Wilma?"

"I made an executive decision, Keller. Tell me you haven't got a problem with that."

"No, but—"

"'People call me Dot,' I say, and that's generally enough. If anybody asks, I just say it's a long story. Tell people something's a long story and they're usually happy to let you get away without telling it."

Keller waited in the car while Dot went to the front desk to register, wishing she'd parked in back, or at least somewhere other than the waiting area opposite the front door, wishing he'd remembered to bring his Saints baseball cap. He felt more visible than he wanted to be, and tried to remind himself that no one at the Laurel Inn had ever laid eyes on him.

She came out brandishing two key cards. "One for each of us," she said, "just in case we get separated between here and the room. The girl who checked me in must have been a Chatty Cathy doll in a previous life. 'Oh, I see we've got you in two-oh-four, Ms. Corder. That's sort of a celebrity suite for us, you know. The man who shot the governor of Ohio stayed in that very room.'"

"Oh, Christ. She said that?"

"No, of course not, Keller. Help me out here, will you? Where do I park?"

■ ■ ■

Something made him knock on the door of Room 204. The knock went unanswered. He slid the key into the slot and opened the door.

Dot asked him if it looked familiar.

"I don't know. It's been a while. I think the layout's the same."

"That's a comfort. Well?"

For answer he tugged the spread off the bed, lifted a corner of the mattress, and burrowed in between the mattress and the box spring. He couldn't see what he was doing, but he didn't have to see anything, and at first his hand encountered nothing at all. *Well, that figures,* he thought, *after all this time, and—*

Oh.

His hand touched something, and the contact shifted the object out of reach. He wriggled forward, his feet kicking like a swimmer's, and he heard Dot asking him what the hell he thought he was doing, but that didn't matter because he'd moved the extra few inches and his fingers closed on the thing.

It took an effort to get out again.

"Damnedest thing I ever saw," Dot said. "It looked for a minute as though some creature in there had a hold of you and was dragging you under, like something out of a Stephen King novel. By God, I don't believe it. Is that it?"

He opened his hand. "That's it," he said.

"All this time, and nobody found it."

"Well, look what I had to go through just now."

"That's a point, Keller. I don't suppose too many people go mattress diving as a sport, like all those idiots walking around in the woods with metal detectors. 'Look, Edna, a bottle cap!' How many people do you suppose slept right on top of that gizmo and never had a clue?"

"No idea."

"I just hope one of them wasn't a real princess," she said, "or the poor darling wouldn't have had a wink of sleep. But I don't suppose the Laurel Inn's a must-see for European royalty. Well? Aren't you going to see if it works?"

He flipped the phone open.

"Wait!"

"What?"

"Suppose it's booby-trapped."

He looked at her. "You think someone came here, found the phone, fixed it so it would explode, and then put it back?"

"No, of course not. Suppose it was booby-trapped when they gave it to you?"

"I was supposed to use it to call them."

"And when you did—boom!" She frowned. "No, that makes no sense. You'd be dead days before Longford even got to town. Go ahead, open the phone."

He did, and pressed the Power button. Nothing happened. They got back in the car and found a store that sold batteries, and now the phone powered up just the way it was supposed to.

"It still works," she said.

"The battery was dead, that's all."

"Would it still retain information, though? With the battery dead?"

"Let's find out," he said, and pressed buttons until he got the list of outgoing calls. Ten of them, with the most recent one at the top of the list.

"Well, I'll be damned," Dot said. "Keller, you're a genius."

He shook his head. "It's Julia," he said.

"Julia?"

"Her idea."

"Julia? In New Orleans?"

"Suppose the phone's still where you left it, she said, and suppose it still works."

"And it was and it does."

"Right."

"Keller," she said, "you keep this one, you hear me? Don't send her off to walk the dog. Hang on to her."

36

They sat in the car, and he read the phone numbers out loud while she copied them down. "In case the phone goes ker-blooey," she said. "First thing we can do is toss all the numbers with a five-one-five area code. You think there's a chance on earth Al lives in Des Moines?"

"No."

"What about Harry?"

"Harry? Oh, you mean the guy with hair in his ears."

"If you'd rather," she said, "I suppose we could call him Eerie. You think he was local?"

"He seemed to know the city. He found the Laurel Inn without any trouble."

"So did I, Keller, and the closest I've ever been to Des Moines before was thirty thousand feet, and I was in a plane at the time."

"He knew enough to recommend the patty melt at the Denny's."

"So he lives in a city that has a Denny's. That sure narrows it down."

He thought about it. "He knew his way around," he said, "but maybe he was just well prepared. I don't think it matters. Either way we can forget the five-one-five numbers. If Hairy Ears was local, then he was way down on the totem pole. They wouldn't pick up someone locally and let him know much."

"Point."

"In fact," he said, "if he was local, he's probably dead."

"Because they'd clean up after themselves."

"If Al would send a team of men to White Plains to kill you and burn your house down—"

"Keller, that was me. Remember? I was the one who did that."

"Oh, right."

"But I take your point. We'll concentrate on the out-of-towners."

The most promising number, with three calls to it, had a 702 area code, and turned out to be a Las Vegas tip line for sports bettors. Another was a hotel in San Diego. Dot said the third time was the charm, and tried the third number, and got *coo-wheeeet* for her troubles.

"The only way to look at it," she said, "is it's enough of a miracle that the phone was still there, and we'd be asking too much if we expected it to do us any good. I've got one more number to try, and then we can go back to the Laurel Inn and stick this damn thing under the mattress where it belongs."

He watched as she dialed, held the phone to her ear, raised her eyebrows as the call went through. Someone answered it, and she promptly pressed a button to put the call on speakerphone.

"Hello?"

She looked at Keller, and he hand-gestured *Come on,* wanting to hear more. In a voice a little higher than her own, she said, "Arnie? You sound like you got a cold."

"You sound like you got a wrong number," the man said, "not to mention the brains of a gerbil."

"Oh, come on, Arnie," she cooed. "Be nice. You know who this is?"

The phone clicked.

"Arnie doesn't want to play," she said. "Well?"

He nodded. It was the man with the Hairy Ears.

"Well, no wonder he hung up," Dot said. "It turns out his name's not Arnie after all."

"There's a surprise."

"It's Marlin Taggert. That's Marlin like the fish, not Marlon like Brando. And he lives at seventy-one Belle Mead Lane in Beaverton, Oregon."

"There was an Oregon map in the car."

"This car? Just now?"

"The Sentra."

"You think he left it there?"

"No, how could he? And it wasn't the car I rented, it was the one I switched plates with at the airport. Never mind, it's got nothing to do with anything. It's an actual coincidence."

"And a real interesting one, too, Keller. Brightens my whole day."

"Sorry. Where's Beaverton? Is it near anything?"

"Tell you in a second," she said. "There you go. It's just outside of Portland."

And just like that they knew his name and where he lived. They were in a Kinko's on Hickman Road, where they'd set her up at a PC for $5 an hour. He'd been watching over her shoulder, so he didn't have to ask how she did it, but that didn't render the performance any less remarkable. Google had led her to a site where all you had to do was enter a phone number and it would see if it could find it; once it determined that it was available, you had the option of buying it for $14.95. After a quick credit-card transaction, it coughed up the data.

"I knew the government could find out anything," he said, "but what I didn't realize was everybody else can, too. You'd think he'd have an unlisted number."

"He does. Unpublished, anyway. It said so, right there on the screen, at the same time it was offering to sell it to me for fifteen dollars."

"Can't argue with the price, can you?"

"There's probably a way to get it for free," she said, "if I'd wanted to devote the time to it. And no, you really can't argue with the price. I figured the absolute minimum it would cost us was thirty pieces of silver. I wonder who flies to Portland?"

"I'll go," he said. "There's no reason why you have to."

She gave him a look.

"What?"

"We're both going to Portland, Keller. That goes without saying."

"You just said—"

"What *airline,* Keller. And I don't have to wonder, not since God created Google."

They spent the night at the Laurel Inn after all, but in separate rooms. It was Dot's idea, after she'd gone to the United website and booked them on a flight the next morning. "We have to stay someplace," she said, "and we've already got the one room."

His room was on the ground floor in the front. He checked in and had a shower, then went up to 204. She was drinking a bottle of Snapple from the vending machine and making a face every time she took a sip. She asked if he knew a decent place for dinner, and he said the only place he could think of was the Denny's across the street, and he didn't think it would be a good idea to go there.

"It's probably not the only Denny's in town," she said, "but let's not go to any of the others, either." She found a steakhouse in the

Yellow Pages that billed itself as Iowa's best, and they agreed it was pretty good.

Back in his room, he watched cop show reruns on A&E. It seemed to him they were episodes he'd seen before, but that didn't matter. He watched them anyway.

When he got home, he thought, he'd upgrade their TV, spring for a big flat-panel set like the one he'd left behind in New York. Get TiVo, too, and a decent DVD player. No reason not to, not if he had all that money in a bank in the Caymans.

He could think of a batch of reasons not to call Julia, but in the end he went ahead and called anyway. She said hello, and he said "It's me," and she said "Nicholas." Just her voice saying his name, and he felt his chest swell up.

He said, "It worked. The thing was there, and it had what it was supposed to have, and she says you're a genius."

"All pronouns and nonspecific nouns. Because we're on the phone?"

"The night has a thousand ears."

"I thought it was eyes, but I suppose it could be ears, too. A thousand eyes, a thousand ears, and five hundred noses."

"Because it worked," he said, "I've got more places to go."

"I know."

"I won't call until—"

"Until it's over. I understand. You'll be careful."

"Yes."

"I know you will. Give her my best."

"I will. She says you're a keeper."

"But you knew that."

"Yes," he said. "I knew that."

In the morning they had breakfast at the airport while they waited for their flight for Denver, where they ate again before the flight to Portland. The rental car there was booked in his name, and he showed his driver's license and paid with his credit card. He didn't have to worry about either of them, or any of the pieces of ID he was carrying, including the passport he'd shown at check-in. They were legitimate and authentic, even if the name they carried was not the one he'd been born with.

It was easy to locate Belle Mead Lane on the street map Keller bought, but not so easy to find it when you were driving. The development it was in, on the western edge of Beaverton, seemed to specialize in thoroughfares that twisted this way and that, often winding up more or less back where they'd started. Add in a rich complement of dead-end streets, plus some fantasy roads that existed only in the mind of the cartographer, and the whole business got tricky.

"That's supposed to be Frontenac," he said, glowering at a street sign, "but it says Shoshone. How do you suppose Taggert finds his way home at night?"

"He must leave a trail of bread crumbs. What's that off to the left?"

"I can't see the sign from here. Whatever it is, maybe it goes somewhere."

"Don't count on it."

"Here we go," he said a few minutes later. "Belle Mead Lane. Number seventy-one, wasn't it?"

"Seventy-one."

"So it'll be on the left. Okay, that's it."

He slowed for a moment across from a red-brick ranch with white trim, set back on a spacious and well-landscaped lot.

"Nice," Dot said. "Be a showplace when the trees get some size to them. I call it a positive sign, Keller. He's got to be more than an errand boy to afford a place like this."

"Unless he married money."

"There you go. What heiress could resist a small-time crook with hair growing out of his ears?"

"Well," he said.

"Well, indeed. Now what?"

"Now we find a motel."

"And wait until tomorrow?"

"At the earliest," he said. "This may take a while. He doesn't live here all by himself. But we want to get him when he's alone, and when he can't see it coming."

"It's like when you work, isn't it? You go out and have a look around and plan your approach."

"I don't know any better way to do it."

"No, it makes sense. I guess I expected it to be more straightforward, the way it was yesterday in Des Moines. Go there, get what we came for, and leave."

"We were just picking up a phone," he pointed out. "Our task here is a little more complicated."

"Just finding the damn house was more complicated than anything we did in Des Moines. Will you be able to find it again tomorrow?"

It wasn't hard to find, not once he'd been there and knew when to disregard the map. When he turned onto Belle Mead Lane the next morning, he half-expected to see Marlin Taggert out in front of his house, watering his lawn. But that was Gregory Dowling who'd been watering his lawn, and who might be watering it still, never knowing what a close brush with death he'd had. No one was watering Marlin Taggert's lawn.

"And no one ever has to," Dot said, "because we're in Oregon, where God waters everybody's lawn. How come the sun's out, Keller? Isn't it supposed to rain here all the time? Or is that just a rumor they started to keep Californians from moving in?"

He parked two doors down on the other side of the street. That gave him a good view of Taggert's house, but put them where he wouldn't spot them unless he decided to take a good look around.

Still, they couldn't park here long enough to sink roots. Taggert might not be expecting trouble, but his was a line of work where trouble was never entirely out of the question. Even if there was no one with a reason to wish him ill, he almost had to be a person of interest to law enforcement officers of all descriptions, local and state and federal. He and his boss might have gotten away clean in Des Moines, but Taggert couldn't have lived this long without getting tied into something somewhere. Keller, who'd met the man, was willing to bet he'd done time, though he couldn't have said where or for what.

So he'd be cautious out of habit, whether or not he had anything specific to be cautious about. Which made surveillance complicated. You couldn't park on the block for too long, or come back too often.

That afternoon they returned to the airport, where Dot went to a different rental car counter and rented a car for herself, paying extra for an SUV so that it would be recognizably different from the sedan Keller had rented. With two cars, Keller figured they were that much less likely to be spotted. But even with a whole fleet, they had to be circumspect in their surveillance, or Taggert would simply conclude that he was being watched by a government agency with a whole motor pool at its disposal.

A couple of times a day they took one of the two vehicles and found their way back to Belle Mead Lane. They'd do a couple of drive-bys, park at curbside for five or ten minutes, circle the block a time or two, and then return to the motel. They were staying nearby at the Comfort Inn, and there was a shopping mall with a multiplex theater just half a mile from the motel, and plenty of places to eat. But most of the time they sat in their separate rooms and read the paper or watched television.

"If we had a gun," Dot said, "we could speed things up a little. Just walk up to the front door and ring the bell. He answers, we shoot him and go home."

"And if someone else answers?"

"'Hi, is your daddy home?' *Bang.* But even if you drove from New Orleans to Des Moines with the gun in the car, we still couldn't have brought it to Portland. Not without driving across the whole damn country. You think it would be impossible to buy a gun here?"

"Probably not."

"But you don't want to."

"No. Anyway, how can we shoot him dead and then expect him to talk?"

Saturday morning they had breakfast across the street from the motel. Over coffee they went over what they'd learned in several days of intermittent surveillance:

—A couple of sightings had confirmed that Marlin Taggert, if that was the name of the man residing at 71 Belle Mead Lane, was definitely the man who'd been Keller's contact in Des Moines. The same fleshy face, the same big nose, the same loose mouth, and the same characteristic walk, not quite shambling but not far from it. And, of course, the same Dumbo ears, though they were too far away to see if his barber had done anything to make them more presentable.

—The rest of the family included a woman, presumably Mrs. Taggert, who was younger than her husband and a lot better-looking. There were three children, a boy and two girls, ranging in age from ten to fourteen. The dog was a Welsh corgi, its puppyhood barely a memory. Once they'd seen Taggert and one of his children take it for an agonizingly slow walk around the block.

—There were two cars housed in the Taggert garage, a brown Lexus SUV and a black Cadillac. When Mrs. Taggert left the house, with or without her children, she took the Lexus. Except for the single excursion with the dog, Taggert barely left the house and never ventured off the property, and the Cadillac stayed put in the garage.

"Monday morning," Keller said. "Until then I don't want either of us to go anywhere near Belle Mead Lane. We're not going to catch him alone over the weekend, and just in case he noticed our cars parked on the block or driving by, he'll have a couple of days not to notice them. Then Monday morning we'll take him."

Later he asked Dot if she felt like a visit to the mall, but she'd found something she liked on television. He went to a hardware store and picked up a few things, including a heavy steel pry bar with its end bent into a U, a roll of wire for hanging pictures, a roll of heavy-gauge duct tape, and a pair of wire-cutting pliers. He put his purchases in the trunk and drove around to the theater entrance. He watched a movie, and when it ended he stopped at the men's room, then bought popcorn before sneaking into one of the other theaters to watch another movie.

Just like old times, he thought. But at least he wouldn't have to spend the night in the car.

37

At 8:30 Monday morning they were on Belle Mead Lane, parked where they could see the Taggert house. They hadn't been there five minutes before the garage door rose and the brown SUV emerged from it.

"Taking them to school," Dot said. "If she's coming back right away, we'll want to wait until later. But there's no way to know, is there?"

"There is if she turns this way," he said.

"Huh?"

"Here she comes," Keller said, and as the car approached he opened his door and got out from behind the wheel. He'd brought the Gideon Bible from his motel room, but he left that in his car. He stepped out into the street in front of the oncoming SUV, raising a hand palm-out and waving it from side to side. The Lexus stopped, and Keller smiled the kind of benign smile you'd expect from a studious balding man wearing glasses. He walked over to the side of the car, and when she rolled down the window he explained that he was having trouble finding Frontenac Drive.

"Oh, it doesn't exist," she said. "It's on maps, but they changed their minds and never cut it through."

"That explains it," he said, and she drove away, and he got back in the car.

"I knew it," he said. "There is no Frontenac. The map lied."

"That's wonderful, Keller. I'll sleep better knowing that. But why on earth—"

"She's dressed to meet the world," he said, "not just to dump the kids and come home. Lipstick, earrings, and a purse on the seat beside her."

"And all three kids?"

"Two in the back and one in front. And not a sound, because two of them were listening to their iPods and the other, the boy, was playing something where you use your thumbs a lot."

"Some video game?"

"I guess."

"A nice little family group. Keller, you're having second thoughts about this, aren't you?"

He said, "She'll be gone a couple of hours, would be my guess, but we don't have time to waste. Let's get it done."

Keller pulled into the driveway and they got out of the car. Dot, carrying her handbag, led the way up the flagstone path to the front door. Keller, with the Bible in one hand and the pry bar in the other, was a step or two behind her.

She rang the doorbell, and Keller heard it chime. Then nothing, and then footsteps. He flipped the Bible open and held it in his left hand as if he were reading it, so that it obscured the lower portion of his face. His right hand clutched the pry bar, holding it out of sight at his side.

The door opened, and Marlin Taggert, wearing a Hawaiian shirt and a pair of camo cargo pants, took a look at the two of them. "Oh, Christ," he said.

"The very subject I wanted to raise with you," Dot said. "I hope you're having a divine day, Mr. Taggert."

"I don't need this," he said. "No disrespect, lady, but I got no use for you or the Jesus shit you're peddling, so if you'll just take it somewhere else—"

But that was all he said, because by then Keller had driven the rounded end of the pry bar into the pit of his stomach.

The reaction was heartening. Taggert gasped, clutched at his middle, took an involuntary step backward, stumbled, caught his balance. Keller rushed in after him, with Dot right behind, drawing the door shut after her. Taggert retreated, picked up a glass ashtray, hurled it at Keller. It sailed wide, and Keller went after him, and Taggert yanked a lamp off a table and flung it.

"Son of a *bitch*," Taggert bellowed, and charged Keller, swinging a wild right hand. Keller ducked under the blow, swung the pry bar like a sickle, and heard the bone snap when he connected with Taggert's leg. The man let out a roar and crumpled to the floor, and Keller had the pry bar high overhead and just caught himself in time; he was that close to smashing the man's skull and rendering him forever silent.

Taggert had an arm raised to ward off a blow. Keller feinted with the pry bar, then swung it in an easy arc that caught the man high on the left temple. Taggert's eyes rolled up in his head and he pitched over onto his side.

Dot said, "Oh, hell."

What? Had he struck too hard a blow after all? He looked up and saw the old dog waddling across the carpet toward them. Keller walked toward it, still holding the pry bar, and with a visible effort the dog raised its head to look up at him.

Keller put down the bar, took hold of the dog's collar, put it in another room, and closed the door.

"For a second there," Dot said, "I thought it was about to

attack. But it was just waiting for Queen Elizabeth to take it for a walk."

He checked Taggert, found him unconscious but breathing. He rolled him over, secured his hands behind his back with a few loops of the wire he'd bought, and used some more of the wire to bind his ankles together.

He straightened up, handed the pry bar to Dot. "Watch him," he said, and went looking for the kitchen.

A door from the kitchen led into the attached garage. Keller found a button to raise the garage door, parked his car alongside the Cadillac, and lowered the door. He wasn't gone long, and Taggert was still out when he returned to the living room. The lamp was back on its table, he noticed, and so was the glass ashtray.

Dot shrugged. "What can I say, Keller? I'm neat. And this mope's still out. What do we do, throw water on him?"

"We can give him a minute or two."

"You know, I thought you were exaggerating about the hair in his ears. If he doesn't come to on his own, I'll find a tweezers and start ripping out ear hair. That should bring him around."

"This is simpler," he said, and poked his toe gently into Taggert's shin. He found the spot where he'd struck with the pry bar, and the pain cut right through. Taggert yelped and opened his eyes.

He said, "Jesus, my leg. I think you broke it."

"So?"

"'So?' So you broke my fucking leg. Who the hell are you people? If this is some religious cult, you got a hell of a way of recruiting, is all I can say. If it's a robbery, you're out of luck. I don't keep any money in the house."

"That's a good policy."

"Huh? Look, wiseass, how'd you pick my house? You got any idea who I am?"

"Marlin Taggert," Keller said. "Now it's your turn."

"Huh?"

"To tell me who I am," Keller said.

"How the hell do I know who you are? Wait a minute. Do I know you?"

"That was my question."

"Jesus," he said. "You're the guy."

"I guess you remember."

"You look different."

"Well, I've been through a lot."

"Look," Taggert said, "I'm sorry that didn't go the way it was supposed to."

"Oh, I think it went exactly the way it was supposed to."

"You're probably upset that you didn't get paid, and that's something that can be taken care of. All you had to do was get in touch. I mean, there's no need for violence."

This was taking too long. Keller kicked him hard in the leg, and Taggert screamed.

"Cut the crap," Keller said. "You set me up and left me hanging."

"All I ever did," Taggert said, "was what I got paid to do. Pick up this guy, take him here, take him there, show him this, tell him that. I was doing my job."

"I realize that."

"There was nothing personal to it. Jesus, you ought to be able to understand that. What the hell were you doing in Iowa? You weren't there on a relief mission for the Red Fucking Cross. You went there to do a job, and if I didn't keep telling you 'Not today, not today,' you'd have iced that poor schmuck we saw pruning his roses."

"Watering his lawn."

"Who gives a shit? One word from me and you'd have killed him without even knowing his name."

"Gregory Dowling."

"So you know his name. I guess that changes everything. You'd have killed him without it being personal, is what I'm saying here, and I did what I did, and that wasn't personal, either."

"I understand that."

"So what do you want from me? Money? I got twenty thousand dollars in my safe. You want it, you can take it."

"I thought you didn't keep any money in the house."

"And I thought you were the strong-arm division of the Little Sisters of the Poor. You want money?"

Keller shook his head. "We're both professionals," he said, "and I've got nothing against you. Like you said, you were just doing a job."

"So what do you want from me?"

"Information."

"Information?"

"I want to know who you did the job for."

"Jesus," Taggert said. "Why don't you ask me something easy, like where's Jimmy Hoffa? You want to know who put the hit on Longford, you're pissing on the wrong tree. Nobody's gonna tell me shit like that."

"I don't care who ordered the hit."

"You don't? Who are you after, the shooter?"

"No," Keller said. "He was just doing his job."

"Like you and me."

"Just like us. Except we're alive, and I have the feeling the shooter's not."

"I wouldn't know."

Oh, you'd know, Keller thought. But since he didn't care either way, he didn't bother to push the point. He said, "I don't care about the shooter, or about the person who commissioned the job. And I'll stop caring about you as soon as you give me somebody else to care about."

"Like who?"

"Call me Al," Dot said.

"Huh?"

"The man who made the call to hire me," Keller said. "The man who gave you your orders. Your boss."

"Forget it."

Keller touched the man's shin with his foot, pressed just enough to get the message across. "You're going to tell me," he said. "It's just a question of when."

"So we'll see who's got the most patience," Taggert said.

You had to admire the man's nerve. "You really want the other leg broken? And everything else that comes after that?"

"Once I give you what you want, I'm dead."

"And if you don't—"

"If I don't I'm dead anyway? Maybe, maybe not. Way I see it, if you're up for killing me, you'll do it whether I talk or not. In fact as long as I *don't* talk, you'll keep me alive hoping you can open me up. But once I turn rat and sell the boss out, I'm a dead man walking."

"Not walking," Keller said.

"Not on this leg, you're right about that. Point is, either you kill me or he does. Either way it's the same ending. So I think maybe I'll see how long I can hold out."

"There's only one problem with that."

"Oh?"

"Sooner or later," Keller said, "your wife's going to come home. She was dressed for a day on the town, so maybe she'll go shopping, maybe have lunch with a girlfriend. If we're gone by the time she gets back, she'll be fine. If we're still here, we'll have to deal with her."

"You'd hurt an innocent woman?"

"It wouldn't hurt her much. She'd get what the dog got."

"Jesus Christ, what did you do with the dog?"

Keller brandished the pry bar, made a chopping motion with it. "Hated to do it," he said, "but I couldn't take the chance he'd bite somebody."

"Aw, God," Taggert said. "Poor old Sulky? He never bit anybody in his life. He could barely bite his dinner. Why'd you go and do a thing like that?"

"I didn't feel I had any choice."

"Yeah, the poor old guy might have licked your face. Slobbered all over you. He's got arthritis, he can barely walk, most of his teeth are gone—"

"It sounds like I did him a favor."

"Sometimes I think I'm a hard case," Taggert said, "and then I run into a son of a bitch like you. My kids loved that fucking dog. He's been part of the family longer'n they've been alive. How am I gonna explain to them that their buddy Sulky's dead?"

"Make up some story about Doggie Heaven," Dot suggested. "Kids buy that crap all the time."

"Jesus, you're colder'n he is."

"And speaking of the kids," Keller said, "if you're still holding out when they come home—"

"You'd do that?"

"I'd rather not, but if we're still here when they turn up, you want to tell me what choice I'd have?"

He looked at Keller, looked at Dot, looked down at his own broken leg. "It hurts like a bastard," he said.

"Sorry about that."

"Yeah, I can tell. Okay, you win. Between you and him, either one of you would kill me, but he wouldn't come after my family."

"What's his name?"

"Benjamin Wheeler. And you never heard of him. That's his fucking secret, nobody ever heard of him."

"Call me Ben," Dot said.

"How's that?"

"Never mind," Keller said. "Keep talking. His address, his schedule, everything you can think of."

38

"That's a nice computer his kids have," Dot said, "and a real fast broadband connection. You go to Google Image and type in 'Benjamin Wheeler' and you get a ton of hits. You make it 'Benjamin Wheeler Portland' and it narrows it down." She was holding three sheets of paper, and she showed one to Taggert. He nodded, and nodded again at each of the other two sheets.

Keller took one of the sheets he'd nodded at and looked at a color photo of three men standing next to a horse. A fourth man, the jockey, was on top of the horse, and one of the men was holding a trophy, to be presented to the horse, the jockey, or the owner. Keller couldn't tell which, nor did he know which of the men was Wheeler—although he was ready to rule out the jockey.

He looked at the other photos, and there was only one man who appeared in all three. In one he was with two women, posing for the camera, while the third shot showed him and another man in conversation. In each of the pictures Wheeler was the dominant figure, taller than anyone else, except for the horse. He dressed in expensive suits conservatively cut, and wore them with the ease of a retired athlete. His dark hair was well barbered, his face deeply tanned, and he wore a mustache.

"'Financier, sportsman, and philanthropist,'" Keller read aloud.

"A hell of a guy," Dot said. "On all these committees for civic betterment. Patron of local cultural events. That one woman there is an opera star, and there was a pretty good shot of him shaking hands with the new mayor, but I thought three was plenty."

"You could have a hundred pictures," Taggert said, "and that's as close as you're gonna get to him, because you can't just pick up a Bible and go ring his doorbell. He's got a house that's the closest thing I've ever seen to a castle, up on a hill with an electric fence around the whole property. You got to go through a gate to get close to the house, and the guy on the gate confirms by intercom before he lets anyone in. If you got over the fence, you'd have the dogs to contend with, and you couldn't deal with them the way you did with poor Sulky. Man, I can't believe you killed my dog."

"Then don't."

"They're Rhodesian ridgebacks, a boy and a girl, and if you took a swat at one of them, he'd take your hand off at the wrist, while his sister was having your balls for dinner. Get past 'em somehow and make it into the house and he's got four guys on staff, and they've all got guns and know how to use 'em. When he leaves the house, two of them go with him, one to drive and one to ride shotgun. The other two stick around and guard the house."

"All those precautions," Keller said. "I guess a lot of people must have tried to kill him over the years."

"Why? Mr. Wheeler's respected throughout the state, he calls the mayor and the governor by their first names. As far as I know, there's never been a single attempt on his life."

"No kidding. Where do you keep your guns?"

"My guns?"

"You know." He pointed his finger, wiggled his thumb. "Bang! Your guns."

▪ ▪ ▪

There was a locked gun rack in the den, and the key was where Taggert had said it would be—and, Keller thought, right where any kid would look for it. Keller took the shotgun and slipped a few shells in his pocket. He left the rifle in the rack. He could fire a rifle but wasn't that confident of his ability to hit anything with it. With a shotgun, all you had to do was get close enough to the target. A clay pigeon might present a certain challenge, but a human being standing still would be pretty hard to miss.

"They're for hunting," Taggert said, "and if I've gone out three times in the last ten years it's a lot. Hell, if I was a hunter, you think my dog'd be a corgi? I still can't believe you killed my dog."

"You said that before. You must have handguns."

"Just the one, in the bedside table. For emergencies."

It was a revolver, a .38 Ivor Johnson, immobilized with a cylinder lock. Keller had a vision of an intruder surprising the Taggerts in their sleep, and Taggert yanking the gun out and rushing to the den for the key. Handy.

"It's hard to believe you're a pro," Taggert said. "Taking my guns? You didn't bring your own?"

"You offered me a choice of guns in Des Moines," Keller reminded him. "So I've come to think of you as my regular supplier."

"You took the revolver. Were you even planning on using it?"

"No," Keller said, "but it came in handy later on."

"You could have an AK-47 and you wouldn't have a chance with Mr. Wheeler. You know what I would do in your position?"

"Tell me."

"Put the guns back, let yourselves out, and go home. Mr. Wheeler won't send anybody after you because he'll never know you were here. He's sure not about to hear it from me."

"You can tell him you broke your leg tripping over your dog."

"Jesus," Taggert said. "I can't believe you killed the poor damn dog."

"Let's be clear on this," Keller said. "Packing up and going home, that's not on the table. So what you've got to do is come up with a way for us to get to him."

"Mr. Wheeler, you mean."

"Right."

"You want to use my gun, and you want me to work out how you're gonna do it."

"That's your best shot."

"It's *my* best shot? How the hell do you figure that?"

"It's pretty simple," Keller told him. "That's the only way you stand a chance of coming out of this alive. Say we go up against Wheeler and we wind up dead."

"Which you will."

"If we do, so do you. He'll know how we got to him. We'll tell him if he asks, and he'll figure it out if we don't. How long do you figure he'd let you live, and how far could you run with a broken leg?"

"And if I help you, and you get lucky? Then you turn around and kill me."

"Not if you help us. Why kill you?"

"Shit, why kill Mr. Wheeler, for all you're going to get out of it? Why would you kill me? Because you're some kind of a psychopath, is all I can think of. Look what you went and did to Sulky."

"Jesus," Dot said.

"I still can't believe it," Taggert said. "I can't believe you killed a poor old dog like that."

"I can't fucking stand any more of this," Dot said, and went over to the door Keller had closed earlier. She opened it and made clucking noises, and Taggert turned his head in time to see the old dog waddle into the room.

"My God," he said.

"It's Sulky," Dot announced, "back from the dead, and I bet you can't believe that, either."

39

"If you didn't have to go and break my leg," Taggert said, "this part would be a whole lot easier."

Keller couldn't argue the point. Getting the man from the living room floor to the back seat of his Cadillac took a lot of work on everybody's part. Keller had snipped the wire from around his ankles, which made it a little easier, but security concerns had led him to leave Taggert's wrists tied together behind his back. The whole process, through the kitchen and into the garage, was difficult to negotiate, and Taggert inevitably bumped into something here and there, and yelped with pain.

"What's funny," Taggert said, "is I was ready to beg you to take me in the car. Instead of killing me right there in my own house. On account of I didn't want her to walk in and find her husband dead on the floor. I figured it was bad enough she'd come in and trip over the dead dog. See, this was back when I still thought the dog was dead."

"Now she'll trip over the live dog."

Taggert didn't seem to appreciate the line. It was hard to tell, he was in back where Keller couldn't see his face, not and concentrate on his driving at the same time. Dot would have enjoyed it, but she was in the other car, tagging along in Keller's wake. So there were no cars in the garage at 71 Belle Mead Lane, and the garage door was shut and the other doors locked, and the only signs of their visit were the absence of a shotgun and a revolver, both now in the trunk of the Cadillac, a table lamp that refused to light, and a dent in one wall where the glass ashtray had struck it.

"You want to take your next left turn," Taggert said. "Point is, I didn't want her to see that. Or the kids, if they came home the same time she did. And I thought that was the best I could do, just fix it so I could die somewhere else, because I didn't think I had a chance of getting out of this alive."

Keller waited until the oncoming traffic cleared, then took the left turn. He kept an eye on the mirror, made sure Dot had gone straight through the intersection, heading back to the motel.

"Now you got me believing I might have a shot," Taggert said. "Not a real good one, but I have to say it's better than nothing."

"I suppose you could knock out the power," Taggert had said. "Find a way to take out a power line and you'll do two things at once. The fence won't be electrified anymore, so all you have to do is climb over it. And, if you go in at night, you'll have all the confusion of darkness going for you. No lights in the house, and everybody running around and bumping into each other."

"Unless they've got one of those generators," Dot said, "that kicks in automatically if the power supply's compromised."

"I wouldn't know about that. But I have to say it's the kind of thing Mr. Wheeler would have."

"Suppose we had you with us," Keller said. "Wouldn't that get us through the gate?"

"Only if he knew I was coming, and he told them to let me in. Say if I called him, made up something I had to see him about."

"Like what?"

"Well, I can't come up with anything right off the top of my head. I'd have to think of something."

"You'd have to think up some way to explain what I was doing in the car with you," Keller pointed out. "That might be tricky."

"Say you're my prisoner," Taggert said, and snapped his fingers. "That's it! I'll tell him the guy we set up in Des Moines turned up, and I managed to subdue him and now I want to bring him over for questioning. Then I march you in there and it looks as though you're tied up securely, but you get loose and—"

Keller was shaking his head.

"Okay, this is better yet," Taggert said. "I go over to see him, I make up some story, doesn't matter what. And you're in the trunk."

"I'm in the trunk?"

"The trunk of my car. I park the car, Mr. Wheeler and I go in the house, and when the time's right you open the trunk—"

"From the inside?"

"They got a way to do that now, to save kidnap victims. Or small children who crawl in car trunks when they can't find an abandoned refrigerator to play in. So that's what you do, you pop out of the trunk and go to work."

"Mowing the lawn?"

"You do what you came to do. They'll be off guard, all you got to worry about is the dogs."

"Those Rhodesian ridgebacks."

"I grant you they're vicious," Taggert said, "but do you think they're gonna bother with a parked car?"

"They might take an interest," Dot said, "what with everybody else standing there with guns in their hands, waiting for the trunk to open. You're driving and he's in the trunk? I don't think so."

"You don't trust me," Taggert said. He sounded hurt.

"I don't even trust you to drive," she said. "How are you going to work the gas pedal with that leg?"

"I could use my other foot."

"And the brake?"

"Same thing. I mean, it's not as if I'd have a clutch pedal to contend with. The Cadillac's got automatic transmission."

"You're kidding. What'll they think of next?"

Keller said, "I like cutting the power line. It seems to me you don't run an auxiliary generator all the time, you just switch it on when the lights go out. So you do it in the daytime, and the only thing that goes out is the fence."

"And the TV," Dot said, "and the air conditioner, and everything else with a plug and a switch."

"Still, it's better than at night."

"Then what you want is a rainy day," Taggert said. "So you'll have a decent shot of finding him at home. Day like today, Mr. Wheeler's gonna be playing golf. What? Did I say something?"

Benjamin Wheeler belonged to three country clubs, and when he played a round of golf the drill was always the same. Two of his aides would accompany him, while the other two remained at the house. One man, the driver, would stay with the car; the other, more of an all-purpose bodyguard, would walk to the first tee with Wheeler, then wait at the clubhouse while Wheeler and his playmates buzzed around in their golf carts for eighteen holes.

Rose Hill, according to Taggert, was Wheeler's most likely choice, so that was the first place Dot called. Posing as the secretary of one of Wheeler's fellow golfers, she said she wanted to confirm the foursome's tee time. It was scheduled for 11:15, said a young woman with a snooty English accent, and would there be four? Because she had Mr. Wheeler down as a party of three.

"Yes, three," Dot said. "That's quite right, because Mr. Podston won't be able to make it after all."

She hung up and Keller said, "Mr. Podston?"

"What I almost said," she said, "was Pond Scum. Podston was the best I could do. Eleven-fifteen, that's when they're teeing off, so there's not a lot of time to waste."

You had to pass a gate attendant and assorted other functionaries at the entrance to Rose Hill Country Club, and then a valet would turn up to park your car. Keller drove right past the entrance and followed the map from the club's website. Dot had printed out a copy, and he studied it again and decided the best bet was the seventh hole, a 465-yard par four with a dogleg to the left and woods on the right. A slice would put Wheeler in the woods, and that was where Keller decided to wait for him.

And there was a place forty or fifty yards from the fairway where he could park. He had a feeling it wasn't entirely legal to park there, but any cop who felt compelled to do something about a nice big Cadillac with Oregon plates parked where it wasn't in anybody's way, well, the worst result would be a ticket, not a tow.

The only problem was that the parking spot was on the wrong side of the fairway. To get to the woods you had to cross the fairway, easy enough for Keller, but not so easy for a man with a broken leg. Keller could put an arm around Taggert and take most of his weight, but what would the two of them look like to anybody playing the hole? And you couldn't just wait until a foursome played through, not with the amount of time it would take to get Taggert across the fairway; by the time they were halfway across, the next group of golfers would be at the tee.

One man trotting across a fairway, that was nothing remarkable. Two men, one unable to walk, the other struggling to assist him—even someone as singleminded as a golfer would zoom over on his cart to see what was wrong, and what he could do to help.

And could Taggert make it across, even with support? His entire lower leg, including the knee joint, was swollen and inflamed. They'd removed his shoe earlier, when Taggert complained that his foot had grown too large for it, and now it was larger still, twice the size of the other one.

No, the man couldn't go anywhere.

"You're going to have to wait here," Keller told him. "In the trunk."

"The trunk!"

"It won't be that uncomfortable, and you won't be in there that long. As soon as my work's done, I'll run you to a hospital and you can get that taken care of."

"But what if—"

"If I don't come back?"

"I didn't want to say that."

"Well, it's possible. But there's a latch, remember? You're the one who told me about it. For kids playing refrigerator."

"How am I supposed to reach it with my hands tied behind my back?"

"That's a point," Keller conceded, and clipped the wire on Taggert's wrists. It still was no easy matter getting him into the trunk, and throughout it Taggert reeled off a litany of complaints—his leg was killing him, he could barely move his fingers, his shoulders felt dislocated, di dah di dah di dah.

"It won't be long," Keller said. He put the shotgun on the floor of the trunk, near Taggert's swollen foot, and checked to make sure that the revolver was fully loaded.

"You're leaving me the gun?"

"The shotgun? I don't want to carry it around on the golf course. Too easy for somebody to spot it."

"So you're leaving it with me?"

"Although I suppose they'd just mistake it for a four wood. But it's bulky, I don't want to carry it."

There was a car coming. Keller turned so his face wouldn't show, waited for the car to pass. Meanwhile, Taggert said he was glad Keller trusted him enough to leave the shotgun with him.

"It's not exactly a matter of trust," Keller said.

40

When four golfers played a round together, you called it a four-some. Benjamin Wheeler was grouped with two other men, so it stood to reason that you'd call them a threesome, but you couldn't use that word nowadays without imagining all three of them in bed, twisted into some unlikely position. Keller figured there ought to be a way around it, but he wasn't sure what it might be. A trio? Maybe.

He stood in the woods halfway up the fairway of the seventh hole. He'd left his jacket in the car, and was dressed in a pair of dark slacks and a polo shirt, reasonable attire for a golf course. He didn't think anyone had seen him stride across the fairway, but if they had, there'd been nothing in his appearance to set off any alarms. The question might arise as to just what he was doing there, without cart or clubs, lurking among the trees and bushes.

But then lurking was suspicious by definition, wasn't it? The trick in lurking was to appear to be doing something else, but Keller couldn't think of anything. What would anyone do there other than lurk? Well, look for a lost golf ball, he thought, but the companionable thing to do when you came upon someone so engaged was to help him look for it, and that was the last thing he wanted.

Best, then, not to be noticed at all. And so he kept himself deep enough in the woods to pass unnoticed, surfacing now and then to inspect each arriving group of golfers, making sure Wheeler was not one of their number, and then slipping back once again into the shadows.

In Arizona—Tucson, not Sedona—Keller had once rented a house on a golf course. He hadn't been interested in either the house or the game, but it was the only way he could find to gain access to his quarry's gated community. (If its residents were all bisexual, Dot had suggested, you might call it a double-gaited community.) His one-month sublet had brought with it membership in the on-premises country club, and access to its championship golf course. Keller had made use of the club's bar and restaurant and hobnobbed with its golfer members, without ever quite managing to pick up a golf club or set foot on the course.

Of course he'd watched the sport on television, though never with enormous enthusiasm. He found it more bearable than basketball or hockey, if less involving than football or baseball. The scenery, undulating expanses of green enlivened by tan sand traps shaped like amoebas, was restful to look at, and the announcers spoke in low tones, and sometimes even kept their mouths shut. The only way to improve on something like that, Keller sometimes thought, was to turn off the set altogether.

Now, as Keller watched from the woods, he had no announcers to contend with, and no commercials, either. The tee was two hundred fifty yards to his left, the green almost that far to his right, and what he mostly saw were golfers gliding past him in their carts. Golf was what prosperous men did for exercise, but there didn't seem to be much exercise involved. *A good walk spoiled,* he'd heard the game called, but that was back when there was some actual walking involved in it. Now all you did was ride from one shot to the next.

He had to pay close attention, because he wasn't sure he'd be able to spot Benjamin Wheeler. The face in the photographs was distinctive enough, certainly, but how distinctive would it be at two hundred yards?

For the first time in months, Keller had a handgun tucked into the waistband of his trousers, pressing against the small of his back. He'd left the shotgun in the trunk of the Cadillac, and was just as glad, but he found himself wishing he'd brought the other long gun, the rifle. Not to try a shot at distance, but because the thing had been fitted with a scope sight, and the scope all by itself would be useful now as an aid in spotting his target. Meanwhile he stared hard at every golfer who came along, and none proved to be the man he was waiting for.

Soon, he thought. They'd been scheduled to tee off at 11:15, and how much time was each hole likely to take? Some of the passing foursomes, he noted, took longer than others. Some golfers pulled two or three clubs from their bag before settling on the one they wanted for the shot, then prepared themselves with several practice swings, and finally tossed a handful of grass in the air to give them a read on wind direction and velocity. Others went straight to the ball, stepped up to it, addressed it (*"Hello, ball!"*) and gave it a whack.

And, of course, the better golfers were faster, because the slower ones took more strokes. Keller couldn't really see what they were doing once they got to the green, but it seemed to take some of them forever to get off it.

A certain percentage of them hit slices, with the ball curving around sharply to the golfer's right, sometimes into the light rough a few yards from Keller, sometimes into the deep rough where he was lurking. Each time he retreated deeper into the woods, remaining there until the golfer found his errant ball or gave up the hunt and played another. Now if Wheeler would have the decency to hit a shot like that, and then trot over to look for his ball . . .

Soon, Keller thought.

He spotted Wheeler the minute the man reached the seventh tee.

With glasses, Keller had eyes like a hawk, but even an eagle would have had trouble at that distance. And Wheeler wasn't facing him directly, so it was hard to explain how he was able to recognize the man. Something about his stance, maybe—but since Keller was seeing the man for the first time, how did he know what his stance looked like? Maybe it was pure animal instinct, the predator sensing the presence of his prey.

Once he'd identified the man, he knew he wouldn't have to worry about spotting him again. Wheeler, conservatively dressed in all three of the shots Dot had printed out, hewed to a different sartorial standard on the golf course. His golf slacks were bright purple, and his shirt was a Day-Glo canary yellow. He wore a tam-style cap, too, the kind with wedge-shaped pieces like slices of pizza, with a little button where they met in the middle of the pie, and the slices were scarlet and lime green.

It was amazing, Keller thought, how a man could dress like a banker the rest of the time and then turn into a peacock on the golf course. But it did make it easy to tell the players apart.

Another man had evidently won the last hole, which gave him the honor of teeing off first. He topped the ball and hit a roller down the middle of the fairway, not a lot of distance but a shot that wouldn't get him in any trouble. It stopped fifty yards or so short of Keller.

Wheeler was next. *To me,* Keller urged silently. *Hit it over here, Ben. Drop your shoulder, pull up on the ball, and slice the hell out of it.*

Keller had been watching golfers today for long enough so that it seemed like forever, and of course he'd seen the pros enough times on TV. And Wheeler's form, from what he could see of it, was nothing great. A pro could very likely have found ten things wrong with his swing, from his stance all the way to his follow-through, but evidently the ball didn't know what a bad swing it was, because it took off as if Tiger Woods himself had just swatted it. Straight down the middle of the fairway, and damned if it didn't reach where Keller was waiting and carry a few yards beyond him.

And then of course the third man, who must have been last on the preceding hole, did what he could to be last on this one as well. He hit just the shot Keller had hoped for from Wheeler, a wicked slice that was bad from the moment it left the tee. The golfer knew it, too, letting the club fall, putting his face in his hands. His buddies consoled him, or teased him—it was impossible for Keller to tell which—and then they all mounted their motorized carts and headed down the fairway for their second shots.

Keller had watched the ball land, and moved back into the woods, making sure he was out of sight when the unfortunate golfer got there. But it took him forever to get there, the idiot, because he looked all over the place and couldn't find the damn thing.

"Hey, Eddie, you want help there?"

The offer came from Wheeler. *Yes,* Keller thought. *Yes, please, come over here and give him a hand.* But Eddie said no, he'd find it in a minute, and then he did, and jogged back to his cart for a club, and came back and managed to find the ball again.

Half a dozen strides, Keller thought, and he'd have him. The driver who'd led off, whose ball hadn't carried very far, had already taken his second shot. Wheeler was up ahead, planning his own shot, tossing bits of grass in the air. Nobody was looking at Eddie, who was pretty well screened from their view by the trees and bushes. Half a dozen strides and he'd have him, and he wouldn't need the gun, his hands would do the job, and it would be over.

Because did it really make any difference which of these golfers he killed? Wasn't one as good as the other?

That's just your mind talking, he told himself sternly. *It's crazy, and the good news is you don't need to listen to it.*

41

The eighth hole, another par four, was the reverse of the seventh, with its fairway running along the other side of the wooded stretch. Keller took a shortcut through the woods while the three duffers headed for the green, and he'd found a good spot for himself by the time they turned up on the eighth tee.

This time Wheeler had the honors, and Keller braced himself, willing the man to hit a slice. Once again the woods were on the players' right, and once again Wheeler failed to cooperate. He missed the fairway, but not by much, his ball rolling until it came to a stop in the light rough on the far side, away from Keller.

The next man up, whose name Keller hadn't caught, hooked his tee shot, and wound up a little deeper in the left rough than Wheeler. And then Eddie hit a perfect slice into the woods on the right, the ball coming to rest mere steps from Keller's place of concealment.

It was almost as if the guy wanted Keller to kill him. Almost as if that was what Keller was supposed to do.

Keller backed off, trying not to make any noise. In the movies, someone in his position always wound up stepping on a twig, and all ears perked up at the sound. Keller stepped on a lot of twigs, it was impossible to do otherwise, but no one noticed a thing.

Eddie found his ball with no trouble this time, and had the sense to play a safe shot back onto the fairway. Keller got out the course map and tried to figure out what to do next.

The ninth hole was a par three, and the trick was to get on the green without going in the water hazard. That was no place for Keller to lurk, not without scuba gear. He could see from the map that the tenth hole was similarly devoid of suitable cover, so he made his way directly to number eleven, and got there in time to watch another colorfully dressed group of aging businessmen find various ways to misplay the hole.

He waited, and the next team off the tee was another foursome. What would he do, he wondered, if Wheeler and his pals decided to skip the back nine?

And they might. For all he knew they were in the clubhouse right now, bandying friendly insults back and forth, reliving nine holes of golf you'd think they'd be delighted to forget. Knocking back a couple of rounds of drinks at the bar, chatting with other club members, and networking just enough to keep their club memberships tax deductible.

How long, he wondered, before he could conclude that he'd missed his chance? And if he had, what would he do next?

He reviewed the possible courses of action open to him, and couldn't find any he liked. He reached a point where he was plotting long-range schemes that would keep him in Oregon for a couple of weeks. Then he glanced over at the tee and he'd never been so happy to see a pair of purple pants and a vivid yellow shirt.

Eddie went first, having evidently found some way to win the preceding hole. He sent his tee shot straight down the middle of the fairway, and so did the next man, whom the others seemed to be calling Rich. And so, maddeningly, did Wheeler, whose drive never came anywhere near Keller's stand.

When he had the chance, he moved on to the next hole.

Deep rough edged both sides of the twelfth fairway. Keller had to guess, and guessed wrong. Poor golfers hit more slices than hooks, he reasoned, so he chose the woods to the golfers' right, and Rich and Eddie did hit slices, Eddie's ball just reaching the woods. Wheeler, maddeningly, hooked his drive well into the woods on the opposite side. He was all alone there, searching for his ball among the trees, but Keller was stranded on the other side of the fairway.

On thirteen, the rough on both sides was fairly deep, but there was no tree cover available. The only trees involved were about a hundred and twenty yards out from the tee, a stand of mixed hardwoods stretching for twenty or thirty yards across the fairway. From the tee, you had two choices; you could try to clear the trees on the fly, or you could play it safe and skirt the hazard on the right.

Keller watched from the trees. Rich and Eddie both took the safe route, laying up alongside the trees on the right. Wheeler sent his ball straight down the middle of the fairway, and it looked for a moment as though it was going to sail right over the trees. But it fell short, hit a tree, and dropped like a stone into the middle of the hazard.

Perfect.

Keller waited, positioning himself where he couldn't be seen, holding his breath, as if the sound of air going in and out of his lungs might be audible over the engines of the carts. He balanced his weight on the balls of his feet, felt the comforting pressure of the revolver in the small of his back, and watched helplessly as

Wheeler drove straight up to where his ball had landed, with both of his companions, Rich and Eddie, putt-putting along on either side of him. All three carts parked together, and all three men climbed down and joined in the search for Wheeler's ball.

Well, why not take out all three of them? Make it a real front-page story, "Three Business Leaders Gunned Down at Rose Hill." And how hard could it be? He could walk right up to them without arousing anybody's suspicions, and if he ran out of bullets before he'd finished the job, well, a five iron would do to wrap things up.

But all he did was stand there while Wheeler found his ball and took three more strokes to get it through the patch of woods.

Fourteen, fifteen, sixteen. It was one damn thing after another, and Keller figured the seventeenth hole was his last chance. The eighteenth hole had sand traps for hazards, and no trees in a position to help him out. So either he got lucky on seventeen or his only shot was to follow Wheeler into the locker room and drown him in the shower.

Or he could just forget the whole thing.

And was that such a bad idea? It wasn't as though he had to punch Wheeler's ticket in order to get his reward. There was no client on this job, no advance to be refunded if he failed, no final payment to be collected for a job well done. This was for him and Dot, this was a matter of revenge, this was evening the score.

But did the score need to be evened?

He didn't know Ben Wheeler and Wheeler didn't know him, wouldn't recognize him, probably wouldn't remember his name, if he'd ever known it in the first place. Wheeler had made use of him in a way that had taken Keller's whole life away from him, or at least it had looked that way at the time. But now Dot was alive again, and Keller was a millionaire again, and he even had his stamps back—or would as soon as he went to Albany and collected them. His apartment was gone, his life in New York was over, and he could never again use the name he'd been born with, but he could live with that, couldn't he?

Why, he was living with it already, and living comfortably, too. He liked New Orleans as well as he'd liked New York, and he had work he enjoyed, work that was easier to live with than running around the country killing people. Not once, after a day of installing tongue-and-groove flooring, say, had he felt the need to shrink the image of the day's work in his mind, graying it down, lightening its burden on his memory. He had a woman who was at once exciting to be with and easy to live with, and all he had to do was walk away from all of this purposeless vengeance and he could be back with her, being Nicholas Edwards, living his new life.

Wheeler had won the last hole, and led off. Keller was waiting in the woods on the right, and Wheeler actually hit the ball in his direction. But it wasn't a terribly wicked slice, and wound up in the rough a good dozen yards short of where the trees and dense shrubbery began.

Rich hit his tee shot, and really got hold of it. It went high in the air and took off down the left side of the fairway, carrying almost to the first pair of bunkers. All three of the men at the tee watched its flight, but not Keller, who picked that moment to dart out, sprint to Wheeler's ball, pick it up, and scamper back into the trees again.

He stopped, leaning against a tree trunk while he caught his breath. Any of them could have seen him, all they'd have had to do was glance in his direction, but if they did he'd have heard an outcry. He chanced a look, and they were still on the tee, with Eddie putting one club back in his bag and taking out another, then going through his usual ritual of practice swings before he finally stepped up to the ball. Keller begged him silently not to slice it, and he didn't, knocking a no-harm grounder down the middle of the fairway.

All three men went to Eddie's ball, and waited while he sent it another hundred yards or so toward the pin. Then he and Rich headed for their respective balls, while Wheeler drove straight to where he'd seen his own ball land.

It wasn't there, and Wheeler walked around in circles, the picture of total confusion. You'd think it might occur to the guy to try the woods, but he'd seen where it landed, dammit, and that's where he was going to look for it.

Keeping his voice down, Keller said, "Hey, buddy. This what you're looking for?"

Wheeler looked up, and Keller motioned him over. Could the others see him? It didn't matter, they were looking in another direction, but he moved to his left to put a tree between him and them, just to be on the safe side.

He said, "Thing hit a rock, took a leap like a scared rabbit. Right this way."

"Never would have looked way over here," Wheeler said. "I owe you one."

"I'll say."

"How's that?"

"Wait a minute," Keller said. "Don't I know you? Aren't you Benjamin Wheeler?"

Wheeler smiled in acknowledgment. Then a frown creased his forehead. "You look familiar," he said. "Do I know you?"

"Not exactly," Keller said, reaching for him. "But you can call me Al."

42

"Griqualand West," Julia said, reading over his shoulder. "Is that a country?"

"It used to be," he said. He reached for the catalog, found the right page. "Here we go. 'Originally a territorial division of the Cape of Good Hope Colony, Griqualand West was declared a British Crown Colony in 1873 and together with Griqualand East was annexed to the Cape Colony in 1880.'"

"So that's where? South Africa?" He nodded. "Do you have stamps from Griqualand East?"

"They didn't issue stamps for Griqualand East."

"Just Griqualand West."

"Right."

She studied the album page. "They all look pretty much the same," she said.

"They're all stamps from Cape of Good Hope," he said, "overprinted with a *G*."

"For Griqualand West."

"I think that's probably what they had in mind. Some of the overprints are red and some are black, and there are lots of different variations in the *G*."

"And every variation is a different stamp to collect."

"I guess it doesn't make much sense."

"It's not supposed to make sense," she said. "It's a hobby, and you have to have rules, that's all. Some of the *G*'s are upside down."

"They call that an inverted overprint."

"Are they worth more than the others?"

"It depends," he said, "on how scarce they are."

"It would, wouldn't it? I'm really glad you've got your stamps back."

At the golf course, he'd had a long walk back to the Cadillac, and was afraid someone with a badge might have taken an interest in it by then. But the car was where he'd left it, and he got in and drove to the mall. He parked at one end of it, made a quick call to Dot, then wiped the interior of the car and made sure to take his jacket with him when he left it.

The multiplex movie theater was at the other end of the mall, and he walked there and bought a ticket for a movie about penguins in Antarctica. He'd seen it before, and so had Dot, but it wasn't the sort of film that was spoiled if you knew how it ended. He took a seat in the last row and got caught up in the action right away, barely noticing when someone took the seat beside him.

It was Dot, of course, and she offered him some popcorn, and he took a handful. They sat there, neither of them saying a word, until the entire tub of popcorn was empty.

"I feel like a spy in an old movie," she whispered. "You saw this already, didn't you? Well, so did I. Is there any reason we have to watch the rest of it?"

She got up without waiting for an answer, and he followed her out. "Every last piece of popcorn," she said, tossing the tub in the trash bin. "Except for the old maids. What? You're not familiar with the term?"

"I never heard it before."

"Because they never got popped. Well? We're all set?"

"All set. The car's parked in a good spot, and it'll probably be a day or two before anybody notices it. I left the shotgun in the trunk."

"Is that what you used to—"

"No, it would have been awkward and messy. I used the revolver, and then I left it in Wheeler's hand."

"You left him holding it?"

"Why not? That'll be puzzling, a man with his neck broken and a gun in his hand, and then when they match the gun to the slugs in Taggert, it'll give them something to think about."

"Retribution in Portland's dark underworld."

"Something like that."

"I got us on an early flight tomorrow, and we have to change planes twice. With the time change, it's going to take the whole day to get to Albany."

"That's okay."

"I reserved a rental car, and two rooms in a motel a quarter of a mile from the airport. We'll drive to the storage place in Latham first thing Wednesday morning, and then you can drop me back at the airport."

"And you'll fly back to Sedona."

"With a few more changes en route. I'll tell you something, Keller, I'm too old for this shit."

"You're not the only one."

"When I get home I'm going to stay put. Make a big pitcher of iced tea and sit out on the terrace."

"And listen to Bell Rock."

"Ding Fucking Dong. And on that subject, did you have any trouble with Big Ben?"

"The hardest part was following him around all day. He and everybody else got to ride those little carts. I was the only person on the whole course who was walking."

"Thank your lucky stars, Keller. That's why you're in so much better shape than he is. Did he know who you were?"

He recounted the final exchange. "But I'm not sure it meant anything to him," he said. "Something came into his eyes, but it may just have been that he could see what was coming."

"The Grim Reaper, swinging a sand wedge. And Taggert?"

"Just a matter of doing it," he said. "The man was in the trunk of his car with his leg broken. You couldn't call him a hard target."

"Unless your mind got in the way."

"My mind?"

"You know, after he cooperated and all."

"He cooperated because he had to. He thought it might buy him a little more life, but there was never any question of letting him off the hook. How could we risk that?"

"You don't have to convince me, Keller."

"I tried to make it quick," he said, "but he had a couple of seconds to see it coming, and I can't say he looked surprised. I don't think he expected to get out of it alive."

"It's a hard old world, all right."

"I guess. He didn't want us to leave him where his wife would find him, and we didn't. And his dog's alive."

"And Taggert lasted a good half hour longer than he would have if he hadn't come through for us. Maybe longer, maybe a full hour. And just think how much that is in dog years."

After three plane rides, after ten hours in an airport motel in Albany and a ride to Latham, the two of them managed to get the stamp albums loaded into the trunk of Keller's latest rental car, a Toyota Camry. The car was comfortable, and held the road even better with the extra weight in the trunk.

"You've got a long ride ahead of you," Dot said, "but I guess you're not keen on sending the stamps home by UPS and flying home yourself. No? I didn't think so. Well, have a good trip, Keller. I'm glad you got your stamps back."

"I'm glad you're alive."

"I'm glad we're both alive," she said, "and I'm glad they're not. If you ever get to Sedona . . ."

"Or if you get to New Orleans."

"There you go. Or pick up the phone, if you get the urge. And if you lose the number, just check the White Pages. I'm listed."

"Wilma Corder."

"Known to her friends as Dot. So long, Keller. Take care."

The drive to New Orleans took three full days. He could have driven faster, or put in longer hours behind the wheel, but he made himself take his time.

He spent the first night in a Red Roof Inn off I-81. He left the stamps in the trunk of the Camry, and after he'd been in the room for half an hour he went to the desk and switched his room for one on the first floor. Then he moved the car and brought all ten stamp albums into the room.

The second night, he specified a ground-floor room when he checked in. The third night he parked in their driveway. He used his key and found Julia in the kitchen, and one thing led to another. A couple of hours later, he went out for his stamps.

Donny was happy to see him, glad to have him back. The fiction Keller and Julia had cooked up was a family emergency, a health crisis for a favorite uncle, and Donny asked a few polite questions that Keller couldn't answer, but he managed to slip and slide his way through the conversation. Then the subject shifted to a house Donny thought had real possibilities, and Keller was on firmer ground.

Over coffee Julia said, "According to *Linn's,* kids today aren't interested in collecting stamps."

"They've got Internet porn sites," he said, "and a hundred channels of cable TV, and lots more things to do than when I was a kid."

"More homework, too," she said, "so we can keep up with the Chinese."

"You think it'll work?"

"No," she said. "I suppose a little boy would be a lot more likely to take up philately—did I say that right?"

"No one ever said it better."

"More likely to take up philately if his father introduced him to it."

"'Billy, I'd like you to meet Philately. Philately, this is Billy.'"

"Don't you think that would make a difference?"

"I suppose it might. I didn't have a father around the house."

"I know."

"But if I had, and if he collected stamps . . . but, see, I got there on my own."

"So it's hard to say what might have happened, because it happened anyway."

"Right."

"Well," she said, "maybe you'll get to find out."

He looked at her.

"Maybe it'll be a boy," she said, "and you can teach him all about stamps. And where Griqualand West is, and useful stuff like that. Not right away, I suppose you have to wait until he can walk and talk, but eventually."

He said, "Did you tell me something earlier, and I wasn't paying attention?"

"No."

"But you're telling me something now."

"Uh-huh."

"And we're going to have a boy?"

"Not necessarily. I'd say it's about fifty-fifty. I haven't gone for the ultrasound yet. Do you think I should? I always used to think I'd rather wait, but just about everybody finds out ahead of time nowadays, and maybe it's just goofy not to. What do you think?"

"I think I'd like some more coffee," he said, and went to refill his cup. He brought it back to the table and said, "There was something you were going to say before I left for Des Moines, and then you decided it would keep. Was that it?"

"Uh-huh. And I was right, it kept."

"I might not have gone."

"That's one reason I decided it would keep."

"Because you wanted me to go?"

"Because I didn't want to stop you from going."

He thought that over, then nodded. "That's one reason. What's the other?"

"I didn't know how you'd feel."

"How could you? I'm not sure how I feel myself. Excited, of course, and happy, but—"

"Really? Excited and happy?"

"Sure. How did you think I'd feel?"

"Well, that's just it. I didn't know. I was afraid you might want me to, you know."

"To what?"

"To do something. You know."

"You mean like an abortion?"

"And I knew I didn't want to do that."

"I should hope not," he said.

"But I was afraid you might want me to."

"No."

"It might be a girl," she said. "Can girls collect stamps?"

"I don't see why not," he said. "They've probably got more time for it, because they spend so much less of it at Internet porn sites. You know, this is a lot to take in."

"I know."

"I'm going to be a father."

"A daddy."

"God. We're going to be a family. I never thought, well, I had no idea it was an option. Even if it was, I never dreamed it was something I would want."

"But it is?"

"Yes. We'll have to get married. Sooner rather than later, don't you think?"

"That's not something we absolutely have to do, you know."

"Yes it is. I was thinking we ought to do it anyway, I was thinking that during the drive back from Albany."

"And bringing your stamps into the motel room each night."

"It does sound silly, looking back on it, but I wasn't taking any chances. Stand up, will you?"

She got to her feet and he took her in his arms and kissed her. "I never thought any of this would happen," he said. "I thought my life was over. And it was, and I got a whole new one in its place."

"And you have medium brown hair."

"Mouse brown."

"And you wear glasses."

"Bifocals, and I have to tell you, I can see the improvement when I work on my stamps."

"Well," she said, "that's important."